The Road to Samarcand

**Center Point
Large Print**

**This Large Print Book carries the
Seal of Approval of N.A.V.H.**

The Road to Samarcand

PATRICK O'BRIAN

CENTER POINT PUBLISHING
THORNDIKE, MAINE

This Center Point Large Print edition
is published in the year 2007 by arrangement with
W. W. Norton & Company, Inc.

The text of this Large Print edition is unabridged. In other
aspects, this book may vary from the original edition.
Printed in the United States of America.
Set in 16-point Times New Roman type.

ISBN-10: 1-60285-011-9
ISBN-13: 978-1-60285-011-8

Cataloging-in-Publication data is available from the Library of Congress.

The Road to Samarcand

One

THE *Wanderer* ran faster with the freshening of the breeze; her bows cut into the choppy sea, throwing white hissing spray into the sunlight. The schooner was carrying every stitch of canvas that she could spread, and she was so close into the wind that the boy at the wheel kept glancing up at the sails, watching for them to shiver and spill the breeze; but they remained taut and full, and presently his attention wandered. His gaze went up past the dazzling white triangles of the sails to the great albatross above them.

"How does it manage to keep up without moving its wings?" he wondered, craning over to the left to see it more clearly. "It has never—"

"Keep her on her course, you young idiot," roared an unseen voice, and at the same moment the *Wanderer* yawed a little. The lee scuppers vanished under a cloud of foam, and Derrick gripped the wheel; it bucked under his hands, but he held it firm; the compass steadied, and the *Wanderer*'s bowsprit pointed to Tchao-King again. Derrick stood there, square to the wheel, his eyes fixed on the binnacle, the picture of a model helmsman; but he was red in the face, and he felt acutely conscious of the head that had appeared on deck. The rest of his uncle's tall, lean body followed the head and stood there easily on the sloping deck, swaying to the send of the waves as the captain looked up at the sky, the wind-vane and the rigging.

7

"If you do that again," he said, coming aft, "I'll drown you with my own hands, and then you'll be put on half-rations for the rest of the voyage. Now listen, Derrick, you hand over to Olaf at six bells and come down to the saloon. We want to have a talk with you."

"Okay—I mean, aye, aye, sir," replied Derrick, grinning. But when his uncle had gone below, he frowned. "I wonder what they want to talk to me about," he muttered, changing his grip on the spokes. He turned it over in his mind for some time, but he could think of nothing: soon he gave it up, and concentrated his whole attention on steering the *Wanderer* as she ran through the China Seas.

He heard the ting-ting of the ship's bell, three times repeated, and a moment later Olaf Svenssen came out of the fo'c'sle. He was a big, fair Swede with a face as broad and as red as a side of beef, and like Captain Sullivan he stood for a moment gazing up at the weather and the sails.

"How's she steering?" he asked, coming to the wheel.

"Due northwest by north," replied Derrick, handing over.

"Nort'-vest by nort' it is," said Olaf, taking the wheel. "Do you think the wind will get up any more, Olaf?"

"Not till after sundown. The sun'll swallow it up, Ay reckon. Maybe in the night we'll have a blow, Ay dunno.

But the *Wanderer* can take it, eh?"

Derrick went below. His uncle and Mr. Ross, a tall, raw-boned Scot, were in the saloon, working out the *Wanderer*'s position on the chart.

"Is the sun over the yardarm, lad?" asked Ross.

"Yes, sir, just over," answered Derrick. The schooner had no yards at all, but he knew what the question meant. "Good. Li Han! Coffee and rum."

"Coffee and rum on the spot one time," cried the Chinese cook, bringing in a tray.

"Now then, Derrick," said Sullivan, finishing his coffee, "we want to talk to you."

"Aye, we want to talk to you," repeated Ross, solemnly. "Have a wee tot of rum."

"It's like this," went on Derrick's uncle. "When you joined us in Wang Pu after. . . ." He paused. He didn't like to say "after your mother and father died", and while he was seeking for a better phrase he thought of that sudden death far away in Chang-An, and of those two kind, gentle missionaries who had been Derrick's parents. He coughed and went on, ". . . after the funeral, we had no time to make any arrangements, so we took you along on the *Wanderer* while we considered what ought to be done with you. That is quite a time ago now, and so far we've done precious little about it. But we have come to the conclusion that you ought to go to school. The only question is where, the States or England."

"Or Scotland," put in Ross.

"Or Scotland. But wherever it is (and I had thought of Ireland too) a school it must be."

"Just so," said Ross. "A school first, and then the university, to be bred up to one of the learned professions."

"Exactly," said Sullivan. "Knocking about the China Seas with a lot of rough-neck sailors is not the thing for a boy who ought to be hard at his books, not at all, at all."

"But, Uncle," cried Derrick, "I've had all the education I want, and I want to be a sailor. Can't I just stay on the *Wanderer* with you and Mr. Ross? It's much better than school for a sailor. I'm learning to navigate, and I can splice a rope as well as Olaf."

"No, my boy," said his uncle, firmly. "It won't do at all. I don't say that you aren't very useful—you've got all the makings of a sailor—but it won't do. There are hundreds of reasons, To begin with, you'll have to train in steam to get anywhere nowadays: I doubt whether you would ever get a mate's ticket with this kind of training. And, besides, you have got to be properly educated. Your English cousin on your father's side thinks just the same."

"Just so," said Ross. "Get a good grounding in the classics, mathematics and geography, and then you'll be ready for sea training."

"But, sir, didn't you say that you ran away to sea when you were younger than I am? And everyone knows that you are the best master mariner in the Yellow Sea."

"Weel, lad, that's as may be. Humph. But that's another case altogether. Days were different then. And let me tell you this, when I was a wee laddie I was a great headstrong fule: I did not know the wisdom of my elders. But when I had been first mate of the *Indus* just three years, I saved my pay and I went to Saint Andrew's. I realised that my elders were not so stupid as I had thought when I could walk under a table without bending my head, and so I took my degree."

"Couldn't I do the same, sir? Look, Uncle Terry, just let me stay aboard the *Wanderer* until I'm old enough to go to college, and I promise you I'll—"

"No, no, my poor boy. School it must be, so pipe down and make up your mind to it. You must go and learn how to parse, and the Kings of Israel, and how many beans make five. Besides, the matter is not entirely in my hands—there's your English cousin, and he has a big say in the affair."

"That would be Professor Ayrton, I suppose," said Derrick, gloomily. "My father often talked about him. He was coming out to see us this year."

"Yes, that's the one. He's a great authority on oriental archaeology, a very learned man, and I don't suppose that you will be able to escape the advantages of a liberal education with him on your track. We shall be seeing him a few days after we reach Tchao-King, and we'll have another talk about it then. Now cut along and give Li Han a hand at checking over the stores."

Derrick left the saloon with a heavy heart and made his way to the galley. The idea of being a schoolboy again after the freedom of the schooner was not a pleasant one.

In the saloon Sullivan leaned back and lit his pipe. "I sympathise with the boy," he said. "I'd feel just the same myself in his place. And there's a lot in early training: nothing like it for a deep-sea sailor. Still, I suppose he must be educated."

"Aye," said Ross, "though I don't know anything to beat an apprenticeship under sail to make a sailorman. But this Professor Ayrton probably will not see eye to eye with us there."

Derrick found Li Han counting piles of bags and tins, trying to make them tally with the total in the store-book.

"They want to send me to school, Li Han," said Derrick, sitting on a tea-chest.

"Thirty-nine piculs of rice: exactitude only approximate," said the Chinese cook. "Do they? Very proper too. Thereby you will have inestimable privilege of becoming first-chop scholar."

"I don't want to be a first-chop scholar. A master mariner is good enough for me."

"You are talking jestily. Who wishes to be a meagre sailorman if he can be a learned and enter the government service? Why, in time you might be an official and never do anything for remainder of earthly existence. You could grow long fingernails, and become obese and dignified."

"I don't want to be obese and dignified. I'd rather be a meagre sailorman."

"Ah, but think of the excessive perils and discomforts of seafaring life. Very often sea is unnecessarily

12

agitated by heavenly blasts, and seafaring persons are plunged beneath surface. It is much better to be the meanest official with firm chair under seat. And maritime persons enjoy no prestige, no face, while government officials are very dignified. You should go to school with rejoicement, labour with unremitting zeal, and become pensionable civil servant. Please excuse." He stowed away the chest on which Derrick had been sitting, and went on, "Observe the classics: in the Shih King it says, 'It is the business of scribes and scholars to correct the government of the people.' You pursue ancient advisement, and correct the government. What face! What daily bribes! What squeeze!"

"Yes, there's glory for you," said Derrick. "But as for me, I'd rather be master of a schooner like the *Wanderer*."

"You like some lichees now?" asked Li Han. "Just one or two?"

"As many as you like, Li Han. There won't be any at school, I dare say."

Li Han piled the fruit on a plate. "Exceedingly peculiar thing," he said, "I run after learning all the time, chasing it in adverse circumstance, and you run away from it when it comes on a tray." He lit a cigarette. "This morning I reach the letter S in my dictionary."

"Gee, Li Han," said Derrick, finishing the lichees, "you thought it would take you another week to work through R, didn't you? At this rate you'll come to Z and the abbreviations before the end of the year. That's swell. Is there anything I can do to help, apart from eating the lichees? Because if not, I think I'll vamose."

"Vamose?"

"I shall move my person with distinguished agility from this place to another," explained Derrick, slipping into the Chinese that he had learned before ever he spoke English.

"Vamose—to skip away. Thank you. Will make instantaneous note—colloquial knowledge of English most valuable."

Derrick came on deck and stood watching the *Wanderer*'s wake for some time. The wind had dropped with the sun, and in the calmer sea he could see the schooner's trail stretching far behind her. He looked down, and there, sure enough, was the great dark, torpedo-shaped form of the tiger-shark that had been following since the ship left port. Li Han came up with a bucket of rubbish: he threw it over the side, and at once Derrick saw the little pilot-fish dart forward and follow a lump of spoiled salt pork as it sank. The shark shot out from the shadow of the schooner, and Derrick saw the white gleam of its belly as it turned; there was a swirl in the water, and it was gone. The pilot-fish snapped up the scrap that remained and joined the shark under the stern. Derrick shuddered: sharks were the only things in the sea that he hated. There was something appallingly sinister about the great fish's silent voracious rush.

He looked away and searched the sky and the horizon for the albatross that was nearly always there, a particularly fine one, with such a vast wing-span that it seemed impossible that it should ever be able to fold them and walk on the ground. But it was not there: nor were the gulls which usually appeared to swoop on the scraps that Li Han threw overboard.

Presently he went along to have a word with Olaf. "I say, Olaf," he began, "if you wanted to be a sailor, would you go to school?"

"Well, I am a sailor, ain't I?" said Olaf. "What do you think Ay look like? A film-star, maybe, or a guy that dances on a tight-rope?"

"No, I mean do you think school is a good thing?"

"A good thing?" said the Swede, watching the compass and considering. "Well, Ay reckon they wouldn't teach me much out of a book, eh? Ay can't read only big print, see? And Ay don't want to be squinting down my nose at a lot of words Ay can't understand."

"I mean if you were young and wanted to be a ship's captain."

"Hum. That's another thing. You got to know how to navigate, of course: but Ay don't know that anything else ban much use to a sailor, except the nautical almanac."

"I think you're right, Olaf. They want to send me to school."

"What for, eh? You can read and write and figure, can't you? Ay never was a one for falals and doodads. My old man, he was the master of a whaler, see? And he never knew any more than navigation by rule of thumb." He turned the wheel two spokes, and went on. "Now Ay knew a man in Baltimore, could read out of books in Greek and what you say? Uh, Latin, ain't it? Yes. Well, it worn't any manner of use to him. He fell in the sea and drownded just the same."

"But that might happen to anyone, however much they knew."

"Ay don't know. My old grandma, she was a Finn. Half Lapp, they say; and she was a wise woman. She could read the runes. You know what Ay mean? The old heathen writings, eh? And she could put good luck on a ship with what she knew, and she could sell you a nice little wind if you asked polite. If you went and tipped your hat to her and said, 'Good morning, marm, I've come for a nice little wind like you can make, marm, if you please,'"—Olaf imitated himself being polite, with a horrible smirk and a bob of his head—"Why, then you'd maybe get it. But if you was to say, 'Hey, old girl, give us a wind yust one point off of east and make it snappy,' why, then you would get something more then you bargained for, eh? What she knew, my old grandma! Ay don't reckon she would have drowned in any sea. Ay t'ink she must have been ninety when Ay remember her. Old, she was, with a beard like a man, and she was a little creature you could of broken like that . . ." he snapped his fingers. "But they was all afraid of her, even the old pastor, though he hated her worser'n poison. She used to be able to tell the day when a man was going to die, and she could charm the whales out of the sea. But Ay reckon you can't get that sort of learning in no school. If you could, maybe it'd be some use, eh?"

"Could she really tell when you were going to die, Olaf?"

"Well, maybe. There was only two or three ever asked her, and they died all right. After that, nobody wanted to know. But Ay seen her call an ice-bear over the sea. She was a wise woman all right."

"How did she do that?"

"Ay don't rightly know. We was up in the north of Norway, visiting a sick relation, see? And this relation, he went on keeping sick, in spite of my grandma. So she went out into the tundra and called in the reindeer—a good many Lapps can do that—and she made some kind of a spell then; but still this man, he could not get any better no way. So then she bawled him out and swore so that we all got frightened and asked her to stop, very polite. 'Stow it, Grandma,' we said. 'Stow it, marm, if you please.' And she stopped. She sat by the fire and smoked her pipe for a long while. It was very cold, Ay remember: up there the winters go on seven, eight months, and there ain't no sun. The fjords were frozen deep, too, and the wolves, they came so close you could hear them breathe. After a long while she got up and looked out: there was a double ring of the Northern Lights flashing up all colours in the sky, and she went out. Soon there was a wolf howling close by outside, and another answered in the tundra. My father, he said, 'That's your grandma, son, talking to the wolves.'

"Well, nothing happened for a long while, and they all ban gone to sleep when Ay took a look outside, because Ay wanted to see. And Ay saw my grandma going down across to the fjord. So Ay slipped out and followed her in the moonlight, see? She went right on to the ice and squatted down. She took out a knife, an old stone knife like some of the Lapps have, and she cut runes on the ice. Then she called out across the sea, and far away there was an answer. Ay can't make the proper noise, but it was something like this — Haoo, haoo. She called six, seven times with her hand like that, see, up to her mouth, and each time the answer came nearer. She held her knife by the blade and beckoned with it. And over the ice I see a great white bear coming slow, with his head turning from side to side on his long neck. Eh! He was a big one. Sometimes Ay could not see him against the snow on the ice, because he was white too, see? But there was his shadow there all the time. And Ay was so frightened Ay could not move my little finger, and Ay was cold: cold to the heart. Soon he come right up to her, and he sit down on the ice, and they talk, grunting and nodding. Suddenly something seems to crack in me, and Ay up and run like mad for the house, hollering all the way. I hear the white bear roar as I slam the door, and they all wake up and ask what's biting me? Have I had a bad dream, maybe?

"But soon my grandma comes in and she swear at me and clout my head and say Ay have spoilt everything: but that night this relative got better."

18

"Was it your grandmother that did it, Olaf?"

"Of course it was. The doctor from Kjelvik, he said it was his physic, but we knew it was Grandma. Oh, she was a wise woman, all right, my grandma, and they was all afraid of her because of her learning. When she died, they found she got hair on the soles of her feet, like an ice-bear." He stared up at the sails for some moments, and then said, "If you can get learning like that, you go to school and learn all you can. Otherwise you stay on board and leave it for these ship's chandlers, eh?"

"I wish I could, Olaf. But they seem set on educating me."

"Hm. Well, Ay reckon the Old Man knows best. Still, an albatross can fly clean round the world without learning out of no books, and maybe a sailor can do just the same without being learned no Greek or this so-called Latin."

"That reminds me. I haven't seen the albatross this afternoon, nor any gulls."

"Ain't you? That's funny." Olaf looked over his shoulder to the western rim of the sea. "She don't look quite right, neither," he said. "And the wind dropped a bit too quick. Ay don't like it, not in these seas. Ay t'ink Ay know what it means, without no book-learning."

Derrick looked at the bright horizon where the sun had set. "It looks all right to me," he said.

"You look close. Don't you see no sort of a haze up there?"

Derrick looked again. Yes, there was a haze; not quite a cloud, nor yet a mist. It was strange.

Down below Sullivan finished writing his log. He looked at the tell-tale compass, cast an automatic glance at the brass ship's clock and the barometer and was preparing to refill his pipe when his eye shot back to the barometer. He sprang up, made sure that the barometer was not broken, and let out a long whistle. The thick column of mercury had dropped, as if the bottom had fallen out of the glass. He moved aside to let Ross see, and without a word they ran up the companion-way. Olaf jerked his thumb over to the west and they stared at the sky: they gazed up to the sails, flapping wearily in the dying breeze. They looked at one another and nodded.

"Derrick, take the wheel," ordered Sullivan. "Olaf, bear a hand." He ran to the foremast winch, shouting for the two Malays in the fo'c'sle as he ran. Ross hurried about on deck, battening and lashing everything movable.

"What is it, sir?" asked Derrick, as he passed.

"Bit of a blow coming up, lad," answered Ross, making all fast.

Li Han hastened by with an anxious expression on his face. Derrick felt uneasy. Soon the *Wanderer* showed no more than a scrap of canvas, a single jib; her decks were cleared as though she were going into action, and she had so nearly lost steering-way that the wheel was lifeless in his hands.

On the western horizon a strange cloudbank was

forming rapidly. There was a heavy swell running, but no wind at all. In reply to a shouted order Derrick had put up the helm, and slowly the *Wanderer* came round to face the east. The long swell, which he had not noticed before, took her from behind, and her bare masts groaned as she worked heavily on the sea. Ross and Sullivan stood watching the growing patch of darkness on the sky.

"I think we'll just about get the full force of it," said Sullivan. "The glass is still falling."

"Aye," said Ross. "It won't be long now. I'll take the first trick at the wheel. We'll run before it?"

"Surely. The *Wanderer* can stand very nearly anything."

Ross dived below, and reappeared in his oilskins and sea-boots. The light of the day was fading with every minute, a menacing, unnatural fading of the light. The cloudbank was now a stretch of darkness covering a quarter of the sky. Suddenly Derrick realised what it was: there is nothing in the world like the coming of a typhoon.

"You go below, Derrick," said his uncle. "And don't come on deck without orders."

The swell increased, and Derrick in the saloon had to hold on tight to prevent himself from bowling up and down as the *Wanderer* pitched. There was still no breath of wind to stir the sails, and the schooner seemed to have lost all her life and strength; she wallowed like a log.

Soon the light was obscured as if by a thick fog: a

hot, oppressive darkness filled the air, and the send of the waves grew stronger. The *Wanderer* laboured in the huge, smooth seas, creaking and groaning. Suddenly, and for the first time in his life, Derrick felt seasick: he was cold and clammy one minute; much too hot the next. He was very anxious not to disgrace himself, but he knew that if the ship went on bucketing much longer there would be no help for it.

At last there came a little singing in the rigging; the single jib filled and drew, and life came back into the schooner. Then, after one minute of easy riding, the typhoon struck. In a split second the singing in the rigging mounted to a loud, high-pitched, angry shriek. The schooner leapt and quivered: for one moment she seemed to be staggered by the blow, but the next she was racing before it. Huge seas towered behind her, threatening to poop her at any second, but she fled before them unscathed.

Sullivan plunged head-first into the saloon, followed by a sheet of spray.

"What's it like on deck, Uncle?" asked Derrick.

"Pretty tough," gasped Sullivan. "Not what you would choose for a Sunday-school outing."

"Are we in the storm-centre?"

"I think so. Not far from it, anyhow. You're not worried, are you?" he asked, with a kind smile.

"No," said Derrick, going red.

"Well, I wouldn't blame you if you were. I was, in my first big blow. I went pea-green. But then I was in a Portuguese tramp." He had to shout to make himself heard. "That was a different kettle of fish: feel how this old crate rides, and look at the give in her."

The *Wanderer* lifted to a monstrous sea, standing almost upright on her stern; she twisted and thrust like a living creature. "Look here," shouted Sullivan, pointing to the angle of the bulkhead. The joint between two thick timbers opened and closed an inch at a time. "Teak and ironwood," he said, "with oak backbone and knees. She was made to give so. She can whip anything made of metal." He patted the wood, wedged himself into a bunk, and in two minutes he was asleep.

Derrick, clinging precariously to his seat, watched him with astonishment. An enormous din pervaded the whole space; the ship was being hurled about like a chip in a mill-stream, but still Sullivan slept on, braced against the pitching and the corkscrew roll. Derrick had always wondered at his uncle's ability to snatch a spell of sleep at odd moments, but never so much as now.

The time passed, lost in the prodigious hullabaloo: Derrick hardly noticed that the hands of the clock had crept on and on. He had been rather alarmed: the word typhoon has a very ugly ring in the China Seas, but the sight of his uncle sleeping there, even more than his reassuring words, was wonderfully comforting. Now Derrick could concentrate on gathering the various objects that had broken loose from their fastenings and stowing them away, rather than on the dozens of stories that he had heard of ships lost without a trace—and he could stop thinking about the tiger-shark under the *Wanderer*'s stern.

Suddenly, above the steady roar, there was a report like the firing of a gun. At once Sullivan was awake. "That would be the jib," he said, forcing his way through the wind-locked door. "Stay where you are."

Derrick listening intently, fancied that he heard a change in the voice of the typhoon after some minutes; there seemed to be a shriller note in it, louder and more savage.

.A solid mass of water shot into the saloon as Sullivan staggered in with Olaf over his shoulder. "Lash him into a bunk," he shouted, "and get into oilskins." He disappeared. Derrick lugged Olaf to the bunk, waited for the *Wanderer* to roll, and slid him into it. He took off the Swede's dripping clothes, covered him with a rug and lashed him into the bunk with a dozen turns of a rope. Olaf was unconscious; his shoulder hung strangely, and there was a streaming gash on his forehead. Derrick did the best he could with the sleeve of a shirt by way of a bandage, and hurried into his oilskins and sea-boots. He was hardly ready before Sullivan came down again.

"All fixed, Derrick?" he asked, looking at Olaf. "Ready? Good. You'll have to give me a hand on deck. Olaf will be all right—collarbone, that's all, and a bang on the head. Now listen, we've got to clear away the wreckage of the deck-house. There's a lot of rigging loose, so watch your step. Hang on to the hand-line all the time, and watch for the green seas.

24

Look out for yourself, and don't let go the hand-line."

Derrick nodded. His heart was beating violently. Sullivan handed him an axe, and they went on deck. The moment Derrick left the shelter of the companion-way the wind knocked him clean off his feet, but the hand-line brought him up. The shrieking air was full of flying water: he could hardly see or breathe. Following his uncle along the hand-line he made his way for'ard. They came to the wreckage: it had been stove in by a piece of driftwood, and some of the timbers were pounding furiously. It was plain that they must be cleared at once, before they could spring the deck planking.

Derrick cleared some of the smaller debris: the moment it was free it shot away, carried by the wind. He came to a thick rope, a fallen shroud that held two heavy timbers threshing against the deck. He hacked and hacked at it, but it would not part: he could not hit it square. He let go of the hand-line, held the shroud with one hand and cut at it with the other. At the same moment a heavy sea broke over the stern, a wall of green water swept along the deck, caught Derrick as he cut through the rope and shot him along the deck. He found himself under a cloud of spray, with his back against the capstan. He was still holding the end of the severed shroud. The spray cleared: he saw that he was still alive, but immediately another surge of water buried him. He held tight, snatched a breath of air as the water poured over the *Wanderer*'s bows, and began to work his way aft. Then, as suddenly as he had been swept for'ard, he was swept back: the *Wanderer* was climbing the back of a huge wave, with her nose pointing at the sky, and the water on the fo'c'sle surged back and carried him with it. He was among the wreckage again almost before his going had been seen. He took a turn about the hand-line and went on cutting the loose wood free.

Again and again the great following seas smashed over the schooner's stern, and each time she wallowed under a sheet of water and spray. But each time, after the spray had half drowned them, she would rise, the water shooting from her scuppers, lighten herself and speed on. Derrick grew used to the rhythm of it: he would see the sweep of water out of the corner of his eye as he worked, hang on, hold his breath and crouch until it had passed. At last, as he emerged from a welter of spray, he saw that the whole of the wreckage had been swept away, and his uncle, on the other side of the deck, was pointing aft. Bent double against the furious blast they clawed their way along: they passed Ross and one of the Malays, lashed to the wheel. Derrick, held motionless by the wind, noticed that the big Scotsman had his useless pipe clenched in his teeth, and that he was grinning. Derrick had never seen him looking so cheerful before. Usually he wore a solemn, dour face, but now he had the uplifted expression of a man in a winning fight. He nodded to Derrick, and shouted with all the force of his lungs; but Derrick, who was within a yard of him, only saw his mouth open and close.

Once they were below it seemed that they had passed from one world to another. The relief from the immense noise and the strain made the saloon feel like a peaceful, silent parlour on dry land. Derrick sank down and savoured the delight of breathing air that was not mixed with sea: he suddenly felt extremely weak. His uncle was speaking to him, shouting, but he could not hear, and he found that the infernal howling on deck had deafened him. Sullivan helped him off with his oilskins, pointed to a bunk, to the clock, held up four fingers, and went.

By the madly swaying light Derrick saw that the clock said half-past two. "It can't be right," he thought. "It must be . . ." but before he could even finish the thought he was asleep.

"It's not half-past two," he exclaimed, waking suddenly, as someone shook him by the arm.

"No," said Li Han, "this person did not suggest it was."

After hours of labour Li Han had managed to get a fire going in the galley, and the steaming mug of cocoa that he held out to Derrick was the result of his efforts. Derrick collected his wits as he sipped the sweet, scalding liquid. He felt horribly sore and stiff all over, as if he had been put through a clothes-wringer. There was a deep gash on the back of his left hand—he had never noticed it at the time—and one of his front teeth was gone. But the cocoa was wonderfully good: he had never liked the stuff before, but now it sent down a flood of warmth into him.

27

"Gee, that's good cocoa, Li Han," he said, "you are a swell guy."

"Is approximately one-half rum," replied Li Han, refilling the mug for Olaf. "Other half mostly Yellow Sea."

"That's a good sea-cook," said Olaf, thoughtfully, after Li Han had gone. "Although he's only a poor heathen."

"What's happened?" asked Derrick, suddenly aware of a change in the ship's motion.

"The Old Man put her about at dawn. We're riding it out now."

Derrick hurried on deck. "You take care," shouted Olaf after him, "this ain't no day for a swim."

He saw at once that the worst was over. There was still a huge sea running, and the wind was a full gale, but it was nothing to what it had been, and the *Wanderer* was riding it out with a high and buoyant ease.

But the deck was a dismal sight. The ordinarily trim expanse of holy-stoned wood was a tangle of ropes and cordage, broken spars and storm-wrack: a gaping hole showed where the davits had torn out, and the deck-house was gone entirely.

His uncle was at the wheel now, and Derrick shouted in his ear, "It was a proper typhoon, wasn't it?"

"No, only a little one," said Sullivan.

"But we passed through the storm-centre, didn't we?" asked Derrick, in a disappointed bellow.

"No. Nothing like it. We skirted the edge after all.

28

Now if you've done with admiring the view, go for'ard and bear a hand."

Derrick hurried along the deck as fast as his aches and bruises would let him. To a landman's eye the ship looked derelict, but in fact everything was well in hand. The Malays were at the pumps, and Ross was reeving new halliards: already the essential had been done, but it needed a more experienced eye than Derrick's to know it.

"Good morning, lad," said Ross, as Derrick came up. "Are you fit for a spell of hard labour now?"

"Well, sir, I think I could manage a little gentle exercise," said Derrick, grinning.

"Very good. Then just take a wee look at the shrouds and ratlines yonder, where the spar tore through them. See if you can set that to rights."

"But—" gasped Derrick, with his smile fading as he gazed up into the endless tangle.

"Och, lad, I can see you need a few years of schooling. A sailor would have set about that in no time. Ah weel, I'd best do it myself."

"No, no. I just meant I was wondering where to begin."

"Humph. The best plan is to begin at the beginning and go on until you come to the end."

Derrick swung himself up and started at the nearest dead-eye. "I'll show him," he muttered, jabbing away with a marlin-spike. It was a difficult, tedious job, and Ross knew it well: he was testing the boy. Piece by piece Derrick unravelled the tangle, and presently the ratlines began to assume a reasonable shape. The wind was blowing itself out, and by noon it was easier to work. They ate, enormously, at midday, and after the meal Derrick came on deck again, surveyed his work with satisfaction, and was just beginning to start on the frapping when there was the cry of a sail on the port bow.

"She looks to me like the remains of a junk," said Ross, focusing his glasses.

The *Wanderer* came about on the other tack, and soon they were within hail of the junk. No answer came from her as she wallowed in the dying swell: her decks were awash, and she had been battered almost out of recognition. The high poop had been completely torn away, and only a gaping hole showed where the main-mast had been wrenched bodily out of her.

"There's no one alive on board," said Sullivan, scanning her ravaged decks. "She'll not last the day."

The derelict rose and fell: each time she vanished into the trough of a wave it seemed impossible that she should reappear, but she did, time and time again.

"There's something moving in her bows," cried Derrick, from the rigging. "I saw it twice."

Lowering the only boat that had survived was a tricky job, but there was no broken water, and they managed it. Ross and the old Malay stayed in the boat while Derrick stepped aboard the junk: she was so low in the water that he did not have to climb.

"Look lively, boy," cried Ross. "She'll be going any minute now."

30

In the bows Derrick found a drowned Chinese sailor and a living dog. It was very weak; it could only just move, but it growled and snapped as Derrick shifted the broken planks to reach it. It was a large dog, rather of the build of a mastiff, but with longer legs and a shaggy yellow coat: a thick leather thong held it to the deck. As Derrick tried to cut it free, the dog turned and sunk its teeth into his hand.

"Oh, you—," cried Derrick, remembering some of Olaf's choicer words. He clouted it and cut through the leather. The dog made as if to stand, but it could not. Derrick grabbed it by the scruff, dragged it to the broken gunwale and dropped it into the boat, where it lay snarling.

"That's all it was that was moving, sir," he said to Ross. "I'm afraid the man was dead."

"Humph," said Ross, eyeing the dog.

"Well, that's a fine bit of salvage," said Sullivan, when Derrick hauled it aboard the schooner. "A measly pie-dog. And a yellow one with the mange at that."

Li Han came up from the galley and looked at the dripping beast. "Animal of small value," he said, having considered it from all angles. "Of no value at present, but might furnish succulent stew if fattened."

"That ain't no dog," said Olaf. "That's an infant dromedary, that is."

"You'd better disinfect your hand, Derrick, and sling the pie-dog overboard. I doubt if it would live, anyway."

"Och, I don't know," said Ross, who felt partially responsible for the dog, "the poor beastie might recover."

"Can't we give him a chance, Uncle?" asked Derrick. "I don't think he's a pie-dog—his tail doesn't curl." The water-logged creature seemed to know that they were discussing him: he looked from one to another with a mournful countenance, and wheezed.

"Well, it's your dog by rights," said Sullivan, "and if you think he will be any good, keep him by all means. You'll catch rabies and mange from him, of course, but you won't be able to say that I didn't warn you when you start running about foaming at the mouth and biting people."

Derrick took the dog and stowed it in the chain-locker. It feebly tried to bite, but it swallowed a little food from the dish he brought.

The next morning, when Derrick went to feed it, the dog was on its feet. It backed into the locker, growling continuously, with its hackles up, but it did not go for him or bite when he put the dish down. It was days before it would come out of the locker at all, and even then it would only dart out to eat voraciously, glaring suspiciously from its dish before it backed quickly away into the shadows. For a long while there was far too much to do on board the *Wanderer* for Derrick to spend much time with the dog, or to think of it very often. There were ropes in plenty to splice, new sails to bend, all the shambles left by deck-house to repair and a hundred other jobs before the *Wanderer* looked anything like her old trim self again. But there was plenty of time for all this work, for the typhoon had blown the schooner a great way off her course, and then for days and days on end the wind blew steadily from the west, so that with all her fine sailing powers the *Wanderer* could not make up the distance lost.

It was after a long day's work with a paint-brush, slung over the side in a bosun's chair, that Derrick noticed for the first time that the dog seemed pleased to see him. It moved its tail uncertainly from side to side and came half out of the locker as he approached. It looked like a dog that had never been treated kindly enough to have learnt how to wag its tail or how to express pleasure, and it was still almost sure that it was going to be kicked or beaten.

Then, a day or two after that, when there was at last time for a make and mend, when Derrick was squatting on the deck, repairing the heel of a sea-boot stocking, he saw the dog slowly creeping towards him, stopping, going back, creeping on, gradually approaching nearer and nearer: he took no notice, but went on darning, and at last he felt a hesitant nose touch his elbow. The dog was standing there, looking sheepish, wriggling all over, grinning hideously, and in two minds whether to run or stay. He talked to it quietly for a long time, and gave it a name. "Chang, Chang," he said, slowly putting his hand over its head: Chang looked frightened for a moment, but as Derrick patted it it lay down and eventually went to sleep at his feet. After that it suddenly began to advance in friendliness, and by the time they came in sight of land the dog followed him wherever he went. Chang was a large dog, a very large dog, and now that at last he had found a human being who would treat him decently, his pleasure was larger than the pleasure of most dogs; he kept as close to Derrick as his own shadow, and attached himself to him as only a dog can.

And even before they had made their landfall and were working up the coast towards Tchao-King, the others had withdrawn their unkind remarks about Chang.

"It seems to me, young Derrick," said his uncle, "that you might make something out of that object, after all." He inspected the dog as it stood at Derrick's heel, and suddenly he made a quick swipe with his hand, as if to clout his nephew's ear: at the same moment he sprang backwards, but it was too late. Chang had pinned his white duck trousers, and there was a tear from knee to ankle: the dog stood there, bristling with fury, but waiting for a word from Derrick to go in and kill the aggressor.

"No, no, don't be angry with him," said Sullivan. "That's just what he should have done. Only I wish he hadn't done it quite so quickly."

And Olaf said, "Ay reckon they was all wrong about this so-called pie-dog of yours, eh? Ay said at the time, that's something like a dog, that is, Ay said. Ay ban't so sure it ain't some kind of a special breed, at that."

Only Li Han was still of the same opinion. "Animal is becoming a little fatter," he said. "Yes: soon adequately obese now. Very succulent stew, he will make, very nourishing; and dog-chops, almost the same as chow, for the feast of the Lotus Flowers, very savoury, very unctious."

Two

ALL the way along the coast they met with calms or contrary winds, and the *Wanderer*, instead of the two hundred and seventy miles which she had logged in the first day and night after leaving Kwei Hai, now crept along, making no more than ten sea miles for a long day's arduous tacking. Sullivan was particularly worried about their meeting with Professor Ayrton. "When I wrote," he said, "I underlined the words 'God willing and wind and tide permitting,' but I don't know whether he will understand the kind of winds that we have been having—and even if he does understand, I am not sure whether he will be able to wait. At this rate we shan't make Tchao-King before Christmas. Derrick, go on deck and try whistling for a spell, will you?"

Derrick whistled. Olaf whistled. Li Han beat a gong and the Malays sang their wind-song: Chang howled: but still the sails flapped idly, and far away on the starboard quarter a small junk which had been in sight since dawn came nearer and nearer, propelled by the immense sweeps that her sweating crew pulled to the sound of conchs and drums. "Ay wish my old grandma was here," said Olaf, pausing for breath.

"She'd blow us to Frisco if we was to ask her polite. If the Old Man was to go to her and tip his hat and say, 'Good morning, marm,' or 'Good afternoon,' as the case might be—"

"You don't suppose that's a pirate, do you, Olaf?" interrupted Derrick.

Olaf stared at the junk. "Could be," he said, indifferently, shading his eyes. "They come like wasps after honey along this coast. But they won't meddle with us, not unless they was three, four war junks all together. They tried that once, only two of them, off Tai-nan." He laughed reminiscently. "They won't meddle with the *Wanderer* no more. No *sir*. Besides," he added, "there's that destroyer on the horizon."

"What destroyer?"

"Ain't you got no eyes?" asked Olaf, impatiently, as he pointed to the northwest. Derrick made out a low smudge that might have been smoke.

"How do you know it's a destroyer?" he asked.

"How do I know that's my hand in front of my face? Ay look at it, see? Ay got eyes, see? Of course she ban a destroyer, U.S.N., and she's bound for Manila."

The day wore on, a hot and sticky day without a breath of wind: Derrick sat in the shade of the mainsail, trying to comb Chang's coat into something like respectability. He was an ugly dog, it could not be denied; and if anything the combing made his appearance worse. He had enormous feet, and from his feet and his clumsiness Derrick judged that he was not nearly fully grown: Chang already weighed a good fifty pounds, and if he went on filling out he would soon be more like a lion than a dog. Derrick looked up from his hopeless task, and saw the destroyer bearing down on them. Olaf had been quite right: she was an American destroyer, belching smoke from her four funnels and cutting a great furrow through the oily sea with her high bows. The junk far behind had turned long ago, and was now creeping painfully over the horizon, still sweeping arduously.

"What ship?" hailed the destroyer. "Where bound?"

"Schooner *Wanderer*," answered Sullivan, his great voice roaring over the water. "Thirty days out of Macao for Tchao-King."

"What ship?"

"Schooner *Wanderer*, Terence Sullivan master," he answered louder still.

The destroyer made a sharp turn to port and came alongside. "Captain Sullivan, I've got a message for you," hailed the officer on deck. "It reads, 'Ayrton at Tchao-King to Sullivan, schooner *Wanderer*: am waiting at Tchao-King until 31st, then moving to Peking by way of Tsi-nan.' Have you got that?"

"Yes, thank you very much."

"You missed the typhoon, then?" asked the officer, looking curiously down at the gleaming, orderly decks and the spotless canvas.

"We had a little blow," said Sullivan. "Do you want to pick up a pirate junk? There's one bearing south by east, just about hull-down at this minute. A gentleman by the name of Wu San-kwei, by the cut of his jib."

There was the sound of a bell inside the destroyer, her screws whirled into violent life, and she shot off in a great curve, leaving the *Wanderer* rocking in her spreading wake.

"Perambulating kitchen-stove," said Ross, who had just come up from the hold. "Why don't they clean their flues, or at least lie to leeward of a real ship?" He looked indignantly at the sails, grey from the destroyer's smoke.

"She brought us a message from Tchao-King," said Sullivan. "Professor Ayrton will be there until the end of the month."

"Well, perhaps there's some good in the navy yet," said Ross, looking pleased. "Did you tell her about Wu San-kwei? He's got a nerve, coming out after us with no more than a couple of brass nine-pounders: he must have lost what few wits he had."

The message was particularly welcome. Sullivan had been fretting for weeks about the appointment, but now he knew that even if they made no better pace than they had for the last few days, they would reach the port in time. In the evening he harked back to a subject that he had already discussed quite often. "Now listen, Derrick," he said. "We want you to make a good impression on Professor Ayrton. Get Li Han to cut your hair in the morning."

"Okay," said Derrick.

"And don't say okay."

"Gee, Uncle Terry. . . ."

"And don't say gee," said Ross.

"We don't want him to get the idea that we have made a barbarian of you. You must brush your nails, and you must not eat with your clasp-knife. Have you got any gum?"

"Yes, sir."

"Then toss it overboard. I know what they think of gum at Oxford. And try to look intelligent."

"Like this?"

"No. Not like that. No, perhaps you had better forget that: we don't want him to think you're sickening for something."

Just before dawn all the whistling for a wind had its effect, and by the time that Derrick was sitting in the galley having his hair cut, the *Wanderer* was racing along under all canvas, leaning from the wind so that with every thrust from the following sea her lee rails vanished under the flying spray. The chair slid on the canted deck, and the hair-cutting had proved a tedious and difficult operation.

"Hope results of Western-style hair-dressing satisfactory," said Li Han, anxiously. "Should not have made bald patch or cut ear, however. Please excuse."

"Oh, it's okay," said Derrick, mopping his bloody ear with his handkerchief. "You're a swell barber, Li Han."

"Don't say okay," roared a distant voice.

"Why not say okay?" whispered Li Han.

"Because of my cousin, the one we are going to meet at Tchao-King. It seems that he wouldn't like it. Li Han, do you know what an archaeologist is?"

39

"Archaeology is disinterment of ancient fragments," replied Li Han, promptly, "and piecing of same together to form harmonious whole. Very learned pursuit."

"That's what my cousin does. He's a professor of it."

"Your cousin a professor?" asked Li Han, in an unbelieving tone.

"Yes, of course he is. Haven't you heard them talking about Professor Ayrton?"

"Is the same honourable person?" Li Han dropped his scissors. "Excuse please. Would never have cut ear. . . ."

He was obviously deeply impressed, and he at once opened a can of lichees for Derrick. "Such face," he murmured. "Such estimable learning. Such dignity."

"How would you make a good impression on an archaeologist?" asked Derrick, after thinking for some time.

"Display intelligent interest, and ask acute ancient questions."

"Could you give me an acute question to ask him, Li Han? Just one or two really swell questions that will show him that I've already had enough education."

"Not knowing, cannot say. Regret lamentable ignorance."

"Now you're really useful, aren't you, Li Han?" said Derrick, bitterly. "You mean to say you don't know a thing about archaeology, and you a sea-cook? Some of your hashes have been pretty ancient fragments, all

40

right. You ought to know the subject backwards."

"If I had inestimable privilege of serving worthy learned gentleman," said Li Han, with a sigh, "or even of beholding erudite face, it would be different. But, alas, sea-cook confined to maritime tossing existence is condemned to dog-like ignorance."

"Olaf," said Derrick, going for'ard to where the Swede was sitting on the well-deck, tying a beautiful turk's-head at the end of a short length of rope, "Olaf, if you wanted to impress an archaeologist, how would you set about it? I want some right good advice, now."

The big Swede scratched his head and closed his eyes with the effort of thinking. "Well," he said at last. "Impress, eh? An archaeologist, huh? Well, Ay reckon Ay would strike him just behind the shoulder with a twenty-four pound harpoon. Strike hard and fast, not too far back, see? My old man, he chanced on one of them things northeast of Spitzbergen in the fall of, lemme t'ink, 1897 was it, or 1898? Yes, Ay reckon it was 1898. It chawed up his long-boat something horrible, but they got fifty-three barrels of oil out of it."

"Olaf, you're wrong. An archaeologist is a person who digs for ancient things."

"No. Ay ain't mistaken, son. It's a fish, it is, rather smaller nor a fin-whale, but mighty dangerous, and you don't want to strike it too far back."

"Well, I've got to make a good impression on one, anyway."

"Hum. You watch your step, then. This one Ay talk about, he chawed up a long-boat, like I told you.

41

Chawed it up," he repeated, gnashing his jaws, "just like that."

"What's that rope's-end for, Olaf?" asked Derrick, changing the subject.

"That's for you, son," said Olaf, with a happy smile. "The Old Man, he told me to pick out a nice whippy piece. 'Put a right good knot in it, Olaf,' he says. 'I'll learn the young—to talk proper,' he says."

"Is that what Uncle Terry said, Olaf?" asked Derrick, turning pale.

"His very words. 'I'll larrup him,' he says. 'I'll learn him to talk barbarious,' he says. 'And when I'm tired, you can take over, Olaf,' he says. He's going to lay into you like blue murder every time you say gee or okay," said Olaf, heartlessly tightening the knot.

"Why, gee, Olaf, what am I to say?" cried Derrick, appalled.

"Well, you can say dearie me, or land's sake—no, not land's sake; that's low. But you could say cor stone the crows. That's English. I shipped along with a whole crew of Limeys oncet, and they all said cor stone the crows. There was this German submarine, see? Surfaced off Ushant and shelled us. 'Cor stone the crows,' said the Limeys, particularly the Old Man, who was hit by a splinter on the nose. Then Ay rammed the—and the Limeys all stood along the side and said, 'Cor stone the crows, Olaf's rammed the—.'"

"I never knew you had rammed a submarine, Olaf."

"Oh, it was just luck that time," said Olaf, modestly. "The other ones was more difficult."

"You must have been quite a hero in the war, Olaf. Did they give you any medals?"

"Oh, no. They wanted to make me an earl or a duke or something, but Ay never was one for falals or doo-dads, see?"

"Cor stone the crows," said Derrick.

The *Wanderer* flew on, and the next day at noon she raised the high cape of Tchao-King, by the evening she had threaded her way through the junks and the sampans to the inner harbour, and she was tied up at the wharf of the Benign Wind-Dragon, by the European godowns.

Derrick was standing in the saloon in a high state of preparedness, brushed, gleaming and nervous. His uncle gave him a final inspection, and said, "It's a pity you look as if you had the mange, but otherwise your rig is trim enough. Have you tied up that monstrous beast?"

"Yes, sir," answered Derrick, who could hear Chang's desperate scratching at the closed hatch: he noticed that his uncle had dressed with more than usual care, and that Ross, huge and splendid in his best shore-going ducks, was nervous too.

"I feel just like a nursemaid who's got to display her charge to a crew of critical relations," said Sullivan, fingering Derrick's tie. "You won't behave like a roughneck shell-back, will you? Or go roaring about as if we were in a gale of wind? Or hurl the soup down your shirt?"

"Perhaps it would be better if Derrick were not to keep his mouth ajar," suggested Ross. "He might look brighter with it closed. More intelligent."

"Yes, it looks better closed," said Sullivan, looking anxiously at his nephew. "Now the great thing to remember is not to be nervous, Derrick," he added, leading the way on deck.

The three rickshas threaded their way through the bullock-carts, wheelbarrows and ancient lorries that crowded the streets of Tchao-King: they went slowly, for it was a market-day as well as the feast of Pong Hsiu, but they went too fast for Derrick, and when he arrived at the steps of the Kylin Hotel he felt that he would rather go for a swim with a tiger-shark than face the remainder of the evening.

Yet a few hours later, when their dinner was done and they were all sitting in long cane chairs on the verandah, he was talking away to Professor Ayrton as if he had known him all his life. His cousin turned out to be a tall, thin, frail-looking man, far older than Sullivan and Ross, with a face the colour of yellowed parchment and a somewhat Chinese cast of countenance that was accentuated by the large, horn-rimmed spectacles that he wore. If he had been dressed in a robe rather than a very old tweed jacket and a pair of disreputable flannel trousers he might have passed for a north-Chinese scholar. He had a thoroughly benign face that entirely matched his kind way of speaking: he was as unlike a tiger-shark as could be imagined, and he completely won Derrick's friendship by wel-

44

coming Chang, who appeared ten minutes after their arrival, still dripping wet and trailing his broken leash. Chang did not behave as well as Derrick could have wished: the porter tried to keep him out, but was utterly routed; as Chang blundered at full speed down the long verandah he bowled over one waiter and two low tables, and when he reached them it was instantly apparent that he had been swimming in the horribly malodorous waters of the harbour.

"Never mind, never mind," cried Professor Ayrton, as Derrick tried to induce Chang to go quietly away. "Let him stay. I should like him to stay very much. He looks a most interesting creature." He put out his long, thin hand to pat Chang's head, and with a thrill of horror Derrick thought that Chang would have it off: hitherto no one had touched Chang without bloodshed, except Derrick. But Chang only looked amazed, then rather pleased, and finally he put a large and muddy paw on the Professor's knee. "You're a fine fellow," said Professor Ayrton, addressing the dog and pulling his ears. "You are a—what is the term? A bum pooch. I am sure you are a very swollen guy, and we shall be great budlets." He turned to Derrick. "I have been learning some Americanisms," he said, "to make you feel at home."

Derrick burst into a wild laugh that he tried to disguise as a cough. "Uncle Terry has been laying for me with a rope's end if I said so much as okay," he said, wiping his eyes when he could speak again. "Gee, sir, I certainly never thought I should hear you call Chang a swell guy."

"Swollen, my dear boy. Swollen, or perhaps swelled. In the adjectival use we must employ the past participle, must we not?"

"Yet it seems to me that I have heard the expression swell guy," observed Ross.

"Have you indeed? Perhaps it was some local variant—an elision of the terminal -ed? But I am persuaded that the general usage is swollen. I cannot cite the text of my authority at the moment, but I flatter myself that on this question I am an unusually hep cat. There were several American novels in the boat, and on the way over I perused them diligently: there was an American, a most respectable scholar from Harvard, who assured me that I had a greater command of these idioms than he had himself—indeed, that he had never even heard of some of them. It is a fascinating spectacle, don't you think, Captain Sullivan, this development of a new language? I am no enemy to neologisms, and although I am no philologist it gives me a feeling of intense excitement to see an old language renewed and enriched by countless striking and even poetic expressions. There was an elderly gentlewoman on the boat, from some provincial town in the States—I believe it was Chicago—who referred to the Atlantic, which she had recently traversed, as 'the herring-pond'. I was so moved by the noble simplicity of her remark that I noted it down in my diary that evening."

"Well, Professor, I must say that it had never struck me quite that way. But you wouldn't have him chewing gum and addressing you as 'Hi, Prof,' surely?"

"Were the young man to address me as Prof, he would speedily learn the difference between liberty and licence," said Professor Ayrton. "But as for chewing-gum, for my part I find it a great help to meditation—I almost said to rumination—and an excellent substitute for nicotine. Allow me to offer you a piece."

The Professor was a very agreeable relative to find after such dismal forebodings, and Derrick liked him very much; but he was adamant on the need for school. He thoroughly-sympathised with Derrick's longing to go to sea, and he entirely approved of the *Wanderer*, which he visited for dinner the next day—a dinner that an emperor might have admired, so hard had Li Han and three imported cook-boys laboured in the galley—but although he said nothing definite for quite a long time, Derrick felt sure that he had made up his mind. The Professor was closeted with Ross and Sullivan for days on end, and Derrick began to hope against hope that these long, unusual absences might mean that his uncle was putting up a lively opposition.

But in the end Derrick was summoned to the presence, and Professor Ayrton addressed him in these words: "My boy, we have been discussing your future, and your uncle, Mr. Ross and I have all come to the same conclusion. We are all agreed that school is necessary." Sullivan nodded, and the Professor continued,

"We feel that although for training in seamanship the *Wanderer* could hardly be improved upon, yet nevertheless you should not be loosed upon the world without a firm grounding of more general instruction. You may not suppose that a helmsman would steer any the better for being able to decline *gubernator,* but you are young, and absurd as it may seem to you now, you will find in time that such is the case."

Derrick did his best to smile, for he knew that the Professor meant this as a joke to take away the sting of his decision.

"You will always be able to come back to the *Wanderer* when it is all over," said Sullivan.

"Aye," said Ross, in a comforting tone, "you'll come back with a dozen new-fangled modern ways of sinking a ship, and we'll have them out of you with a rope's end in a week."

"Furthermore," said the Professor, "I intend, with your uncle's consent, to gild the pill of education by a suggestion that may be new to you. How would you like to go to the school by way of Samarcand?"

Three

"SAMARCAND," said Derrick. "Do you know where it is, Olaf?"

"Samarcand? That ain't no port," replied Olaf. "But I heard of it. Samarcand, that's where the Old Man left his fingers. It's somewhere inland."

"Was that where it happened?" asked Derrick. His

uncle lacked two fingers of his left hand, and Derrick had never been able to get him to say how it had come about. "How did he come to lose them, Olaf?"

"Oh, Ay don't know," said Olaf, evasively. "Didn't he tell you?"

"No. I asked him, but getting a yarn out of Uncle Terry is like trying to open an oyster with a bent pin. Were you there, or did he tell you about it?"

"No. Ay hear about it some place or other. And don't you let on, eh? Or the Old Man would break my neck."

"Samarcand?" said Li Han. "It is beyond utmost limits of Sinkiang, in the barbarous regions. Why you ask, please?"

"I'm going there."

"In company of learned Professor?"

"Yes."

"What felicity," said Li Han. "In pursuit of learning would traverse the Outer Wastes with singing heart."

"I'll be pursuing learning, all right. Samarcand is the first stop on the way to school, and the Professor said that he would initiate me into the delights of Greek during the long, peaceful days between here and there. And Mr. Ross will go on teaching me trigonometry and navigation." But in spite of these drawbacks, Derrick was boiling with excitement at the thought of the expedition.

"Mr. Ross going too?" asked Li Han.

"Yes, and my uncle."

"What felicity," repeated Li Han, in a thoughtful tone.

"Then they lay up the *Wanderer*, eh?" said. Olaf. "Maybe Ay better ship with Knut Lavrenssen in the *Varanger*. She ban laying at Pei-Ho." He spoke regretfully.

"Why don't you come too?" suggested Derrick. "Men have to be fed, even in barbarian regions, Li Han."

Li Han smiled, bowed, and rubbed his hands. "Wretched sea-cook too humble to ask," he said, "but would voluntarily dispense with wages for privilege of accompanying worthy philosopher—and juvenile seafaring friend," he added, bowing to Derrick.

"I'll ask for you," said Derrick.

Li Han grinned and bowed repeatedly. "Suggest wily approach," he said, in an agitated voice that betrayed his extreme eagerness. "Perhaps gifts of red silk, piece of first-chop jade? Sumptuous repast for learned Professor, and question popped with dish of rice-birds? Will devote entire savings to purchase of same."

"What could Ay do?" asked Olaf, disconsolately. "Ay ban no good by land."

"You can ride horses and camels, can't you?"

"Horses, eh?" Olaf scratched his head. "They steer by a tiller to the head-piece for'ard, ain't it? But camels, no. Ay reckon camels is out. Ay had a camel once, with a hump."

"You had a camel, Olaf?"

"Sure Ay had a camel. One camel with one hump. A

50

hump like that . . ." he sketched a mountain in the air with his finger.

"How did you come by it?"

"Well, it was peculiar, see? We was in Port Said— Ay was shipped aboard a Panamanian tanker then— and Ay went ashore to get me a drink. Ay was thirsty, because it was hot, see? Ay reckon it was the sun that done it, or maybe the night air. Or maybe it was the tinned crab, but anyways, Ay wake up on the quay with no clothes on and a camel. One camel. Least-ways, there was a rope in my hand, and when Ay haul on it, Ay find this camel the other end. So Ay coax the camel aboard the tanker and go to sleep. Oh, they was joyful to find my camel in the morning. It bit the mate in five places. It clomb into the bridge. It fouled the steering-gear. Then it bit the master in the calf, although he was a Portuguee. Ay had to pay a coal-black Jew from the Yemen four piastres and a Straits dollar to take it off at Bahrein, but even then the master, he put me off at Muscat. Marooned me, see? And Ay sat on the shore without my dunnage waiting for a ship three months. No, Ay don't want nothing to do with no camels."

Before Derrick knew anything about it, it had been settled. The Professor spread out the map. "This, then," he said, making a dotted line with his pencil, "is our proposed route. We follow the Old Silk Road through the Gobi, travel north of Kunlun range, skirting Tibet, north of the Karakoram and the

Pamirs, and so to Samarcand. Of course, we shall make several detours on the way, as there is a mass of untouched archaeological material waiting to be discovered. Imagine the importance of the Buddhist frescoes that the elder Ssu-ma describes, or the repository of jade objects mentioned by the Pandit Rajasthana . . . dear me, it makes me feel quite pale to think of it."

"I am afraid you will have to go south of the Kara Nor," said Sullivan, looking at. the map. "There is a huge swamp that is not shown on the map—the whole region is very badly mapped—and that will mean an extra three days. But that is better than getting stuck in the middle."

"How glad I am," said the Professor, eagerly correcting the line. "How glad I am to have the benefit of your advice. I am new to this part of the world, you know, and if I were to have to make all the practical arrangements I should probably be unsuccessful. Besides, it would leave me very little time for archaeological work. But are you sure that you can spare the time and the energy? I am more than happy to avail myself of your kindness, for my knowledge of such things as transport is largely theoretical, but I do not wish to impose myself upon you."

"Oh, we will be able to manage that side of it quite easily, don't you think, Ross?"

"Aye. So long as there will be none of this modern business —caterpillar tractors, wireless and an army of porters. If we travel as the Mongols have travelled these thousand years and more, we'll get there twice as soon and at a hundredth part of the cost."

"I quite agree with you, Mr. Ross," said Professor Ayrton. "It would be much better in every way. I can almost picture myself riding forth like Genghis Khan and the Golden Horde already, making the steppe tremble under my horse's feet."

"There is one thing that I think I should mention, Professor," said Sullivan, "and that is that this route leads through some very troubled country. The warlords are always at it hammer and tongs on the Mongolian border, and farther on there might be all kinds of trouble with all manner of people who are having little private wars."

"Oh, yes," replied the Professor, "I have read about it; but surely a peaceful scientific expedition has nothing to fear? The Chinese of my acquaintance are all intensely civilised; in fact, the whole nation seems to me to be most advanced, and I am sure that their influence will make the journey safe for us. And I have all the necessary papers."

"Well . . ." said Sullivan, and Ross said, "Humph," but the Professor was far away already, thinking of the discoveries that he would make in that archaeological paradise.

As Ross and Sullivan walked back to the ship, Sullivan said, "I wonder what kind of an idea Ayrton has of the Astin Tagh? Do you think he imagines a Chinese warlord sits around sipping tea and composing verses to the T'ang Emperors?"

"I'm sure he does. He should not be let out alone."

After a while Sullivan said, "It would be very hard travelling for a man of his age, quite apart from the likelihood of trouble on the way. I believe he thinks it's going to be a kind of picnic, or a country walk where you look for jade images instead of birds' nests. I don't know that we should not stop him."

"We couldn't stop him without tying him up," said Ross. "If we don't go with him he'll go by himself, taking Derrick with him. Or else he'll pick up one of these rascally White Russians, who'll have his throat cut the first day they are out alone in the Shamo Desert. No, we'll get him through safe enough. D'ye not remember how we got that little old Frenchman out of Urga?"

"Yes. That was a close call. I wonder if old Hulagu Khan is still in the Town of the Red Knight? We could do worse than get one or two of his men."

"I was thinking of that too. They are good fighters, those Kokonor Mongols."

"Then I was wondering about Derrick. But perhaps I am making too much of it altogether. He's a tough lad, and anyhow a Mongol boy is reckoned a man at his age."

A few days later Professor Ayrton came aboard the *Wanderer*, and they sailed north along the coast to Tientsin. The voyage was uneventful, with prosperous winds, and the Professor, who had never sailed in anything but a liner before, came to understand their love for the schooner. He watched them for hours at a time, and he asked innumerable questions. Derrick noticed that he never asked the same thing twice, but each time he received a plain, clear answer he listened attentively, nodded his head, and stowed it away into his extraordinary memory, a memory that had never failed at any intellectual task but that of mastering what he fondly imagined to be the idiom of America.

Among other things he astonished them by an adequate, if hardly colloquial, command of literary Chinese, and when Sullivan asked him where he had learnt this most difficult of languages, he replied, "No, I have never been in China before. My life has been very cloistered—from college to museum and back again—but I have been looking forward to this expedition for years, and I thought it wise to make a few preparations."

"You must have the gift of tongues, Professor: managing the Chinese tones is beyond most Europeans, unless they are born to it."

"Och, it runs in the family," said Ross. "Did you never hear young Derrick talking Malay, or using the string of Swedish oaths he has picked up from Olaf?"

"Talking of preparations," said Sullivan, "did you ever think of learning to shoot, Professor? It is a very wild part of the world, you know."

"Shoot? Dear me, I had never thought of that. But I imagine that there will always be some practised person at hand who will be able to shoot all that is necessary for food."

"Food? Oh, yes. I was thinking . . . but it's of no importance," said Sullivan.

At Tientsin they berthed the *Wanderer*, laying her up in a mud-berth in the charge of an ancient ship-keeper whose family had done nothing but keep ships in that particular piece of mud since the time of the Ming emperors. The Malays were paid off, but Li Han and Olaf remained through the days of preparing the ship for her long repose in the mud. They grew more and more despondent as the preparations neared their end, and Derrick remembered uneasily that he had promised to ask whether they could go along with the expedition. He could not very well forget it, because Li Han kept reminding him, either by strong hints or else by unexpected delicacies, a shark's fin, an unusually large sea-slug or a basket of loquats, all of which were intended to spur him on. One day as he was passing the Professor's cabin he suddenly plucked up courage and went in. The Professor was reading: he looked up at Derrick and pushed his spectacles on to his forehead.

"I hope I am not interrupting you, sir," said Derrick.

"Not at all, not at all," placing a small stone seal on the page to mark his place. "No, no, not in the least. What were you saying?"

"I hadn't said anything, sir."

"Then you had better begin, you know. We cannot carry on a conversation if you will not say anything."

"I was thinking of saying—"

"But, my dear boy, do you not see that such a dia-

56

logue would lead to no useful result? We should sit gazing at one another indefinitely. However, now that you are here, let me read you a most interesting account of Shin Mei's travels in the Gobi—he was Ssu-ma's grandson, you know."

"But, Professor—"

"Ah, yes, I know. You are going to say that this has no bearing on the matter. But you are mistaken. It is about the Mongolian fashion of beginning a conversation.

Listen. . . ."

Half an hour later Derrick was still listening.

"There, you see?" said the Professor at last. "Is it not extraordinary that just as I reached that point you should have come in with the intention of beginning a conversation too? Tell me, what was it to be about?"

"I was going to ask if Li Han and Olaf could come on the expedition. Li Han is a very good cook, and he says he would come without any pay for the privilege of cooking for a—for a worthy philosophical scholar. Those were the words he used. But he hasn't the nerve to ask. And Olaf is very keen, too. He is a wonderful seaman. Please could they come, sir?"

"Olaf is the very large person with a voice like a bull in pain, is he not?"

"Yes, that's him."

"That is he, Derrick. And Li Han is the cook. Did he cook our dinner when first I came aboard the *Wanderer*, and all the wonderful meals since?"

57

"Yes, sir. And he can read and write English as well as I can."

"Really, as well as that?"

Derrick went red. "No, I mean—but really, he is very clever. He told me what archaeology was right away, when I asked him."

"Did he, indeed? Do you remember his definition?"

"He said it was disinterment of ancient fragments."

The Professor smiled. "Well, upon my word," he said, "an erudite sea-cook—and such a cook, too. Hotcha," he added, after some thought.

"Hotcha, sir?"

"Yes. Hotcha. It is an expression that denotes vehement approval."

"Then they can come? Oh, gee, Professor, thanks a lot."

"Come? Where?"

"Why, to Samarcand, with us."

"Oh, yes. Of course. You refer to the expedition. I remember now: you mentioned it before. But, my dear boy, that has nothing to do with me, has it? You must suggest your plan to Mr. Ross, or to your uncle. I am sure that he will be delighted. But before you go, let me read you a fascinating passage that I chanced upon this morning." He hunted through the pages and up and down the close-packed columns of Chinese print, but before he could find his place Ross and Sullivan came in.

"Ah, here you are," said Professor Ayrton. "We were just talking about you. Derrick was asking me whether

58

we should not take some of your crew along, and I proposed that he should refer the question to you."

"He was, was he?" said Sullivan. "Derrick, perhaps you will have the kindness to wait for me in the saloon."

As Derrick passed the galley Li Han popped his head out and asked, "Bad news?" Derrick nodded, and rapidly outlined the situation. Li Han passed him a small mat, saying, "Provision against wrath to come."

The wrath came, very quickly, and a great deal of it. Sullivan was a big man, with red hair and blue eyes; but when he was angry he seemed to be a great deal taller, his hair blazed, and his eyes emitted sparks that were very disagreeable to behold. He picked Derrick up by the shoulder with one hand, held him there for some time on a level with his face, then put him down and said quietly, "Listen to me, young fellow. Suppose an ordinary seaman were to go to the owner and say, 'My dear sir, don't you think it would be an excellent idea if the main to'garns'l were struck? It is blowing rather hard.' And then if he were to go to the captain or the mate and say, 'Mr. Mate, the owner would like the main to'garns'l struck,' what do you think the mate would say? If I were the mate, the man wouldn't walk for a week, if he ever walked at all: but in your case, young fellow, I think I can promise you that you won't sit down for a week."

Afterwards, he said: "It may comfort you to know that we were going to take Olaf and Li Han anyway: you can go and tell them, if you like."

Li Han greeted him with an anxious face. "Soothing embrocation?" he said. "A little Tiger Balm? A cup of nourishing tea? Repose the weary frame in this chair."

"Thank you, Li Han, but I think I'll stand up for the moment. You're coming, and so is Olaf. And I heard them say that we shall start for Peking on Thursday morning."

Sullivan and Ross had a strange knack of knowing people in the most unlikely places: Derrick had almost ceased to be astonished when his uncle was greeted with open arms by odd-looking men of all races and colours—there had been the Portuguese monk in Macao, the Dyak chieftain on the Limpong river, the enormously wealthy Armenian merchant in Canton, the one-eyed Ibn Batuta navigating his Arab dhow through the Hainan Strait—but here in Peking he was astonished once more, for instead of leading him to some walled-in, many-courted Chinese house, his uncle stopped at a neat, trim villa that would have looked perfectly in place in the suburbs of Lausanne, but which looked wildly incongruous in the shadow of a pagoda and surrounded on all sides by the upward-curving tiles and dragon-trimmed roofs of its Chinese neighbours. It was a Swiss boarding-house, and Sullivan walked in as if he had known it all his life. It stood just under the walls of the Inner City of Peking, the Tartar City, but once you were inside you found it hard to believe that you were in China at all. Everything, from the meals to the eiderdowns and the

60

shining brass bedsteads, was entirely European. Li Han was immensely impressed, and Derrick suspected him of burning joss sticks in front of the steel-engraving of President McKinley that adorned his room; but this he was never able to prove.

Once they were installed, Ross and Sullivan were busy most of the day with the preparations for the journey, Professor Ayrton spent nearly all his time in the library of a Chinese archaeological society, where he was an honoured guest, and Olaf disappeared into one of the disreputable haunts which sailors always manage to find; Li Han was actively engaged in learning the correct Mandarin dialect of Peking, for he was from Foochow, and he could hardly make himself understood here in the north; so Derrick explored Peking on his own. He would close the green front door behind him, walk down the three whitened steps, and he would instantly find himself in another world, the noisy, smelly world of China, with its hordes of blue-clad people, coolies carrying great loads on a long bamboo pole, barbers operating in the street, dignified citizens being carried past in covered chairs, old men going to fly their kites in the open spaces and young men with little bamboo bird-cages in their hands, walking to air their birds. He would go a few hundred yards through these people, turn to the left through the enormous gate-house, and find himself in a different world again, the world of the Tartar City. Here in the great serais and marketplaces there were far-wandering Persians and Arabs, Mongols of every tribe, Turkis, Uzbegs, Manchus, Tibetans with their fierce mastiffs, as big as Chang, and obviously of the same original breed. There was a continual roar of voices in a hundred languages and dialects, and here a Chinese looked almost as foreign as Derrick did himself: but there were so many strange figures, from the green-turbaned hadjis from Shiraz to the fur-clad Siberians and the Koreans with their white top-hats, that nobody took any notice of him, and he could wander about at his ease. Here, for the first time, he saw the hairy, two-humped camels of Central Asia, the shaggy, nimble ponies of the Kara Altai and the Kirghiz Steppe, and here, for the first time, he saw the Tartars drinking the fermented milk of their mares. His uncle had given him a list of the most important Mongol words, and as he walked about he both memorised them and tried to hear them as they should be said, in the conversation that surrounded him on every side.

But soon the first excitement of discovery died down, and although he had Chang with him all the time, he began to feel lonely, and to long for a companion: he was very glad, therefore, when after their usual prim and orderly breakfast, his uncle said that he had a journey in front of him, and that Derrick could come.

There was an ancient and disreputable Ford outside the boarding-house, and with some surprise Derrick saw his uncle crank it and climb into the driving seat. It seemed a strange vehicle to carry them through the crowded streets of Peking and of the Tartar City. But after a few minutes Derrick noticed with delight that his uncle was unsure of himself for once. At the wheel of the *Wanderer* and in any other place where Derrick had ever seen him, he had been calm, competent and almost infallible; but now he betrayed a strong tendency to take advantage of every changing breeze and to tack up the street in a zig-zag calculated to strike terror into the mind of the beholder. He had some difficulty with the gears, too, and he appeared to have only two speeds, either a boiling crawl at five miles an hour, or a hair-raising dash at sixty-five or more. At the first speed they raised bitter complaints from the bottled-up traffic behind them, and at the second they scattered the pedestrians like chaff before a hurricane. They left a wake of furious oaths behind them, but by extraordinarily good luck no corpses.

"That's better," said Sullivan, in a voice hoarse with replying to the compliments that had been addressed to him throughout Peking. They were well out of the city now, speeding along the empty road to the north. "That's much better now," he repeated, mopping his brow. He peered down at his feet. "This one is the brake," he said, pointing it out to Derrick. "And this one . . ." he was saying as the car left the road and cut a huge swathe through the tall millet that was growing alongside. Derrick ducked under the windscreen: he felt the car give a violent bound as it leapt the ditch and regained the road without stopping, and he raised his head to hear his uncle continue, ". . . is the accelerator. When I press it, we go faster." He pressed it, and the keen air whistled past the car in a rising shriek.

"What happens if you take your foot off, Uncle?" bellowed Derrick, as the car began to rock violently from side to side.

"Nothing, apparently," said his uncle, peering down again. "It's always the same with these contraptions. First they won't go, and then they won't stop."

"Perhaps if you were to try the other foot?" suggested Derrick, clinging to his seat.

"Now I don't want any advice on driving a car," said Sullivan, testily. "I happen to be a very good driver—not like those inconsiderate road-hogs in Peking."

"There's a sail ahead," said Derrick, after ten miles of the road had flown by. There was, indeed. A heavily laden wheelbarrow with its high rattan sail was creeping slowly along the middle of the road a quarter of a mile away.

"I can see it, can't I?" said Sullivan, experimenting with various levers.

"I only meant perhaps it would be a good thing to slow down—so as not to startle the man, and to give him time to get out of the way."

"Nonsense. There's plenty of room on his windward side. You can give a toot on the siren, if you like."

Sullivan rushed down upon the wheelbarrow with a fixed, set expression: Derrick hooted and then closed his eyes. But the crash never came: there was only an enraged bellow that died rapidly away behind them, and when Derrick opened his eyes again he saw that

64

the countryside was passing at a more normal speed.

"I've got the hang of the thing now," said Sullivan, in a pleased voice. "*This* one is the accelerator. The other one controls the lights, or the heating, or something. Very unusual car, this: not the rig I am used to at all."

They passed a temple, and Sullivan turned round to look at it. "Luff, luff," shrieked Derrick, as the car headed straight for a high stone wall.

"I was going to luff," said Sullivan, wrenching the indestructible car back on to the road, "and if you don't pipe down, Derrick, you'll find yourself overboard before you can say knife."

The fields had given way to open grassland, and in the distance there appeared a ruined triumphal arch. With an unholy crash of gears Sullivan plunged off the road and the car bounded over the dried-up turf towards the arch.

"Did you hear me change down?" he said. "I knew I would master the old musical box before long."

As they hurtled towards the arch he said mildly, "This brake doesn't seem to be holding. Just try that lever in the middle, will you?"

Derrick heaved upon it with all his force; his head crashed violently against the dashboard, and the car came to a shuddering stop, its nose one inch from the arch.

"Very neatly docked, though I say it myself," said Sullivan, getting out.

They waited by the slowly cooling car in the shade

of the arch, and presently they saw a distant plume of dust in the north. It came nearer, and soon Derrick could make out the three horsemen who were approaching them. The drumming of hooves on the hard earth came nearer and nearer, and in another minute the three Mongol ponies dashed up. Their riders pulled them to a dead stop and leapt to the ground: they were short, squat Mongols, with bowed legs and high-cheekboned faces. They were no taller than Derrick, and once off their horses they looked strangely incomplete. All three were armed with rifles slung over their backs and long knives in their belts: they wore bandoliers criss-crossed over their chests, and they walked awkwardly in their long felt boots as they came over to salute Sullivan. Sullivan answered them with a flow of guttural words, and the leader handed him a piece of red silk, a brace of partridges and a small object closely wrapped. Sullivan turned to the car, brought a box from under the seat, and gave the Mongols a piece of red silk, three automatic pistols and a charm in the shape of a bronze horse.

The presents having been exchanged, the Mongols lit a fire in the lee of the ruined arch and began to prepare a meal. Speaking quietly to Derrick, Sullivan said, "These are the three sons of Hulagu Khan, the chief of the Kokonor Mongols. I sent to ask his help for transport animals, and perhaps for a tribesman or two, if he could spare them. Now he has sent his three sons with orders to do everything they can to help, in memory of a good turn that I did him long ago. It's a way they have in these parts, and a very good way, too. I'll introduce you, but remember that they don't like a young man—and you're a man by their reckoning—to talk unless he is spoken to."

He spoke to the Mongols, obviously explaining who Derrick was, and then he said to Derrick. "This is young Hulagu, this is Chingiz, and this is Kubilai." The Mongols, hearing their names, bowed each in turn to Derrick, and Derrick bowed back, wondering what was going on behind their impassive, expressionless faces. The eldest broke a piece of bread, dipped it in salt and handed it to Derrick.

"Don't say anything," murmured Sullivan. "Bite it clean in half and give it back."

Derrick did so; the Mongols gave a hint of a smile and divided the remaining piece among themselves. Then there was a silence until their fire had blazed away to glowing embers: one of the Mongols went back to the tethered horses, took some strips of dried horse-flesh from under the deep saddle, impaled them on the long iron skewers that he carried threaded in his felt boot and burnt them roughly on each side over the fire. He handed them round, and Sullivan whispered, "It would be a good thing if you could eat your piece in seven bites."

It nearly choked Derrick, the raw, warm flesh, but he got it down, and immediately afterwards the Mongols scattered the ashes of their fire, remounted, and stood by while Sullivan attacked the car. Derrick marvelled to see how they controlled the half-wild ponies: they seemed to fit the saddles as though they grew from the horse. Chingiz, the youngest, sat on his madly bucking mount—it had never seen a car in its life, and it was terrified—as though it were no more than a wooden rocking-horse. By something not unlike a miracle the car started at once, and they went back to Peking in a cavalcade.

The next day the Mongols began their active assistance. They stayed in the Ka-Khan serai in the Tartar City, and they sent out word for horses, camels and ponies: the dealers flocked to them; they selected, judged, chaffered with unwearying patience; and at the same time they sent out messages with the caravans all along the route to their friends, warning them to have more beasts ready in due time.

Often when Sullivan was busy he would send Derrick to the serai with some message: he made Derrick repeat it over and over again until he was sure that it would be understood, and although the eldest of the Mongol brothers could make himself quite well understood in Chinese, Sullivan insisted that Derrick should stick to their language through thick and thin. He said it was the only way to learn, and he was right: within a remarkably short time Derrick could understand the gist of much that was said to him, and he could bring back an answer as well as carry a message.

A few days before everything was ready he went down to the Tartar City to tell Hulagu about a small alteration in the plans: but he found the serai deserted except for a few pie-dogs that ran when they saw Chang. It was a horse-racing day, but Derrick had not understood that when they told him some time before. He walked round the great hollow square of the serai, peering into the deeply-roofed verandah that ran clean round it, and looking for someone who could tell him where he might find the sons of the Khan. In the darkness of the stables he saw a dim figure squatting over a saddlebag, and walking noiselessly over the trodden straw he went into the stable. He had left Chang far over in the other corner, sniffing about on the traces of a Tibetan mastiff. The man's back was towards Derrick as he crouched over the saddlebag, and until Derrick spoke he was unaware of his presence. Derrick greeted him in Mongol. The man froze, motionless for a second; then he turned and stared at Derrick without a word. Another man appeared from the shadows, and they both stared at Derrick. Derrick began to feel uneasy: he was beginning to repeat his greeting in Chinese when the first man grunted a word to his companion, and they both hurled themselves on Derrick. Derrick let out a yell and struck out wildly: his fist landed on the first man's head—it felt like wood— and they fell in a writhing mass, with Derrick underneath. He felt crooked fingers gripping at his throat, and then heard a yell and felt the weight above him diminish as Chang wrenched one of the men off him.

But the other was still on him: Derrick's head was covered with the black cloth of his kaftan, and through the cloth the strong fingers were pressing deep into his throat. His breath was coming short, and there was a thundering in his ears. He relaxed utterly, went dead under the man's weight, and then suddenly, with all his force, writhed, brought his knee up into the man's belly and rolled clear. He could see now, but what he saw was the man coming for him again, with a long knife gleaming in his left hand. Derrick was in a corner: there was no escape, and a fleeting glance showed him that Chang was completely taken up with his enemy. The man came in with a quick, silent, purposeful rush, and Derrick threw himself on his back, kicking up with both his feet. One caught the man in the wind, but although he was winded he fell squarely on top of Derrick, pinning him down, and although he was gasping for breath he brought his right forearm across Derrick's throat, pressing with all his weight. Derrick noticed, with a split-second of horror, that he had no right hand—the arm was a stump—but there was no time for horror: Derrick grabbed the man's left wrist with both his hands and tried to twist the knife away. But the man was too strong by far, and twice he stabbed, driving the keen blade into the ground an inch from Derrick's head. Derrick tried to bring up his knee again, and the man caught his leg in a wrestler's lock. Slowly they strove and writhed together, glaring into one another's faces with inhuman hatred, and then by a quick turn the man wrenched one of Derrick's hands free and pinned it with his knee. Derrick lashed with his legs, vainly trying to unseat his enemy. But the man held firm, and with a furious backward jerk of his left arm he wrenched his wrist free from Derrick's remaining grasp.

The clatter of hooves in the courtyard made him pause for an instant, cocking his head to the sound. Derrick heaved with all his force, arching his back in a last violent effort, but instantly the man pinned him again, and whipped back the knife. Then he stiffened, half rose and spun away from Derrick. The knife flew in a long curve to the middle of the serai, and the man fell, drumming with his hand upon the beaten ground.

Chingiz wiped his knife carefully on a wisp of straw and then pulled Derrick to his feet. Derrick stood, swayed and fell flat on his face.

When he came round, Chingiz was squatting beside him, holding a bowl of water. Chang stood on the other side of him, growling like thunder. Chingiz held up Derrick's head and put the bowl to his mouth: Chang bared his teeth; he was not sure of the Mongol, and if Chingiz made one false move, Chang would be at his throat.

"Shut up, Chang," said Derrick, weakly, between his gulps. Then he stood up, shook himself, and found that he was still all in one piece. He grinned palely at Chingiz, tried hard to remember the Mongol for thanks, failed, and held out his right hand. Chingiz looked at it with some surprise, hesitantly advanced his own, and was astonished to find it gripped and firmly shaken up and down.

Derrick averted his eyes from the huddled form beyond him and reached for Chang's scruff. He hauled the dog forward, put his paw into Chingiz's hand and said, "Listen, Chang. Listen. This is Chingiz. Chingiz. Do you understand? He has saved my life, and you do not growl at him, *ever.* Good Chingiz. You understand?" Chang was not a fool: he knew what Derrick meant, and he looked at Chingiz with a new expression, barked twice and licked his hand.

They walked out of the square into the box-like rooms where Chingiz and his brothers stayed. Derrick's wits were coming back, and with them what little Mongol he knew. He tried to thank Chingiz many times, but Chingiz would have none of it. They sat drinking out of the jar of koumiss—the Tartar's fermented mare's milk—and with that inside him Derrick felt twice the man. He listened attentively while Chingiz, with many repetitions, misunderstandings and false interpretations, explained to him that the men were common serai thieves, notorious men from Yarkand. "Thief," he kept repeating, drawing the edge of his left hand over the wrist of his right, and suddenly Derrick understood why the man who had attacked him had only had one hand.

Then they talked of many other things. Chingiz said a great deal that was incomprehensible, but the upshot of it was that everybody in the serai was away because of the races, and that he himself had only come back because he had left his money behind.

"I am glad you came back," said Derrick, and when Chingiz understood at length what he meant, Derrick

72

saw his expressionless face suddenly dissolve into an open and very pleasant grin.

Later Chingiz fixed Derrick with a meaning look and said, "Sullivan?"

Derrick hoped violently that Chingiz meant what he seemed to mean—that Sullivan should not be told. He had very much wanted to suggest it to the young Mongol, but he had not liked to. He shook his head, smiling, and said, "Much better not to tell him. He might stop me going about —you know how it is?"

Chingiz understood this first go, and replied, "Yes, much better. Old men are difficult. Hulagu and Kubilai are often difficult although I am a man." He held up his fingers to show his age. "Not a boy," he said firmly.

Derrick pointed to himself, and held up the same number of fingers. He was surprised, for he had thought Chingiz much older than himself, but they were both very pleased with the discovery, and when they parted in the evening they shook hands like old friends.

Four

OLAF looked discontentedly at the train of animals. The expedition was ready to start, and a line of pack-horses, Mongolian ponies and camels stood waiting in the serai. "Those ain't camels," he said to Derrick. "They got two humps."

The tall, hairy beasts stared contemptuously about

73

them, craning their necks from side to side.

"They are camels all right," said Derrick, mounting his beautiful chestnut pony—a gift from Chingiz—"You lead them with a string. The other sort are dromedaries."

"Ay don't know nothing about dromedaries," replied Olaf, "but Ay ban't going to have nothing at all to do with these here vicious monsters. They ban't natural. Ay reckon Ay can steer a horse with a nice mild temper; but camels with two humps—cor stone the crows."

Li Han hurried into the square, carrying a last bundle to tie to his already groaning sumpter-horse.

"You look gloomy, Li Han," said Derrick.

"Gloomy is understatement," answered Li Han, with a hollow laugh. "Whole being is pervaded with funereal melancholy."

"What ban biting you, then?" asked Olaf.

"Have consulted most learned and expensive astrologers in entire city," said Li Han, wringing his hands and dropping his bundle, "and unanimous prognostication is utterly lugubrious. The soothsayers, the casters of the sacred sticks, the diviners of fêng-shui and the readers of the auspices all cry with one voice that journeys commenced today must meet ill-fortune and encounter physical violence. All types of esteemed seers and prophets say the same, alas, alas."

"You don't believe all that rot, do you, Li Han?" asked Derrick, who believed at least half of it himself, in spite of being a missionary's child—one cannot go to sea and be brought up in China without superstition soaking in through one's skin.

"In words of immortal Duck of Bacon," cried Li Han, trying in spite of his agitation to tie the bundle to the unwilling horse, "there are more things in heaven and earth, esteemed Horatio, than are dreamed of in your philosophy."

"Who ban this Horatio?" asked Olaf, curiously.

"Could we but cause the Old Man to delay," moaned Li Han, taking no notice, "to procrastinate, to sit in silent contemplation of the Temple of Heaven for a day. No hope, alas, alas."

"Never mind, Li Han," said Derrick, "think of the face you will gain in the Professor's company."

"Yes, immense face will be gained. But doubt whether biggest face in Asia is of much use with no head behind it. I deplore violence, especially physical violence to the person."

"He ban gotten cold feet," said Olaf, with a snort of laughter that made the camels start.

"You mustn't be a coward," said Derrick.

"Have been most timid of cowards from day of birth," replied Li Han, without shame, "and this is an inauspicious day."

"No it ain't," said Olaf, "it ban Thursday."

Ross and Sullivan came out, followed by Professor Ayrton, who was muttering about his lost spectacles.

"All shipshape?" asked Sullivan, running his eye over the beasts. "Derrick, go and give Hulagu a shout, will you? Professor, they're on your forehead."

"Forehead? Oh, yes, the spectacles. Why, so they are. Thank you very much." For forty years Professor Ayrton had been losing his spectacles on his forehead, and for forty years he had been intensely surprised and grateful to find them there.

The three Mongols, mounted and armed, with two of their men to mind the camels, took their places, and when Li Han had lighted eleven Chinese crackers to ward off the demons of the road, the expedition moved off. They wound through the streets of Peking, a strange procession in strange surroundings, but in that city they passed unnoticed. At length they came out of Peking, and in the clear light of the early morning they went away towards the north, as straight as they could go for the Great Wall of China.

For day after day they marched along the ancient road, spanned here and there with triumphal arches to commemorate emperors dead these many hundred years. They passed through cultivated country, with the sorghum standing high on either side, and sometimes they met with other caravans coming down from the north, who told them the news of the road. Then, on the fourth day, they came in sight of the Great Wall, stretching like a ribbon away across the rolling country farther than the keenest eye could reach, a wall with innumerable towers; and on the fifth day they passed through the Hsiung Gate, a great dark tunnel through the wall, guarded by four enormous towers that were already ancient two thousand years ago.

Soon the country changed: they travelled over vast plains of thin, wiry grass, and Derrick saw, for the first time, the black yurts, the felt tents of the Mongols who grazed their herds on the rolling steppe. Li Han saw them and shuddered, for now he knew that he was in the land of the barbarians against whom his ancestors had built the wall.

On and on they marched, starting before the first light and going on through the long and dusty day. They were making a great detour round the north-western provinces of China, and Sullivan explained it to Derrick as they pored over the maps one evening, while the campfires of the Mongols twinkled against the dark horizon.

"Here, you see," he said, pointing at the map, "is a part of the world which a peaceful scientific expedition must avoid if it wants to go on being peaceful, scientific and an expedition. There are seven or eight different warlords knocking sparks out of one another all over this area, so we have got to go round and strike the Old Silk Road to Sinkiang here," he pointed with his pencil.

"Won't this lead us through Hsien Lu's province, Uncle?" asked Derrick, studying the map.

"Who has been telling you about Hsien Lu?"

"I heard about him in the serai," replied Derrick. "He's the bandit who rules over Liao-Meng, isn't he?"

"Well, in point of fact he is the Tu-chun appointed by the government—the warlord or military governor or whatever you like to call him. But it's as near as

77

makes no difference to being a bandit. He is the sole ruler of Liao-Meng for all practical purposes, and what he says goes, whatever the central government may think. But we don't have to worry about him. Mr. Ross knew him fairly well at one time, and they say his country is quiet now. Anyhow, it will save three weeks going through Liao-Meng, and we haven't all the time in the world."

"How did you come to know him, Mr. Ross?" asked Derrick.

"If you question your elders," said Ross, "you will end on the gallows. But perhaps for once I will gratify your curiosity. I first had the pleasure of beholding Hsien Lu's face in a bar in Cheringpitti, after I had picked two Malays and a Japanese off it."

"What were they doing on Hsien Lu's face, sir?"

"I did not think to ask them, but I suppose they were trying to improve it in some way. It was a very plain face, as I remember it."

"Please would you tell me about it from the beginning?" Derrick saw that for once Ross was in a yarn-telling mood, and he was determined to profit by it—it was so rare that the opportunity was not to be lost.

Ross stretched, yawned and lit a long cheroot. "We had put the *Wanderer* into dry-dock," he began. "And if I remember rightly it was in the year after we had come through Sinkiang with—well, anyhow, it was when your worthy uncle was off on one of his characteristic wild-goose chases, and I was left alone to do all the donkey-work. We were having her copper-bottomed, and it was hot in this perishing mangrove swamp where we were berthed. So one day I walked into Cheringpitti with the intention of taking a little light refreshment in Silva's bar, the only decent place in the town. As I approached, I heard a violent shindy going on inside; and when I went in I saw that everyone was hiding behind the bar or under the tables. The reason for this, I soon discovered—for I have a very logical mind—was that four men were skirmishing about in the far end of the room, throwing bottles about and shrieking in a very tiresome way. There was no service to be had: I was thirsty, and this vexed me. I thought for a while, and I decided that the only way to be served was to restore order. I got up, and carrying my table by way of a shield I approached the men at the far end. Before I reached them, three of them had got the fourth down in the corner. Well, to cut a long story short, I induced them to leave. The two Malays were easily persuaded one went through the door—which was closed, by-the-bye—and the other, after I had broken his knife arm, went through the window. But the third one, a little Japanese, had a jujitsu hold on the fellow underneath, and although I reasoned with him until my table came to pieces, he would not let go. He was slowly killing the man on the floor, and he was chewing his ear at the same time: I am afraid I had to take him to pieces, more or less, before I could make him stop. Then, when I had finally picked him off and tossed the remains through the window, I saw Hsien Lu's face for the first time. I

79

raised him gently to his feet by his unchewed ear and asked him whether he wanted any trouble; but he did not. On the contrary, he seemed quite pleased to have got rid of his friends, and after he had had his ear attended to he came and shared a drink with me. I saw a good deal of him while he remained in those parts, and I often heard from him afterwards. When he was chief of the Black Flag bandits in Ho-nan he sent me that pair of chronometers: but now he is Tu-chun of Liao-Meng, a reformed character and a very respectable citizen."

"From what I have heard," said Sullivan, "he's still a bandit under the skin."

"What warlord is not? But Hsien Lu was always a clean fighter after his own lights, and he always kept his word to me whenever we had any dealings, so I do riot feel called upon to judge him too harshly."

"But why—" began Derrick.

"You'll certainly end on the gallows," said Ross. "Now it is past midnight, and if you are going out after partridge with Chingiz at dawn you had better turn in."

"And if you see Li Han before we are up in the morning," added Sullivan, "tell him that if he serves up boiled badger again for breakfast I'll rub it in his hair. He bought seven of them cheap in Peking, and I know there are still three more uneaten. I can't bear it any longer. Do your best with the partridges, Derrick. There is nothing so good as a cold roast bird—and after these eternal badgers . . ."

It seemed to Derrick that he had only just closed his eyes when Chingiz was beside him, shaking him awake: the first white streak showed in the eastern sky, and there was hoar-frost on the ground. Their ponies danced in the cold, and Derrick's chestnut, always a handful, came near to unseating him before he had sent his feet home in the deep, shoe-like Mongol stirrups. He clutched the pommel, felt Chingiz's eye upon him, and gave the pony a cut with his whip. Away they went, at a full, stretching gallop over the smooth, rolling plain, and there was no sound anywhere under the sky but the drumming of hooves. Derrick turned in his saddle and saw Chingiz just behind him, sitting his pony as if he were in an arm-chair, with his falcon on his wrist. They reined in to a canter, and rode side by side until they flushed a covey of partridges. They stopped and listened: over to the right another covey was calling. Derrick dismounted, slung his weighted reins over his pony's head, and loaded his gun, a beautifully balanced sixteen-bore that Sullivan had given him.

"Let's walk them up," he said.

Chingiz looked puzzled; he shook his head and said, "You go. I have another way."

Derrick nodded and began to walk over the thin grass towards the sound; presently he caught sight of the covey, walking about slowly and feeding. They saw him and started to run; he walked more quickly, and flushed them at about fifty yards. He picked two birds on the outside of the covey and cracked right and left at them. He could have sworn that he had hit one at least, but they flew on untouched. On the way back to the ponies he put up another covey. "This time I'll make sure," he thought, firing into the brown. A single feather floated down, but the birds whirred on. He was not in the best of tempers when he rejoined Chingiz, and he thought he detected a smile on the Mongol's face.

"You should shoot them on the ground," said Chingiz. Derrick did not reply, except by a grunt. He thought, as he remounted, that Chingiz meant it as a joke, and he did not think that it was very funny.

They rode for some time, and then, when they sighted another covey Chingiz said, "I will show you our way." He unhooded his falcon: it stretched its wings and blinked in the sudden light. Chingiz waited a minute, then he raised his arm, untied the jesses, and the falcon took to the air. It flapped once, then rose with outstretched wings on the wind, higher and higher. Chingiz galloped forward to flush the partridges: they rose with a whirr, so close that Derrick could see the red of their tails. The falcon shot forward, high over the partridges, rose still higher, and then closed its wings and stooped in a great downward curve, faster and faster, with a sound like a rocket. The partridges were gliding ten feet above the ground on stiff, decurved wings: suddenly they were aware of their danger, and they scattered as if the covey had exploded. The falcon, aiming its dive on one bird, altered its direction but a half-stroke of one wing: it was moving so fast that it was a blur in the air. Then there was a burst of feathers from the partridge's back: the bird hit the ground and bounced as if it had been hurled from the sky, and in a second the falcon was on top of it again.

They rode up fast, and the falcon rose from its prey. Chingiz, without drawing rein, leaned from his saddle and picked up the partridge: he smoothed its feathers and passed it to Derrick. It was a fine cock bird, beautifully marked and plump.

The falcon hovered above their heads, staring from side to side. Chingiz whistled, called and held up his arm; the fierce bird floated gently down and sat there preening until Chingiz slipped the hood over its head.

Derrick looked at it with admiration; he felt the ill-temper draining out of him, and he was sure that next time he had a shot he would do better. They rode on until they came to a little dip in the plain. "You stay there," said Chingiz, "and I will go there." He made a sweeping motion with his arm.

Derrick stood in the hollow and watched Chingiz gallop out in a wide curve: then he understood that Chingiz meant to drive the birds over him. He crouched in the hollow, with his gun ready. His pony stood grazing twenty yards behind him. He watched one covey rise and go away in the wrong direction, and then he saw Chingiz rise in his stirrups and wave his arm. The partridges rose almost at his feet—Derrick saw his pony shy—and came straight towards the hollow. Derrick picked his birds carefully, picked them with the greatest care as they veered away in easy shot to his left; he waited, waited, and then pressed the trigger. Nothing happened. He had forgotten the unfamiliar safety-catch on the new gun. The partridges saw him, rose again with a sudden whirr and vanished over the plain.

He was still staring after them when Chingiz rejoined him. Derrick gave him a forced smile, and before Chingiz could say anything he handed him the gun, with the safety-catch off, and ran over to his pony, shouting that he would see if he could drive some birds over the hollow for Chingiz to try for.

Derrick rode out: the plain was full of birds; they were so very rarely shot here that they were not at all shy, but it was some time before he started a covey that went in the right direction. However, he did succeed in the end, although he was rather far from the hidden dip. He watched the birds go. They stopped whirring and glided on and on towards the hollow; but they did not quite clear it. They pitched just this side of it, landed and regrouped. They were walking about, quite calm and unconcerned, within five yards of Chingiz as he crouched there. He waited until they were well bunched together and then blazed both barrels right down the middle of them. Only two birds flew away: the remaining nine lay slaughtered on the ground.

"Good shot?" said Chingiz, as Derrick returned.

"It was the most unsporting thing I have ever seen in my life," said Derrick in English; but Chingiz understood very well from the tone of his voice that he was angry. Chingiz shrugged his shoulders, let the gun fall carelessly and walked over to the partridges. He threw them one by one over to Derrick, counting them as they came. Suddenly Derrick let them drop. "Why should I carry them?" he asked, with an ugly oath he had learnt at sea. "You murdered them, so you might as well carry them."

Chingiz turned a baleful look upon him. "What is the matter?" he asked.

Derrick searched for a Mongol word that might mean unsporting, but he could not think of one, and the best he could do was to use some expressions that he had heard in the serai. He was not sure of their meaning, but he was pretty sure that they were unpleasant, and he was not surprised to see Chingiz frowning heavily.

Derrick was already feeling rather sorry that he had let his bad temper get the better of him, but when he saw Chingiz give his new gun a contemptuous kick as he stalked past it, he could not resist saying still another word, which for all he knew was ruder still. It was hardly out of his mouth before the Mongol was on him, hitting right and left and kicking for his stomach. Derrick stopped him with a short jab to the nose and they backed away. Chingiz drew his knife with one lightning movement, hesitated for a second, struck it into the ground, and came in again. Derrick was ready for him and let out a straight left which stopped him short, and then a swinging right to the ear. The

Mongol had no sort of guard, and for a moment it was easy to keep him at a distance, smashing in a quick succession of blows. One caught him on the point of his jaw and he fell flat on his back: he lay there for a second, spitting blood, and then he was up. Derrick never knew what hit him, but he had a vague impression of being gripped by both ears while his head was battered against the ground like the hammer of an alarm clock. At some time, too, a head or a knee had hit him in the stomach, and teeth had met in his forearm; but that was all lost in the swirl of darkness, and when he came slowly out of it he had a faint notion of having been run over by a steam-roller.

He was lying on his back, staring at the sky: for a moment he did not move, and then, between him and the sky he saw Chingiz, standing over him with his long knife in his hand.

"Better?" asked Chingiz.

Derrick did not reply, but gathered himself to spring.

Chingiz shook his head and smiled. He waved his head, said something in Mongol and pointed to Derrick's arm. Derrick looked, and saw that his sleeve was already rolled up: Chingiz squatted down, squeezed Derrick's arm so that the veins stood out and made as if to cut one gently with his knife.

"No," said Derrick, getting to his feet. "I'm better now." He understood, with immense relief, that Chingiz had meant to let some blood, as the Mongols did for horses, so that he should recover; but still, he did not much care for the operation.

"Better?" asked Chingiz again.

"Yes, quite better, thank you very much," said Derrick, and after a moment he said, "I'm sorry." He was, indeed: he felt ashamed of himself, and he knew that he had got what he deserved. He had got a good deal, he discovered: his left eye was already so swollen that he could hardly see out of it, and it was swelling still; his ears felt as if they had been wrenched off and roughly sewn on again, and he had parted company with one of his eye-teeth. Furthermore, there was no hair left at all over quite a large area of his scalp.

He was feeling his head when he caught Chingiz's eye, and laughed. He pointed to the gap in his teeth, and Chingiz showed his ear, now swollen to the size of a muffin, and standing out at right angles to his head. They were both in very bad shape: Derrick lent Chingiz his handkerchief for his bloody nose, and Chingiz held his cold knife-blade against Derrick's purple eye; they patched one another up as well as they could, and walked slowly over to the unmoved ponies. Suddenly Derrick noticed that although Chingiz had brought the gun, he had left the partridges. Derrick ran back for them, meaning to show that he had been in the wrong, but Chingiz was there before him, and as they bent to gather the birds they cracked their heads together with such force that Derrick went over again, half stunned. This really amused Chingiz, and almost for the first time Derrick heard him laugh; he stood there rubbing his head, wheezing and doubled up with laughter, pointing first to his own

87

head, then to Derrick's and then to the partridges. Derrick was sure that it was very funny, but for the moment his head was so battered and reeling with the shock that he could not see the point of the joke.

As they rode slowly back, Derrick tried to explain why it was so dreadful to shoot sitting birds, but Chingiz could not understand.

"You want to eat them?" he asked.

"Yes," said Derrick.

"So you kill them?"

"Yes," said Derrick, "but not on the ground."

"Why not?" asked Chingiz, amazed, "it is easier, and you kill more. So you eat more, and waste no powder."

Derrick tried again, and finally Chingiz jumped to the conclusion that it was something to do with Derrick's religion. He knew that Christians did many strange things, and he was sure that this business about the birds must be one of Derrick's taboos. In that case, everything was quite understandable: he at once offered to throw the partridges away, and it was with some difficulty that Derrick prevented him.

They were late back, and the expedition was already under way, with only a few of the more difficult camels still to load: everybody was busy, and Derrick was able to pass off the appearance of his face with the tale of having fallen off his horse. Chang, who had been forbidden to come—he was no sort of a gun-dog yet—welcomed him ecstatically, and immediately seemed to suspect Chingiz, but none of the others took any notice except Li Han who, in the course of the afternoon, said, "Horsemanship more difficult than seamanship, it seems?"

Derrick grunted. It was wounding to be thought a bad horseman, particularly by a sea-cook. Derrick prided himself on being a fairly good rider.

"Ay reckon you fall off almighty hard, eh?" said Olaf, peering curiously into his visage. "Maybe Ay learn you a thing or two about staying aboard a horse." Olaf was sitting, or reclining, sideways on a strange blueish mare that had been selected for him, as being mild almost to the point of imbecility. "First," said Olaf, "Ay master the animal with the power of the human eye . . ."

This was too much. "I didn't really fall off," Derrick burst out.

"A rough-house, eh?"

"Yes."

"You ain't ban mixing it with that Mongol?"

"Yes."

"Sadie Mack! You ban lucky to be alive, Ay reckon. You want three-inch steel plate all round you before you start mixing it with those guys."

"I knew it," said Li Han. "I knew it. Soothsayers were correct. Physical violence now commencing." He shuddered.

They travelled on for many days, holding their west-ward course towards the Gobi. In time they came back into cultivated agricultural land, with many fields and villages; but it was plain that an army had passed through the countryside, and that there had been fighting. There were many burnt houses on their road, and once they went through an entire village, a large village, that was no more than a smouldering heap of ashes.

The Chinese peasants had mostly fled, and those few who remained hid from them. It was difficult to get any sort of information until they came to the walled town of Chien Wu, which was untouched: they went straight to the great Buddhist monastery of Chien Wu, and there they learnt that the army of the rebel leader, Shun Chi, had marched through not long before, pillaging and burning on their way to Liao-Meng, beyond the low hills on the western horizon.

"I don't like this," said Sullivan. "Shun Chi is a blood-thirsty brute, with unpleasant ideas about foreigners. He strung up three French missionaries not so long ago: but that was in Fan Ling, far away to the south. He has no right to be up here at all."

"We had better get in touch with Hsien Lu," said Ross. "He will give us an escort through Liao-Meng and on to the Old Silk Road."

"Yes. That's the thing to do. We had better go ourselves: I would not like to trust to a messenger, and there is no point in taking the whole expedition until we have got our escort. There is no telling what lies between here and the Liao-Meng hills."

In the morning they spoke of it to the Professor,

pointing out that he would be quite safe behind the strong walls of Chien Wu.

"Safe?" said the Professor. "From what? Oh, yes, these bandits and so on. You are quite right, I am sure; though really I apprehend very little danger from them myself—the Chinese are a very highly civilised race. Why, only yesterday evening the abbot of this delightful monastery had a long chat with me, and he spoke most intelligently about the archaeological significance of some stelae that are to be seen in a nearby village. I am sure that there can be little danger, particularly for foreigners, who are not concerned with their political differences; but go by all means, if it will make you any easier in your minds. After all, we must take every precaution for the boy's sake."

"Tell me, Professor, did you not notice the burnt-out village the other day?"

"It was not a mere antiquarian interest," said the Professor, still thinking of his stelae, "the abbot was keenly aware of the importance of what he describes as the obvious Hellenic influence, so unexpected at such a date—but you were speaking of the village. Yes, I did notice it. Most unfortunate: most unfortunate. It was probably the effect of carelessness with matches, or the end of a cigarette. I remember a colleague of mine in St. Petersburg who set fire to his waste-paper basket by carelessly throwing an unextinguished cigarette into it. The fire communicated itself to the papers on his desk and thence to his beard, which was badly singed: indeed, he was obliged to reduce it to no more than a goatee, whereas before it had reached to his waist—a great comfort, he assured me, in the Russian winter. However, these unfortunate people are no doubt being cared for by the proper authorities: perhaps there is a subscription to which we might contribute."

"You saw nothing else?"

"No. I think not. Oh, you are referring to the small temple on our right. Yes, I noticed that. Was there, anything of particular interest there?"

Sullivan was referring to the corpses in the village, but he said, "Oh well. . . . No, I don't think it was an important temple. But if you don't mind, Professor, I would rather you put off going to look at your stelae until we come back with the escort."

Ross and Sullivan left at noon, well armed and mounted: they took Hulagu and Kubilai with them, and they said that if they found the Tu-chun in his capital, as they expected, they would be back in five days with the escort.

Time passed pleasantly enough while they were away. Professor Ayrton rejoiced in the company of the abbot, who had a large and important library as well as a collection of rubbings of inscriptions from all over China. Derrick and Chingiz explored the city, which, although it was not very large, had enough in its walls to occupy them for some time; but when some tribesmen rode in from the north and Chingiz recognised a cousin among them, he was obliged to spend the greater part of the day with them, not only

92

from the call of kin, but to hear all the latest news about the steppe, the desert and the northern provinces. So Derrick was left to his own devices: Li Han and Olaf would not let him go with them, for they had been bitten by the gambling fever, and they disappeared early each morning into one of the teahouses near the wall, where they played fan-tan hour after hour. They said he was too young, and that anyhow he had not got enough money. "Besides," added Li Han, "gambling for lucre is most pernicious, debilitating, nauseous and immoral pursuit, quite unfitting for cousin of worthy and virtuous philosopher."

The worthy and virtuous philosopher was fretting about his stelae. "It occurs to me," he said to Derrick, as he sat after breakfast in the guests' courtyard of the monastery while a great deep gong boomed inside the temple, "It occurs to me, my dear boy, that your uncle will want us to push on with all speed as soon as he comes back. That will mean that I shall have no time to inspect these stelae. I should be very loth to miss them."

"Then why don't we go and look at them, sir?" said Derrick.

"An excellent suggestion. But your uncle and Mr. Ross seemed quite concerned about the possibility of danger."

"Oh, I'm sure there isn't much," replied Derrick confidently. "These friends of Chingiz have all the latest news, and they say that Shun Chi's army is retreating. It never touched the country to the north of here, and that is the direction of your village, isn't it? But anyhow, nobody seems to know for sure which army is which, or where either of them are. Most likely both of them are miles away." Derrick was growing rather tired of being cooped up in Chien Wu, and he welcomed the idea of going out, even if it would only be to see archaeological remains. The Professor needed only the smallest encouragement, so before lunch they left for the village with a monk to guide them and Li Han to prepare their rice.

The ride was delightful: for mile after mile the road led through neat, intensely cultivated fields. Tall trees on either hand gave them shade, and there was enough breeze to diminish the strong heat of the sun, but not enough to raise the dust.

"I am afraid your uncle has been over-anxious," said the Professor. "What could be more peaceful than this?"

They came to the village, and the monk led them to a small temple, built on the site of a much larger and more ancient building. He showed the Professor several great slabs of stone, some upright and some fallen, but all carved and covered with half-erased inscriptions. Professor Ayrton was entranced: he took innumerable photographs and rubbings, eagerly explaining the dismal objects to Derrick, who listened dutifully for half an hour, with as much show of interest as he could manage. Fortunately lunch came quite soon: it was perhaps the worst meal that Li Han had ever cooked, for he had been trying to hear the Professor and attend to his work at the same time. But they were hungry after their ride, and the soggy rice vanished from their bowls: by the time they were sitting in the shade and sipping their tea it was no more than an unpleasant memory. The Professor was in fine form, and Li Han listened spell-bound to his remarks on the stelae and on archaeology in general: once, as the afternoon wore on, Derrick suggested that they ought to be going back; he whispered it to Li Han, but the sea-cook turned upon him with such a venomous "Shshsh" that he abandoned the idea and dozed against the wall.

They were at last preparing to return to the monastery when there was a trampling of feet, and a company of soldiers marched into the courtyard. Some were dressed in a ragged blue uniform, and some still had their peasants' clothes upon their backs; most carried rifles of various kinds, and at their head was an officer who wore the tattered remnants of a Western uniform and carried two revolvers, as well as a sword. He stared hard at them for a moment, and then came forward to demand, in a loud, hectoring voice, what their business was and who they were. The Professor answered him mildly, and the officer at once assumed a more bullying tone. Professor Ayrton showed his passport, his permit from the Central Government and several letters of recommendation. The officer pretended to be able to read them—Derrick noticed that he held them upside down—and snapped, "Come with me. You are under arrest."

"But my good man," said Professor Ayrton, "why? For what reason? What is your authority?"

The officer glowered at him, fingered his revolvers, changed his mind, and shouted an order. The soldiers rushed forward and seized the Professor and Derrick. The monk and Li Han had already disappeared: they might have melted into the thin air, for Derrick had never seen them go.

It was useless to resist, so they allowed themselves to be hustled along to a closed Peking cart: their captors threw them in and mounted guard outside.

The Professor put on his spectacles and rummaged through his notes. "How very annoying," he exclaimed, when he had looked through them. "I have left several pages under a stone in the temple. I will just go and . . ." Still speaking, he put his head out of the cart: the guard instantly hit him with the butt of his rifle, and he fell back unconscious: Derrick pulled him into a more comfortable position, and held his head on his knees. A few minutes later there was a shouting outside; the cart lurched into motion, and the troops moved off.

Derrick was worried, far more worried than he had ever been before. He did not know what to do, or where they were going, or whether the soldiers were bandits. He listened to the voices of the troops through the creaking and rumble of the cart, but those who were nearest to him were peasants from a province

96

whose dialect was incomprehensible to him.

They went on and on. It was horribly stuffy inside the closed cart, and Derrick began to feel very thirsty. The Professor was still knocked out, but his breathing and his pulse were steady: that was the one comfort Derrick could find in the whole situation.

Hour followed hour, and Derrick had ample time to reflect upon all the disagreeable possibilities that might await him. Whether the soldiers were bandits or not, it was almost certain that they would hold their prisoners to ransom, for the warlords were utterly lawless in these remote provinces, and they obeyed the governments orders or defied them as they pleased. And Derrick knew what happened if the ransom were not paid.

Then another thought seized him, and a worse one: there were several warlords who hated all foreigners, and would even forgo a ransom for the pleasure of killing them—killing them in the Chinese manner. And the worst of all these was the rebel leader Shun Chi: it was he who had raised the cry "All foreign devils to the sea," and it was he who had so recently killed the three completely inoffensive European priests.

Derrick shuddered as he remembered what he had heard in the serai of the fashion of their death. If these men who were marching outside the cart belonged to Shun Chi, then there was very little hope: and these men had been bitterly hostile from the first—if they belonged to Shun Chi, of course they would hate foreigners at sight.

Once the cart stopped. It sounded as though they were in a village or a town, and from the shouting Derrick thought they were changing the horse. He cautiously put his head out to ask for water; he half-expected a blow, and when it came he dodged it by an inch.

After that he sat for hours and hours in the bottom of the cart, holding the Professor's head. When the cart stopped next he was grasped by two men and dragged out. It was dark: he could not tell where they were, but as he was pushed into the camp he saw the outline of steep hills against the western sky.

Two men held his arms, hurried him over the rough ground, and thrust him into a tent: there was a man there, sitting at a table, writing. He was obviously their leader, and several officers stood behind him. Derrick staggered forward, blinking in the light. The man at the table glared at him, and Derrick glared back.

He was a short man, thick and middle-aged, but he was the toughest-looking man Derrick had ever seen, and there was a very dangerous expression in his eyes.

For a moment Derrick almost lost his courage: but then he saw that the man's left ear was hardly there at all; at some time it had been chewed off. He felt a violent thrill of relief, and he cried, "You are Hsien Lu!"

Five

"So what?" snapped Hsien Lu.

"Is Mr. Ross here?" asked Derrick. "My uncle and Mr. Ross have been looking for you."

"What you mean?" said Hsien Lu, narrowing his eyes. "Mr. Ross—" began Derrick.

"Sandy Loss? You know Sandy Loss?" cried Hsien Lu. "You say Loss? The pilate, live Canton-side one time?"

Why is he talking pidgin-English? wondered Derrick. Then he remembered that he himself had cried out in that language first. "Yes, I know Mr. Ross— Sandy Ross—" he replied, in Chinese, "he is my uncle's partner. But he is not a pirate."

Hsien Lu stood up and came round the table. He was still appallingly ugly, but the wicked look had gone out of his face. He pulled up a chair and sat staring in Derrick's face. "You are Sullivan's nephew," he said at last, searching in his memory. "What is your name?"

"Derrick."

"Dellick. That's right." The Tu-chun smiled and clapped his hands for tea. "But how do you come to speak Chinese?" he asked, with a sudden return of suspicion.

"My parents were missionaries," explained Derrick: he was feeling suddenly very weary, and he wanted above all to ask for the Professor to be taken care of;

99

but the Tu-chun went on, "Where is Loss?"

"In Liao Meng, I think—but please could I go and see to my cousin? He was hit on the head. He is an old, learned man, and he was hit on the head like a—like a beast," cried Derrick, with a sudden burst of rage at the memory of it.

Hsien Lu murmured a quick order, and two officers hurried from the tent. "Never mind," he said to Derrick, "he will be looked after. Now tell me where they started from, and where they were going."

Derrick had lived in China nearly all his life: he knew that he would never be able to sit down in the presence of an elder, let alone a Tu-chun, however weary and faint he might be, so he gathered his wits, concentrated his attention, and answered Hsien Lu's questions as clearly and as briefly as he could. The warlord went on and on; he wanted to know a great deal, and Derrick had to stifle gigantic yawns. Soon he was conscious of the Tu-chun's voice alone, coming as from a great distance: he jerked himself into wakefulness, and answered "Yes" at haphazard. He kept himself alert for some time, but then again the voice went booming on: it was somewhere in the distance, and it seemed to be stating that Ross and Sullivan had blown up four competing pirate junks in the harbour of Pu Ying itself, the stronghold of the society of the Everlasting Wrong: but that might have been a dream; it came and went in snatches, and in another moment Derrick was fast asleep where he stood.

He woke up suddenly, and it was the morning. He

was in a strange bed, and for some time he could not remember where he was. Li Han stood beside him, offering a cup of tea: on the other side of the tent Professor Ayrton lay on a comfortable palliasse, already sipping at a bowl of tea. His head was bandaged, but he seemed quite recovered. He nodded to Derrick and said, "Good morning, my boy. How do you feel?"

"Fine, thank you, sir. How is your head?"

"It spins like a teetotum, but it appears to be whole, which is a blessing. I must admit, however, that I deserved the blow. I am afraid that my ill-timed enthusiasm for the abbot's stelae overruled my caution. We might easily have been caught by Shun Chi instead of the excellent Hsien Lu, and then we should have been in a pretty mess, as I believe the phrase goes. What a deserving man the Tu-chun appears to be: he came to me by candlelight to offer his compliments and excuses, and he assured me that if it would afford me the slightest pleasure he would arrange to have the soldier who was so impetuous with his rifle-butt tortured to death in front of this tent at sunrise, together with the officer. He seemed quite disappointed when I declined the entertainment, but I made up for it by complimenting him on his English—which he appears to have picked up in the Philippines, by the way—and by telling him that of all the military men I had ever met in China he was by far the most swollen guy. It gratified him very much."

"I'm sure it did, sir," said Derrick, taking his tea. "How did you get here, Li Han?"

"During arbitrary arrest of worthy sage," said Li Han, bowing towards the Professor. "I imitated humble but cautious earthworm in nook, or cranny, of temple wall, and subsequently pursued brutal and licentious soldiery at discreet distance for more than twenty li. On perceiving honourable welcome accorded by Tu-chun when all was understood, ventured to insinuate self into tent and proclaim humble presence."

Hsien Lu hurried into the tent; he was so moved that he could hardly complete the long drawn-out ceremonial greetings before he said, "Shun Chi has taken Ross and Sullivan. They were ambushed on the way to Liao-Meng. I must go and give orders. If you have any charms, Ayrton lao-yeh, use them now." He hurried away.

There was a profound silence.

"What do you think will happen, sir?" asked Derrick, at last.

"I hesitate to think," replied the Professor, seriously. "This Shun Chi hates all foreigners, except for the Russian agitators who are egging him on to clear China of all Europeans and Americans. It is just possible that he will hold them to ransom, but . . ." his voice tailed away uncertainly.

"Will Hsien Lu be able to smash Shun Chi's army?"

"No. That is the worst aspect of the whole affair. Shun Chi has already driven Hsien Lu out of Liao-Meng. Formerly Hsien Lu could cope with him, but recently Shun Chi has received modern arms from the

Russians, together with military advisers and experts in the use of the new weapons; whereas Hsien Lu has to rely on old-fashioned rifles and the usual Chinese tactics of wearing hideous masks in battle and letting off crackers. He cannot possibly face Shun Chi's machine-guns. And now they say that Shun Chi has three tanks, and that he is advancing with them to bring matters to a decisive close."

"I suppose they took us for Russians when they captured us."

"Yes. That was why they were so unpleasant. Hsien Lu has captured one—he is going to cut off his head this afternoon."

"Couldn't you beg him off?"

"I doubt it. And after all, the man has asked for it. It seems to me a very wicked thing to bring modern arms into this part of the world to enable this rascal Shun Chi to slaughter anyone who opposes his ambitions. Before these Russians came the Tu-chun and the rebels were comparatively harmless: they more or less played at war, and very rarely killed anybody. The armies used to take the field with umbrellas and teapots, and they would stop the battle if it came on to rain. But now it is all different: there is really savage warfare breaking out, and thousands of innocent people are going to be murdered."

"Why do they do it?"

"They have ends of their own to serve. I have a mind to question this prisoner: he might give us some useful information. If the Tu-chun will promise me his life I may be able to get something out of him. A man will do a lot for his life."

"But do you speak Russian, Professor?"

"Yes, indeed. I studied for many years. in St. Petersburg before the revolution, and I have a White Russian colleague at the university with whom I always speak in that language. I dare say that I could pass for a Russian myself, if the need arose."

After a short consultation with Hsien Lu they went to the tent where the prisoner lay. He was a tall, fair man, dressed in the Mongolian style, with high boots and a sheepskin jerkin. For a long while the Professor spoke to him, but the man only replied in monosyllables.

"I shall have to try something else," said the Professor, leaving the tent. He walked up and down, thinking. Then he said, "We shall go back now. When I turn to you and say something that you do not understand, you must reply 'Da, da.' Then a little later I will tell you to do something and you must say 'Ochen chorosho, tovarich' and leave the tent. Repeat that several times, will you?"

When Derrick was word-perfect they went back to the tent. The Professor spoke in a low, urgent voice to the prisoner: the man seemed to come alive; he answered many times—long, whispered sentences that sounded like questions. The Professor appeared to be reassuring him; he turned to Derrick and said something, looking at him with hidden meaning. "Da, da," said Derrick. And then, a little later, the Professor turned to him and said something that sounded like an order. Derrick said, "Ochen chorosho, tovarich," and hurried out.

He had a long time to wait. He paced up and down until the sun was high up in the sky. At last the Professor came out, with a triumphant look on his face.

"Is it all right?" asked Derrick.

"Hush, boy," whispered the Professor, leading him out of earshot. "Yes, I have got the information I wanted. But I am afraid I was obliged to resort to a most distasteful form of deception to get it. However, perhaps its importance will justify the deceit."

"What did you tell him, sir?" asked Derrick.

"I told him that I was a secret agent working on his side —that I had been sent to Hsien Lu to deceive and entrap him. At length, when it appeared that you too understood Russian he believed me, and he told me that he was the man who was entrusted with the care of the new consignment of machine-guns and bombs that had been sent to Shun Chi for his final attack on Hsien Lu. He was supposed to join the four other Russians in the rebels' camp in order to supervise the operation of these weapons."

"Then without him they won't be able to use them?"

"No. I am afraid that is not the case. The other men know enough about these guns and bombs to manage without him. It is a very bad business, Derrick: the day after tomorrow Shun Chi will attack Hsien Lu. He has lorries and tanks, and with these he can bring up his forces more rapidly than the Tu-chun can retreat. And once he attacks, with these new mortar-bombs and the tanks, I think that it will be all up with Hsien Lu, and as for the fate of your uncle and Mr. Ross . . ." he stopped, and shook his head.

For a long while neither of them spoke. Then Derrick said, "I have an idea, sir. It may seem a feeble one, but it is an idea."

"Tell me. I have been racking my brains, but I can think of nothing that is not obviously foolish."

"Well, couldn't you go and say that you are this Russian? You could take his papers, and you could manage the language all right."

"Yes, and then?"

"Why, then you could throw a spanner in the works somehow."

"But how? That is the point. The first part would not be too difficult. Stavrogin—that is the prisoner—has never seen the other Russians who are with Shun Chi, and we are much the same size and build, though he is younger than I am. Yes, I think they might take me at my face value. But what could I do then?" The Professor wiped his spectacles: he was deeply distressed.

"Perhaps you could get Shun Chi to let you talk to Uncle Terry and Mr. Ross. You could pretend to question them, and they might give you some better idea; they are very good that way."

"Yes, I am sure they are. Yes. That is undoubtedly the best course of action: at all events it is better than waiting here impotently doing nothing. I am obliged to you for the suggestion." He sat down with his head

106

between his hands. "There are difficulties," he said, after some thought, "many of them. I hardly know one end of a machine-gun from another. And the same applies to a bomb. They have so far come so very little into my life, you see. In the last war they kept me at home all the time for liaison work in unusual languages, you see, and I never saw a shot fired. Dear me, this is a singular position for an elderly archaeologist. But, as you say, we must do something. And apart from anything else, I should like to hamper this fellow Shun Chi if it is at all possible. Hsien Lu is a very good fellow in his own rough way, and he has a due respect for learning; whereas this Shun Chi. . . ." He went on to inveigh against the rebel leader's total lack of culture, while Derrick thought furiously.

"We must get cracking," said Derrick. "There is no time to be lost."

"Very well, my boy. I will speak to Hsien Lu. Really, you seem to have a most practical mind in these difficult circumstances. I suppose it is your sea-training."

The warlord welcomed their proposal. He agreed to spare the prisoner's life, according to the Professor's promise, but he stripped the unfortunate man to the skin, and gave the Professor his clothes.

"You will have to wear these," he said, "and here are his papers. I hope you will be able to ensnare the despicable Shun Chi, but if your esteemed intelligence succeeds in this project, I beg that the first consideration should be the safety of Mr. Ross. I owe him a debt of gratitude, and if necessary I will attack with my whole army to set him free, although I have little hope of prevailing against Shun Chi's ignoble strategy."

He gave them all they asked, horses, weapons and a guide, and he added a little packet of quick poison, so that they should die easily if Shun Chi caught them.

Derrick was determined to go too, whatever the Professor might say. He privately asked the Tu-chun whether there were any Mongols in his camp, and when the Tu-chun said that there were four, Derrick begged to be allowed to change clothes with the smallest of them. He was accustomed to Mongol clothes—he had often worn Chingiz's—and when Li Han, working feverishly, had altered them a little they looked natural enough. He greased his face as a Mongol does against the wind, using old and dirty grease, and he pulled the sheepskin hood low over his face. When the Professor saw him, he did not recognise him until he spoke, and his objections died away.

"I should not permit it," he said hesitantly. "You ought to ride back to Chien Wu with Li Han. But I must admit that I would be very glad to have you at hand: I am not very much use in these emergencies. The danger of your being discovered is certainly very much less." He stared hard at the Mongol figure in front of him. "But if there is the slightest unfortunate incident, you must give me your word to ride straight back to Chien Wu, where Olaf will be able to get you out of the country. At the slightest mishap, and at the slightest untoward word, you understand? Fortunately Hsien Lu has given us the best horses in the country."

Derrick promised, but with the mental reservation of deciding for himself just how dangerous the situation could become.

They left Li Han in the camp, with orders to return to the walled city, and the Professor entrusted him with his notes on the stelae, which, he said, were already worth the whole trouble of the expedition. Hsien Lu rode with them to the foot of the hills on the way to Liao-Meng and the rebels' camp. When he parted from them he wished them good fortune and stood watching them for a long while as they followed the winding road up into the hills. Once Derrick looked back, and far down the road beyond the Tu-chun he saw a toiling figure mounted on an ass.

By nightfall they were at the top of the hills, and in the morning they looked down into the province of Liao-Meng. It was just before the rising of the sun that Derrick stood there looking down into the unknown land: he was wondering where in all that stretch of country his uncle lay when he was startled by the braying of an ass. He whipped round, and saw a donkey tethered with the horses. There was a little fire sending up a straight pillar of blue smoke in the still air, and beside it squatted a familiar figure. It was Li Han, brewing the Professor's early morning tea.

"Please excuse pertinacious disobedience," said Li Han, bringing forward the steaming bowls, "but I conceived cunning and lovely stratagem for discomfiture of rebels."

"Hotcha," said the Professor, and then in Chinese. "Speak freely, worthy sea-cook."

"Have prepared several hundred lumps of sugar," said Li Han, bowing, "each one inscribed with Chinese characters for Good Fortune, Long Life, Fertility and Victory. These, if inserted into petrol of mechanical transport belonging to ignominious rebel Shun Chi, will cause practically instantaneous and insuperable carbonisation of working parts."

"Is that really so, Li Han? Where did you find that out?"

"Magnanimous engineer of trampling steamer imparted said information at Hong Kong when he required my unworthy aid in sabotaging car belonging to evilly disposed one-eyed merchant who had acquired engineer's wages by means of felonious trick. We dissolved one lump of best refined sugar in petrol tank, and lo, automobile un-mobile in five minutes, with incapable roarings of disabled engine and violent explosions from long pipe, accompanied by unpleasantly smelling clouds of smoke."

"What a beautiful idea," said Derrick. "But how can we get it into Shun Chi's gas?"

"Now for best part of stratagem," replied Li Han. "Ignorant and superstitious soldiery will buy inscribed sugar-lumps as charms to increase potency of petrol. They will insert said lumps themselves, to their ultimate confusion and downfall. I shall also realise three thousand per centum profit on prime cost of sugar," he added, in a tone of rather hollow cheerfulness.

As they continued along the downward road into Liao-Meng their guide became more and more uneasy. At last he pointed to a distant clump of pines, told them that the rebels' camp was just beyond it, and turned about.

"We are well rid of him," said the Professor, looking after his disappearing figure. "The only men of any use to us are brave men." He nodded to Li Han, who bowed repeatedly, grasping the mane of his little ass.

Some way out of the rebel encampment they separated, and Li Han went forward to peddle his lucky charms to the soldiers. The Professor took a last look through the Russian's papers. "Yes, they are all here," he said, folding them up. "I think the first part should be easy enough. How do I look?" He looked a strange sight in his tall sheepskin hat, with the incongruous horn-rimmed spectacles under it, and at another time Derrick might have been amused. But now he answered quite seriously, "Quite all right, sir. But perhaps you should look more sinister if you could manage it. You have rather a mild expression, you know."

"Ah, I must remember that," said the Professor, with a savage leer. "And you must not forget your part. You are a dull, taciturn young Mongol servant; you speak neither Chinese nor Russian, and you know nothing about anything."

"That shouldn't be too difficult," said Derrick, with a faint grin. "And if anybody speaks to me in Mongol I can answer a few words convincingly enough. I can pretend to be an Usbeg or a Kazak: they won't have any of them here."

They went on, on and on to the clump of trees: they passed a few pedlars with baskets of fruit for the soldiers, and as the road led round the trees they came to a well-fortified camp, surrounded by barbed wire and guarded by sentries. The Professor rode boldly up to the main gate: the sentries saluted, obviously expecting him, and they passed through the barbed wire. Derrick followed the Professor, looking neither to the right nor the left: he felt his heart hammering, but he kept his face expressionless and dull.

In a moment they were past the sentries, and an orderly ran to take the Professor's reins. He dismounted, gave Derrick a pack to carry, and asked in a loud, surly voice where Shun Chi was to be found. Before the soldier could answer a group of men came from a nearby hut, and Derrick saw that four of them were Europeans and two Chinese. The Professor blinked nervously: the men greeted him in Russian, and after a fit of coughing he replied hoarsely, holding his handkerchief up to his mouth. There was a general shaking of hands, and the orderly began to lead the horses away. Derrick was at something of a loss; he could not understand what the Professor was saying, and he did not know what to do. The Professor took no notice of him, but walked away with the men towards the hut, speaking much more confidently as the minutes went by: Derrick stood for a moment, then followed the orderly to the horse-lines and watched him bring their fodder. To the remarks of the Chinese he shrugged his shoulders and replied gutturally in Mongol. The man did not trouble with him any further, and Derrick wandered nonchalantly into the rebel camp.

Presently he came to the flattened, greasy space where the lorries were lined up, and at the far end of the lorries he saw three tanks, with a group of men crowded round them. He went slowly towards them, and from the middle of the crowd he heard a well-known voice extolling the powers of the charms that were for sale. Wriggling in among them, he saw Li Han standing on a box of ammunition, holding up his lumps of sugar. He saw Derrick, gave him an imperceptible nod, and looked significantly towards a stone house in the middle of the camp.

Derrick made no motion of reply, but slipped backwards out of the crowd, and walked in an oblique direction towards the middle of the camp. There were many soldiers about, but they took no notice of him: he looked for all the world like a Mongolian horseboy, not a rare object in those parts. Only his face was out of character, for he could not put on the high, jutting cheek-bones or the wide-set, slit-like eyes of a Mongol; but there was little of that to be seen under the grease and his pulled-down hood. He walked with his legs stiffened and bowed, rolling in his gait; he chewed a piece of straw, and appeared to take little interest in anything around him. Slowly he approached the stone house and took its bearings: it was at the far end of the horse-lines, and there were a dozen ponies tethered to rings in its outer wall. On the side of the ponies there was a small square window, but none on the other sides. In the front of the house, on the side away from the window, there was the iron-studded door, and in front of that several armed guards lounged in the sunshine, smoking and playing dice. It seemed that the place had once been a shrine to one of the local deities, but Shun Chi had strengthened it out of all recognition.

Derrick went twice round it, getting the geography of the camp well into his mind; then he strolled along under the window. He waited until no one was by, and leaning against the wall he whistled the first tune that came into his mind, whistling very softly. It was Annie Laurie that he chanced upon, and he had hardly drawn breath before the answering song came back in a loud Scots voice. "I'll lay me doon and dee," sang Ross inside the stone house, "I'll lay me doon and dee—if you don't come very soon, I'll lay me doon and dee." He sang with very little melody, but with immense conviction.

With a quick glance round, Derrick vaulted on to the saddle of one of the tethered horses: standing on tip-toe on its back he could just see through the window. His uncle and Ross lay on the ground, tied hand and foot, and one of the guards was busy checking the song with his rifle-butt.

The horse moved uneasily, but just before Derrick fell he thought he saw Sullivan wink at him. It was fortunate that he fell when he did, for just then a party of soldiers came round the corner of the house. Derrick walked away: it would not do to arouse suspicions by staying there. The window was too small to get through, he reflected, even if it had no bars; but at least he knew that they were alive, and he felt very much happier. He went round the camp and then wandered to the place where the Professor was engaged with Shun Chi and the Russians. On his way he passed Li Han, who gave him a faint nod to show that all was well, but went by quickly without a word: Li Han's face was a queer, greenish colour.

Derrick went on and squatted in the shade outside the hut: he looked quite natural there, and nobody took any notice of him. From where he sat he could see the line of tanks and lorries. The soldiers were busy round their petrol tanks, unscrewing the caps and putting in the inscribed charms. And inside the hut Derrick could hear the Professor's voice, strong, firm, and apparently quite confident: he felt happy that the Professor had everything well in hand.

But if he could have understood what they were saying, Derrick would have been far less cheerful. The Russians would keep talking about the machine-guns, their rates of fire, their cooling-systems, their spare parts—all things of which the Professor knew nothing whatsoever. He was as non-committal as possible, but he was dreading the moment when they would ask him a direct question that could not be evaded. He tried desperately to turn the conversation; he talked of the weather, of some recent archaeological discoveries near Kiev, of the museums in Moscow, of anything except machine-guns and mortar bombs.

"Tell me, Ivan Petrovitch," said one of the Russians to him, "what is the news from Aksenova?"

"Quite inconclusive so far," replied the Professor warily, wondering whether Aksenova were a person or a place. "Very inconclusive indeed."

"Still? I thought it would have been settled long ago. But speaking of Aksenova reminds me, Tovarich, we have a present from there, have we not, comrades?"

"Ha, ha," replied the comrades, while the Professor sweated with apprehension, "indeed we have."

"And here it is, Ivan Petrovitch," cried the first man, rising from the box on which he had been sitting and opening the lid. "Vodka, little brother! This will make you feel at home, I believe, comrade."

"Yes, I suppose it will," replied the Professor unhappily, watching him pour it into the tea-bowls.

"To the brotherhood of man!" cried the Russian.

"To bigger and better bombs," answered the Professor, raising the bowl. The fiery spirit nearly made him choke, but he got it down, gasping like a stranded fish.

"Why, one would think you had never drunk vodka before, little uncle," said one of the Russians, and they all laughed heartily. The Professor laughed too, but rather later than the others. He felt the vodka burning inside him, and he wondered how his digestion, always a troublesome creature, would

116

care for it. After a few minutes he began to feel better, much better. He grasped the bottle and poured himself another stiff drink. He tossed it off in one gulp, to the toast of "Confusion to evil men," which they all repeated.

His brain seemed to be working excellently now, running on oiled wheels. "Now, comrades," he said, in a loud, firm voice, ringing with authority, "I have something to say to you. I have been sent here with two missions. One you know. But there is another. It is believed that one of you here, one at least, has been acting in a subversive manner, and I am going to investigate the matter," he cried, banging the table with his fist so suddenly that they all jerked in their seats. "I shall make a confidential report. And you all know where that will go." He paused for a moment, hoping that they did know, for he certainly did not. The Russians looked thoroughly ill at ease. He continued, after an ominous silence, "My report will, of course, depend upon what I see of your behaviour while I am here. And there is another matter which a man whose name I need not mention has asked me to look into. Two Europeans have been captured. I wish to interrogate them."

"Certainly, Ivan Petrovitch," said one of the men placatingly. "If you will come with me, Ivan Petrovitch, I will show you the way. This way, comrade."

The Russian led the way to the stone house: his manner had suddenly changed; he spoke fawningly and humbly. The other three watched them go in a downcast silence. "Dimitri Mihailovitch will try to put him against us," muttered one of them.

"I can assure you, comrade," said Dimitri, putting his hand on the Professor's sleeve, "that my conduct has been most conscientious, whatever faults the others may have committed. If you could see your way to mentioning my name favourably, I have a little money. . . ."

The Professor directed a stern and impressive look upon the wretched Dimitri Mihailovitch, who wilted as he stood, and wished that his tongue had been cut out before he had tried to bribe one of the incorruptible higher authorities.

"What nationality are these prisoners?" asked the Professor, without any reference to the Russian's last remark.

"One American and one British, comrade. They are very violent, and—"

"Do you speak English, Dimitri Mihailovitch?"

"No, comrade."

"What ignorance!"

"But nor do the others, comrade. They do not know a single word, Ivan Petrovitch, little father. Shun Chi knows a little, but he could get no information out of them. They are very worthless prisoners, Ivan Petrovitch. He is going to execute them this afternoon before we move off to attack Hsien Lu tomorrow morning."

"I see. Just what is the position of Shun Chi as regards authority?"

"He is under our thumb, Ivan Petrovitch. Under our thumb, comrade. Without our help he is like a pricked balloon—pouf!"

"You mean that he takes his orders from us?"

"Well, not exactly, comrade. He requires a little humouring at times, Ivan Petrovitch, when he is fixed on some object."

They reached the door of the stone house: the guards fell back and saluted. They went in. On the threshold the Professor paused. "Where's that wretched servant of mine?" asked the Professor.

"There he is, Ivan Petrovitch," said the Russian, pointing at Derrick, who had been following them. He ran back and seized Derrick by the sleeve. "Here he is, comrade," he said, hurrying Derrick along.

The three of them went into the stone house. The Professor looked at Ross and Sullivan. "Untie these men, Dimitri Mihailovitch," he said, "I shall adopt a more conciliatory form of questioning than has apparently been tried. One often gets better results that way."

"Certainly, comrade. Just as you say, Ivan Petrovitch: I am entirely of your opinion." The Russian busily untied the ropes, and Derrick bent to help him. Ross and Sullivan glared sullenly at them as they got up and rubbed the circulation back into their cramped limbs.

"Now, comrade," said the Professor, "you will see how I question people. I shall play the benevolent liberator, and you will see that I get far more out of these men by apparent kindness than any amount of torture.

Be so good as to fetch me some tea and a bottle of that excellent vodka. I am thirsty."

"Surely, Ivan Petrovitch, instantly, instantly. . . ." The Russian hurried away.

"Well, here we are," said the Professor in English, but still speaking in a loud, authoritative voice for the benefit of anyone who might be listening outside.

"I'm uncommonly glad to see you both," said Sullivan, straightening himself unsteadily.

"Aye," said Ross. "If you'd been just a wee bit later, you would have been in time for the execution. It's due with all due pomp in three hours' time. It would have been quite a sight: they mentioned boiling oil and the Thousand Cuts as part of the show."

"We'll have to miss it," whispered Derrick. "We've come to get you out."

"Have you though?" said Sullivan. "I would never have guessed that. Would you, Ross?"

"Why, no. I thought they had come to sell us tickets for the church bazaar." It was as well that he said this in an angry, whining tone, like a man who refuses to give any information, for a moment later the Russian came in with the vodka, closely followed by the others with pots of tea.

"Thank you, comrades," said the Professor. "These may be very valuable prisoners. I believe I recognise the villain on the right. It is most important to get all they know out of them, even if it takes some time. You need not wait. While I am busy you may get all the machine-guns ready for inspection. And I shall probably wish to speak with Shun Chi again later—make all the necessary arrangements."

"Tell me, Professor," said Sullivan, when they were alone again, "how did you manage it?"

Professor Ayrton gave him a quick outline of the position. "And now," he said, at the end of it, "I am wondering what to do for the best."

"Yes," said Sullivan, thoughtfully. "That is the question. What do we do now?"

Six

FOR some time no one spoke. Sullivan drummed his fingers on the floor: at last he said, "I have it. Is Li Han still around?"

"I'm not sure," said Derrick, "but I think he is."

"Good. We left the three sons of the Khan at the village of Tu Fu just before we were taken. They will wait for us five days. If Li Han takes a message to them at once, and they ride like the wind to Hsien Lu, they can tell him to bring his men up into the hills where the road leads into Liao Meng, to the place called the valley of the Three Winds. It is a perfect place for an ambush—plenty of cover and a steep slope—and it is just about there that their engines should give out. I'm right, aren't I, Ross?"

"Yes, just about seven li should do it."

"The next thing to do is to disable the new machine-guns and the bombs. Do you know what pattern they are?"

"I am afraid I do not—these things are quite outside my province. But I have the blueprints here, if they would be any use to you."

"That will be as good as seeing the actual machines," said Ross, unfolding the plans. "Derrick, keep an eye open through the crack of the door."

Ross, who knew more about machinery than all the rest of them put together; looked closely at the plans. "They have got some important new ideas here," he said. "Any government would give a pretty penny to see these plans. I dare say they are trying them out here as a test under war conditions. We'll keep these. Look here, Professor, do you see this locking-pin? And this tension nut above it? If you loosen these thoroughly, the gun will jam after the first few rounds, and in all likelihood the whole thing will explode, blowing the gun and the gunner to—to wherever Communist bandits go."

"I see," said the Professor, poring over the blueprint. "This object is to be loosened, and this nut also. Turned to the left, I take it? Derrick, you had better inspect the plan too, in case I make a mistake. I recall that I did so once, with a plan of a mechanical excavator. It buried the foreman and seventeen undergraduates, as well as the umbrella of my colleague Bloom. He was disproportionately vexed: he said that the umbrella, had belonged to his father, the expert on Middle European Hebrew symbolism, you know, and—"

"Forgive me if I interrupt, Professor," said Sullivan, "but what about the bombs?"

"What bombs? Oh, yes, the bombs. Dear me, I was almost forgetting the bombs. Here is a full description of them. Nasty, ugly, dangerous machines, in my opinion."

"This is a cinch," said Sullivan. "You see the variable fuse, Ross?"

"Yes. Set that to zero and they'll blow every man jack to pieces the minute he tries to use them."

"It's a cinch," repeated Sullivan. "Look, Professor, you must unscrew the cap here, and set the marker to the figure nought. Then put on the cap again and leave the bombs strictly alone. In no circumstances touch this pin, or you will be blown up."

"Oh," said the Professor, uncertainly. "Blown up?"

"Blown right up sky high, so have a care."

"I will, I assure you. This is the pin that is not to be touched. Derrick, come and look at this pin, and if you see me touching it, remind me that I should not touch it, then walk—no, run—quickly off."

Derrick was looking at the plan, and Ross was pointing out the vital pin, when Dimitri Mihailovitch walked silently in. He saw the blueprint in Ross's hands, and an expression of intense suspicion shot across his ugly face. He swung to Professor Ayrton and opened his mouth to speak, but Sullivan had been gliding sideways through the shadow towards him, and before a sound came out of his mouth Sullivan leapt on him, covering his face with a large and powerful hand. There was a momentary struggle: the Russian was bent violently back; they heard a strangled cry, a crack like the breaking of a stick, and Sullivan put the inert body gently down.

"I'm afraid I had to break his neck," said Sullivan. "If he had fired that would have been the end of us all."

"That complicates things," remarked Ross quietly, pocketing the Russian's revolver.

Derrick was tough: he had seen death before: but now he felt pale and sick with horror. The Professor could hardly speak.

"Take a drink," ordered Sullivan, passing the vodka.

"You must excuse my agitation," said the Professor in a trembling voice, wiping his spectacles nervously. "I am unused to . . . dear me . . ." his voice trailed off into silence.

"Now, to continue," said Sullivan, "when you have done those things, you will have to remain with Shun Chi's army until they reach the gorge in the hills, or they will get suspicious. You must keep on the extreme right, and at the first shot you lie down dead. We will have men there and ready to take care of you."

Ross suddenly looked at him with a question in his eyes.

"Yes. We'll be there," said Sullivan. "We are going to tie you up, Professor, and take your clothes and the Russian's. Derrick will have two horses ready untied behind. When we have been gone an hour Derrick will come in and find you tied up and will give the alarm. There will be no suspicion of a plot with this dead

Russian here. Then you will arrange the machine-guns and the bombs. Repeat what you have to do."

The Professor was correct in every detail.

"Derrick," said Sullivan, after a moment's thought, "give me the bearings of the camp again. Right: that's plain. As a precaution you must send Li Han off with the message as well. Now is everything clear? Good. Then I'll trouble you for your clothes, Professor, and the blueprints. Derrick, get the horses ready. Do not stand by them—walk clean away, and come back here to give the alarm in one hour. Got it? Right. Professor, I am going to jam this gag into your mouth, so if there is anything that is not quite clear, say it now."

"I have it all plain in my mind," said the Professor. "Good luck and God-speed." He opened his mouth for the gag, and lay still while they bound him.

"Go on, Derrick," said his uncle, softly, patting him on the shoulder, "you can take it, can't you?"

"Yes, sir," said Derrick. "Good luck."

He sauntered out: the guards were rolling dice at some distance from the door, and they did not even look up as he passed. He turned the corner of the house and came to the place where the horses stood. He quickly chose the best and untied them: he noticed that his hands were trembling, but he forced himself to remain calm. He lengthened the stirrups to suit the long legs of his uncle and Mr. Ross, and he tightened the girths. While he was doing this he became aware that someone was watching him from behind. Cautiously he sidled round the horse and peered under its belly. It was only Li Han. He gasped with relief, gave the girths a final pull, left the reins hanging through the loop and turned away. He gave Li Han a jerk of his head, and the Chinese followed him.

Derrick went slowly to the place where he knew that Li Han had left his ass, and there, pretending to be examining the little creature's hooves, he murmured his news and the message. Li Han nodded, mounted his donkey and rode slowly out of the rebel encampment.

Now Derrick had to pass the next hour somehow. He marked the position of the sun and walked about as easily as he could. He listened with all the force of his being for the shots at the gate which would mean that Ross and Sullivan had been detected—shots either at the house or at the gate of the camp. But when ten minutes had passed he was almost sure that he would not hear them now. He knew he must not go round by the stone house to see if the horses were gone, as that might possibly give the game away, but he longed to know for certain, and the next long wait was the most anxious that he had ever passed in his life. At last the sun had moved an hour's space across the sky, and Derrick, walking hurriedly, as if he had a message, went to the stone house. The guards were still playing dice as he passed them. He paused for a second on the threshold, smiled at the Professor, and then let out a yell that echoed throughout the camp.

The guards came rushing in with their rifles at the ready. For several minutes there was a confused hurly-burly, with everyone shouting at the tops of their voices. The din attracted Shun Chi himself; he came stamping through the crowd with his Russian advisers, knocked the guards out of his path, and on hearing the news that his prisoners had escaped, he foamed at the mouth. When he could speak he swore that he would have the head of every sentry at the gate if they had let the prisoners through. In a moment the report came that the sentries, seeing two Europeans dressed like Russians, had let them through without thinking twice about it. In another five minutes heads were rolling outside the camp, and the guards who had been outside the house had melted away into hiding. The officer who was supposed to be in charge of the men who should have been guarding the horses brought the news that two were missing: Shun Chi shot him where he stood.

Meanwhile the Russians were untying the Professor, and as soon as the gag was out, the Professor cried, "That fool Dimitri. I will have him shot, liquidated, sent to Siberia. Put him under arrest at once. The fool, he would insist on having the prisoners untied to question them. He said they would not answer to harsh treatment. I told him that it would be better to flog the answers out of them. Where is the son of a yellow dog? This is sabotage. He was in the pay of the capitalists. I'll know who paid him! I'll flog the answers out of him. Bring him here!"

"They seem to have killed him, Ivan Petrovitch," said one of them apologetically.

"So much the better," growled the Professor. "They have saved me the trouble." He turned to Shun Chi. "Well, Tu-chun," he snapped, "this is a pretty piece of work. They will be half-way to Liao-Meng by now, taking the south road to avoid Hsien Lu's army. If they are not caught before sunset, someone will have to answer for it." He glared about him impressively and caught sight of Derrick. "Here, you," he shouted, falling upon him with a rain of blows, "why weren't you here to protect your master, idle, worthless dog." He kicked him out of the house, and after a little more cursing and stamping about, he cried, "I said that the machine-guns were to be ready for inspection. Where are they?"

"If you will come with me, comrade," said one of the Russians, "I will show them to you. They are all ready. We have explained the working mechanism to the soldiers."

By the side of a long row of wooden crates the machine-guns stood, all neatly aligned.

"You have explained them thoroughly?" asked the Professor, looking at them blankly.

"Oh, yes, comrade, very thoroughly," said the Russian. "They understand them very well. My interpreter learnt in less than a morning."

"Your interpreter? Don't you speak Chinese?"

"Why, no, Ivan Petrovitch. You know that none of us speaks Chinese except the dead capitalist spy, Dimitri Mihailovitch."

"Of course. I remember. Who is your interpreter? How many are there here?"

128

"There were only two, comrade. A Chinese clerk who deserted last week, and the officer of the guard who lost his head just now."

"And you have made no effort to learn Chinese in all this time? You are content to be here now, unable to instruct the soldiers or to communicate with the Tuchun?"

"But you know what our orders were, and what our work is, Ivan Petrovitch," said the Russian, excusing himself; but there was a certain wondering tone in his voice that the Professor did not like.

"Nevertheless," he said, "I think that a little more zeal —however, let us get on with the inspection. These are all the guns?"

"Yes, comrade. Perhaps you can solve a little difficulty for me, Ivan Petrovitch. I find that when they get heated, the stop-pawl sometimes refuses its function. What is the best way of disengaging the return-spring without removing the condenser?"

"Well," said the Professor, "I think I will go on with the inspection now. It would take time to show you, and I have none to spare just now. We will talk about it in the evening."

"But if you pointed it out on the blueprint, comrade, I would see in a moment."

"I have not got it with me."

"But, comrade, excuse me. I saw you put it in your pocket."

"Later, later," cried the Professor, feigning to be absorbed in the machine-gun before him.

The Russian looked at him for a moment, and then said, "Do you think I should detach the draw-bolt?"

"Yes," said the Professor. "Now I want you to go and tell the others that I want a report from all of you immediately on the—on the rate of fire in the hands of inexperienced recruits, and on the difficulties you have met with in training the men. I want them at once, together with a return of breakages. You can be doing that while I look over these."

"Very well," said the Russian, leaving them.

When he was well away, the Professor sat down on the ground by the first machine-gun. It looked very unlike the blueprint.

"I believe the locking-pin and the tension nut are under this casing," he said. "Of course, they would not leave such delicate parts exposed. Pass me that spanner." He worked at the nuts. "Yes, here we are," he said, removing the casing. "Now we turn to the left here, and again here, and the deed is done." He looked up with a smile, wiping his forehead with a greasy hand.

"Don't look round, sir," murmured Derrick, "but there's something rather odd behind. The Russians are standing by their hut, and they are watching you through their binoculars."

"Are they, indeed? Confound their impertinence. I am very much afraid that that fellow who was here is growing suspicious. I could not altogether avoid his technical questions, and I probably answered stupidly. However, I have a petard on which to hoist them if they provoke me." He seemed to Derrick extraordinarily calm.

"They are getting excited," said Derrick. "One is coming our way now."

"I suppose I have done something very unprofessional with this machine," said the Professor, peering thoughtfully at a piece of metal.

The Russian came up, affecting to stroll idly. "It is getting very hot, comrade," he remarked, looking sharply at the dismantled gun.

"I don't find it so," snapped the Professor. "Have you prepared your report?"

The Russian did not reply directly. He said, "You seem to be having some difficulty with that interruptor." There was a false, cunning note in his voice.

The Professor threw down his spanner and stared menacingly at the Russian, who dropped his eyes and muttered, "Don't be offended, Ivan Petrovitch, I'm not criticising . . . I will go and write my report at once."

"They are not quite sure yet," said the Professor, when he was out of earshot. "If I knew a few technical terms in Russian—or, indeed, in any language—I could probably keep them off for the few hours that are necessary. But I am very much afraid," he paused to tighten a nut, "I am very much afraid that they will force me to hoist them before long. Are they still watching?"

"Yes. All of them."

"Humph," said the Professor, moving on to the next gun.

"What do you mean by hoisting them?" asked Derrick, in a worried murmur. He could not understand how the Professor could remain so cool right under the gaze of their enemies.

"I mean hoisting them on their own petard. You have read of the engineer being blasted at the pale-faced moon, have you not? No? Then you must agree with me that school is quite certainly imperative." He was working steadily on the fourth gun. "I mean that I will double-cross the bum galoots. They suppose themselves to be very wise guys: but they will find that they are deceived, and that we are wiser."

"How do you mean?" asked Derrick, hardly able to control his own nervousness.

"Keep a cool head, my dear boy. I know that this is very trying for you, but endeavour to be calm. I will tell you—it is a scheme worthy of a Greek hero, and it is not wholly un-Greek in its element of treachery. But I will condense it into four or five words. They do not speak Chinese: I do. I hope very much that I shall be able to accomplish my design without bloodshed, but if I cannot, then I must regretfully sacrifice the knaves. Are they still there?"

"Yes."

"When you are speaking to an older man, Derrick, it is better to say 'sir.' Even in times like these one should try to keep one's self-command, and the little civilities are like so many bulwarks, as I believe the nautical term goes. Now just help me fasten this disagreeably oily piece, and I will go and pay a call on Shun Chi. They are still watching?"

"Yes, sir."

"Then there is no hope for them, the unfortunate knaves. Now the next screw. . . ." It seemed that he would never finish: Derrick watched him go on and on, patiently adjusting the scattered parts, until he could hardly bear it any longer. But at last the Professor straightened his long and bony frame, wiped his face and said, "Now, Derrick, I want you to stand where you can watch the Tu-chun's tent. If you see anything unpleasant happening to me, you must give me your word to escape at once, without trying to do anything to help me. I want your word, and I will not go otherwise." He spoke gently, but Derrick knew that he was in deadly earnest. He gave his word, and the Professor said, "There is, in point of fact, no danger at all. All this is only to make me feel a little more confident." He smiled, and turned away.

Derrick watched him walk to the left, out of the Russians' sight, and then turn sharply to the Tu-chun's tent.

The rebel leader was in a black mood, but he greeted the Professor with as much courtesy as he could manage, which was not a great deal, for he was an ill-conditioned, brutish fellow, who had risen from the gutters of Hu Wan through the various stages of petty thievery, brigandage and banditry to his present position. He was a false, treacherous man, of the kind who can be relied upon to turn against his friends and allies at a moment's notice if it serves his ambition, or if his fears are aroused.

"I have some disturbing news for you, Tu-chun," said Professor Ayrton. "There is treachery in your camp."

"What?" cried Shun Chi, grasping his revolver. "Who?"

"You have had no suspicions?"

"The sentries this morning?"

"Worse."

Shun Chi went pale. He had been a traitor all his life and he felt treachery all around him.

"Tell me at once," he begged. "I will give you . . ." —he looked wildly round the tent—"I will give you a thousand taels of gold."

"I want no gold, Shun Chi. The cause I serve needs no gold. When I came here I was told to expect to find four Russians. I found one. He is dead. The others are foreign devils hired by Hsien Lu. They knew that I had detected them, or at least that I suspected them—their papers were stolen or forged— and they were certain that as soon as I inspected the machine-guns and the bombs I should be certain of their treachery, so they hatched a plot with the prisoners—who were almost certainly confederates—to have Dimitri Mihailovitch and me murdered. You had better have them arrested at once, before they bribe the sentries and escape too. But they must not be killed: my chiefs will want to see them. I cannot promise any further support for your army if these men are killed. Now you must excuse me, Tu-chun: if I am to repair the sabotaged machine-guns and the bombs in time for tomorrow's attack I shall need every minute. Just have them tied and gagged, and let no one near them—they have too many accomplices here already."

For a moment it seemed as if Shun Chi were going to have an apoplectic fit. The veins stood out on his forehead and he gasped for breath. But by a violent effort he mastered himself enough to scream for his guards and to rush out of the tent.

The Russians were standing by the machine-guns, peering into their works. They started guiltily when they saw the Professor. If the rebel leader had not already been wholly convinced, he would have condemned them in that moment, for they looked like men detected in a crime. "Sons of pigs," he shouted, "you are at it even now. You are dead men." He screamed orders to his guards, and in spite of his greed for more tanks and guns his fury overcame him, and in a moment the Russians rolled headless on the ground.

"This is a foretaste of victory," said Shun Chi, with an evil smile. "Tomorrow I shall do the same to Hsien Lu and every prisoner we take, if only you can get the guns ready in time."

"Rest assured, Tu-chun: I shall have them fully prepared for you by the hour of the Rat," said the Professor, "and the bombs, too."

"Well," said Derrick. "I never thought it would come off quite like that."

"I was afraid it would," said the Professor, seriously. "I did my best for them, but there was no help for it. It was their lives or ours."

They worked hard. They soon grew accustomed to the machine-guns, and by nightfall they had successfully wrecked every one of them. The Professor attended to the bombs by the light of a hurricane-lamp, and by midnight the serried racks of bombs were all set to explode as soon as their pins were pulled. The Professor put the last one in its place and got up to stretch. "I never hope to spend a more thoroughly uncomfortable evening," he said. "It quite surprises me that I am still in one piece. Never again shall I permit myself to come into such a position that I am obliged to handle these infernal machines. They are utterly revolting in cause, effect and appearance." With these words he lay down and tranquilly composed himself to sleep.

Derrick listened to his even breathing and wondered how he could possibly sleep. He knew that he would never go off himself, and his mind ran busily over the possibilities of the coming day, the great number of things that could go wrong, and those which might go right. They were to keep to the extreme right of the gorge, he repeated: he must remember that.

Yet somehow he must have gone to sleep, for there was the Professor shaking him awake. "It is the hour of the Rat," he said.

136

The first part of the column was already moving off towards the hills when the Professor and Derrick came from their tent. Shun Chi was waiting, for them with his staff. "You shall come with me," said the Tu-chun, after greeting the Professor: he pointed to a light tank that stood drawn up immediately in front of a lorry containing all the rebel's most valuable loot.

Shun Chi was a firm believer in leading his army from the rear: he had no intention whatever of running into any danger that he could possibly avoid, and he offered this place in his tank to the Professor as the most valuable favour that he could devise.

Derrick's heart sank as he followed the Professor into the cramped and stuffy tank: he had thought of a great many possibilities, but not of this one. Now there would be the whole body of the army to get through if ever they were to reach their friends.

The Professor, too, looked worried; but he could not refuse without arousing the warlord's suspicions, and he sat down with a calm, thoughtful expression.

The tank jerked into motion with a roar: the whole column was in motion now; there was a vile smell of oil and of petrol fumes, and the infantry kicked up a cloud of dust so dense that it drifted thick through the slits and eyepieces of the tank.

Derrick sat awkwardly on a box on the floor of the tank, wondering just what would happen to them when the engine gave out and it became obvious that the machine-guns had been doctored. He noticed that one of the guns was in position on the tank, and that a rack of bombs stood close at hand and ready. "The moment anyone grabs one of those," he thought, looking at the bombs, "it's all up with us."

Very quickly, it seemed to Derrick, they drew nearer to the hills. He could see quite well out of one of the traverse slits, and long before he expected it he saw the opening of the valley of the Three Winds. This was where the road started to climb at a very steep. angle, and this was where things ought to start to happen. The gorge came nearer and nearer. He heard one of the lorries farther up the line spluttering and backfiring. He looked apprehensively at the Professor, and passed his tongue over his dry lips. The Professor smiled back at him calmly, and then leant casually over to Shun Chi, pointing to the heavy revolver at his belt.

"That is an unusual pattern," he remarked. "May I look at it?"

"Certainly." The warlord handed it over. "I took it from the body of Tzu Mo. I have shot seventy-three men with it, and fourteen women." He smirked with pride; but he did not mention that of the seventy-three, sixty-nine had had their hands tied behind their back.

The Professor turned it over in his hands, and released the safety-catch. The front of the column was well into the gorge: Derrick heard several motors misfire and stop. One exploded, and in the silence that followed he heard the sharp crack of a rifle.

"Seventy-three men and fourteen women," repeated

the Professor. "Indeed?" Then, without any change in his voice, he said, "I shall kill you, you evilly minded scoundrel, if you make the slightest movement. Put your hands up in the air at once. Derrick, take away the disgusting fellow's weapons."

The driver looked round to say that the engine was misfiring, and he looked straight down the barrel of the automatic that the Professor was holding in his other hand. "Stop the engine," said the Professor, "and come in here." The man obeyed, and the Professor made him creep low between himself and the warlord to the far end, where Derrick disarmed him and tied his hands behind his back. The driver lay with his face to the ground, and there only remained the man in the turret. "Pull him by the leg," said the Professor. But when Derrick pulled there was no reply. He pulled again, harder, and the man slid gently down into the body of the tank: he had already received a bullet between the eyes.

The sound of firing was general now. All along the column the machine-guns crackled into action: each fired three or four rounds and then jammed. More than one blew up, and soon nearly all the firing was coming from the other side. A solid iron cannon-ball came trundling briskly down the line and bumped heavily into the tank: Hsien Lu's artillery was finding the range. A spatter of rifle bullets ricochetted off the tank, making a din like a gong.

Several more bullets hit the tank, and there was a deafening bang as one whipped in and flattened itself behind Derrick's head. Some marksman at close range was finding the slits and eye-holes.

"I think we would be prudent to leave this place," said the Professor, mildly. "Can you see any reasonable shelter outside, Derrick?"

"Yes, there's a rock jutting out about twenty yards away, sir, and there is a path leading up to where Hsien Lu's men are firing from."

Another bullet made the inside metal ring. "Perhaps we had better hurry," said the Professor. "It would be intolerably vexing to be hit by our friends at this juncture." Derrick fumbled at the screw handles of the steel door. "You know," said the Professor. "I have half a mind to shoot this loathsome fellow before we leave. I have taken a prodigious dislike to him."

"You aren't going to, are you, sir? He's unarmed."

"No. I am not. But it would be a taste of his own medicine, and one so rarely has the opportunity of expressing one's dislike so forcibly. It makes one feel quite bloodthirsty, you know." A hail of bullets struck the tank: the din was unceasing now.

"I've got the door open," said Derrick.

"It would be rash to go out now," said the Professor, shouting above the racket. "Perhaps you had better wave something out of the turret, as a sign."

The noise of battle increased farther up the gorge, as the men of Hsien Lu's army who had no rifles—the majority—put down their umbrellas, put on their hideous masks, drew their swords and rushed down the slope, shrieking out blood-curdling threats: but in the immediate neighbourhood of the tank the fire diminished. When no bullets had hit the tank for some minutes, the Professor reluctantly abandoned the idea of shooting Shun Chi and backed out of the steel door. He slammed it, and they raced for the shelter of the rock. The next moment the door flew open, and Shun Chi appeared with a bomb in his hand. He grinned savagely. They were within easy range: he was sure of them. He ripped the pin out with his teeth and flung up his arm. Instantly there was a blinding flash, a shattering explosion, and the tank lurched over in a cloud of acrid smoke. Derrick and the Professor were flung to the ground by the blast, and when they looked round the tank had already caught fire. From the shelter of the rock they looked again, but they saw no sign of Shun Chi, for there was not a square inch of the Tu-chun left.

Seven

THE battle was soon over. The decimated rebel army fled in the wildest confusion and Hsien Lu was left the victor, with hardly a man wounded and the richest booty that he had ever won.

They marched on to the city of Hai Lin, the capital of Hsien Lu's province of Liao-Meng. The rebel garrison yielded without a blow, and from the Tu-chun's palace Sullivan sent word to Olaf and the Mongols to join them: within a few days the Professor's archaeological expedition was reformed and stood ready to continue its peaceful and scientific progress. Olaf brought Chang with him. The poor dog was a bag of skin and bone: he had been trying to find Derrick for days and days, and in all that time he had not eaten; it was only by the greatest good fortune that he had returned to Chien Wu the evening before Olaf set out. Chang welcomed Derrick with boundless delight, and within a few days he began to fill out again to something like his former sturdiness.

The Professor was his former academic self again; he had got over his transient thirst for blood, and he was eager to continue with his journey. But he had reckoned without Hsien Lu. The warlord would by no means allow them to depart until he had shown his gratitude. Every day they sat down to immense banquets, rich with the strangest and most sought-after delicacies. In time Derrick grew weary even of the nests of sea-swallows; he was tired of eating, and he never wished to see another meal again. Li Han, however, was in his element: for years he had cooked for others, and now others were cooking for him; he had acquired a great deal of face, and he sat among the lesser officials, growing almost as stout as a mandarin. They gave him the nickname of Jelly-Belly Wary—Jelly-Belly for his rapidly increasing girth, and Wary for his caution in war.

Olaf, too, ate like a starving man, day after day. "Ay reckon you can't never have too much to eat," he said greasily. "Ay ban so long at sea, Ay ban right sick of hard tack. Fill up against the next long voyage, Ay say:

142

there ain't no telling when you'll have the next chance." He sighed with repletion and looked enviously at a pile of crimson prawns. "Ay t'ink," he said thoughtfully, "that Ay could manage one more."

Derrick watched him demolishing the heap of prawns. "You'll surely burst if you go on," he said.

"Well, Ay reckon that ban a hero's death," replied Olaf, skewering another prawn. "You make a long arm, now, and sling along the fried noodles."

Chingiz and his brothers scorned the endless feasting. They preferred horse-flesh and koumiss; but they were deeply interested in the weapons that had been captured from Shun Chi.

The tanks did not interest them: they thought them greatly inferior to horses; but they spent many hours with the machine-guns before regretfully deciding that they were no use on horseback. They were charmed with the bombs, but Sullivan would not let them have any.

"These Mongols," he said, "are good enough at murdering one another as it is, without giving them the power to wipe out whole tribes at a time. They must forgo the advantages of modern civilisation."

At length Hsien Lu could no longer keep them from the road. He loaded them with presents and sent them on their way with an escort large enough to guard the ransom of a king. He gave them many things, and he would have given them more if Sullivan had not pointed out that they could not cross the Gobi with seven enormous wagons. The Professor had three

143

brass Buddhas, made in Birmingham, a cuckoo-clock and some bronzes. As he was showing them to the others he observed, "These four bronzes are recent forgeries; these here are also forgeries, but they were made in the Sung dynasty to represent Han bronzes. Think of that: well over a thousand years ago they were already forging antiquities when our kings could hardly read and write, and went about knocking people on the head."

"As for knocking people on the head, Professor," said Ross, who was suffering badly from indigestion, and was feeling somewhat liverish and argumentative, "you have shown a very pretty talent for that. And as for forging antiquities, that does not seem to me a very creditable sign of civilisation."

"I should say that that remark showed a very super-ficial reflection," said the Professor, who was also a little liverish, "if it might not be thought ill-mannered. I shall content myself with observing that the forgery of antiquities proves the existence of a widely spread appreciation of them. I would further add, sir, that I have seen Han forgeries of Chow ritual vessels, made, I repeat, at a time when. we were painted blue and ran about howling like a pack of savages. Confucius takes notice of this in the seventh chapter of—"

"But, Professor," interrupted Sullivan, "if they appreciate art so much, how do you account for these horrible brass Buddhas?"

"Well, there I must admit that you puzzle me. The cuckoo-clock can easily be accounted for as a Western curiosity, but I confess that I am surprised by these deplorable brass objects. It is strange that even a soldier, a man of violence," he said, with a sideways look at Ross, "should be so wanting in artistic taste. It puzzles me, particularly when I look at these remaining bronzes, these three incense-burners on the right, which are certainly Han, genuine Han, beautiful things, every day of two thousand years old." As he contemplated the incense-burners his good humour came back, and he said, "With the exception of one bronze that I saw in Moscow when I was a young man, and another in a private collection in America, those are the finest I have ever seen. Quite apart from their beauty, their inscriptions are of extraordinary interest"

"It is odd," said Sullivan, who was still looking at the Buddhas, "because Hsien Lu is no fool. No sort of a fool at all. I noticed that when he gave them to you he said that in spite of their appearance you would find in time that they had a certain inner value."

"True. He was referring, no doubt, to their religious significance. But to return. to these bronzes, I will stake my reputation that they are genuine. This version of the familiar extract from the Great Wisdom, for example, runs . . ."

The Professor would have gone on indefinitely, but he was interrupted by the arrival of the carpenter who had come to make special cases to fit the incense-burners, and while the Professor was giving his instructions the others escaped. The Professor had each of the bronzes swathed in silk before they were packed: he did the same for the Buddhas, in order not to hurt the Tu-chun's feelings, and he had them all loaded on one particular camel, where he could keep his eye on them.

After one last gargantuan banquet which lasted all night the expedition set out. They were bloated and weary—Chang was so fat that he could hardly run—but the new and excellent horses and pack animals that Hsien Lu had given them covered the ground at a great pace, and even on the first day they travelled a long stage. A little before nightfall a galloping messenger caught them up with a letter from the warlord to say that he had caused the Professor's enormous stelae to be uprooted and that they would be sent down to the nearest port to be shipped off as a trifling token of his esteem.

The next evening a second messenger pursued them with several jars of ginger and medicinal rhubarb, in case they should need it on their journey. And on the day after that no less than five arrived with presents of fur-lined clothing, as the Tu-chun thought they might take cold on the high plateau. Silk, weapons, antique porcelain, ivory, wonder-working pills, felt boots, remedies against old age, toothache and jaundice, small patent stoves, charcoal burners and a catalogue of the Army and Navy Stores (which Hsien Lu believed to be in verse) raced after them over the high and dusty roads of Liao-Meng, until their spare baggage animals were loaded down to the ground, and every evening they would scan the horizon apprehensively for the cloud of dust that would herald the coming of a new alarm-clock or an incredibly fragile set of Imperial egg-shell china.

They rode for day after day through Liao-Meng, and at last the fields thinned out, the vegetation grew more sparse, they passed no more trees, and finally they left the last dwelling behind them. They entered upon a vast plain, covered thinly with brown grass and extending to the rim of the horizon all round the uninterrupted bowl of the sky.

Three times, as they crossed this huge expanse, armed bands appeared in the distance: once the advance guard of their escort had a brush with the bandits, and once they passed a heap of bones, among which still blew the torn remnants of plundered bales of merchandise, fluttering in the desolate wind; but they were not seriously molested, although they were travelling through a district infested by all manner of disbanded soldiers from broken armies, brigands and embryonic warlords trying out their hands on stray passers-by or caravans that were weakly armed and irresolute.

There came a day when, in the far distance, a low building appeared. On this flat plain it showed for miles and miles, and it seemed as strange and remarkable there as a ship in full sail. They reached it early the next morning, and the column halted. Derrick saw a broad, rough road running straight as an arrow from one edge of the world to the next, and the building stood at its side. They were on the Old Silk Road at last, a road of immeasurable antiquity, once used by innumerable caravans, but now almost deserted.

Here they were beyond the range of the Chinese bandits, and here the escort turned back, carrying the expedition's last presents and letters to Hsien Lu, now far away in the east. It seemed strange when the soldiers were gone: they had grown used to their company.

Derrick explored the low stone building with Chingiz. It appeared to have been built solely for the convenience of horses: there were magnificent stables, but only a few bare rooms for men.

"I wonder why they built this?" said Derrick.

"He had it made for horses and messengers," replied Chingiz.

"Who?"

"Why, my ancestor, of course," said Chingiz, looking surprised.

"You often speak of your ancestor," said Derrick, "as if you only had one. Who was he?"

"He was Khan of the Golden Horde, Emperor of China and Lord of the World."

"Hm," said Derrick, looking sideways at Chingiz. He was almost sure that the Mongol was either boasting or pulling his leg; but when he mentioned it to Sullivan, his uncle said, "Oh, yes. He is descended from the great Khan, all right. Chingiz Khan, or Gengis, as some say, took one of his wives from among the Kokonor Mongols before he was a great man at all: if I remember rightly, it must have been when he was about your age."

"And was he Emperor of China and Lord of the World?"

"Well, he broke through the Great Wall and took Peking, but I rather imagine that it was his grandson Kubilai who was the first Mongol emperor of all China. As for being Lord of the World, well, he certainly didn't rule in Kansas City —nor in Dublin, for that matter—but he certainly made a good attempt at it. He did rule from Peking to Persia, and maybe beyond: but you ought to ask the Professor if you want to get all the details straight. All I know is that he built this house, and hundreds more all along to beyond Samarcand, and that he had good horses in every one of them and men ready to go out at a moment's notice to carry messages at a full gallop to the next place, so that he could pass the word from one end of his empire to another in no time at all—or not much, anyway."

"Yes," said the Professor, when they talked about the Great Khan that evening, "he was a very successful man in his way. That is to say, in his wars he caused the death of eighteen million people. He made at least eighteen million homes miserable, and he ravaged a larger tract of country than any man before or since: he did it so thoroughly that what was once useful land is now desert, and will be desert for ever. He was a very successful man in that he accomplished all that he set out to do. But if I were descended from him, I should regard it as my greatest shame, and I should conceal the fact. You may smile, Derrick," he said very seriously, "but suppose you had a small house of your own, and some fields that gave you your living, and suppose that you belonged to a country that threatened no one. And then suppose one morning you found a troop of savage, hostile men feeding their horses on the crops that were to keep you through the winter, taking away and slaughtering your cattle and then coming to your house, bursting in, stealing all the things you valued and had possessed, perhaps, all your life —things that had been earned or made by your father and grandfather and handed down to you—robbing and then burning the house for fun. Then suppose they killed your children and your wife, and carried you away to work or fight for them for the rest of your life. You would not consider those men very admirable characters, would you? No, nor do I. However hard you try to imagine that misery you will not realise a hundredth part of it: but if you do your best, and then multiply that wretchedness by eighteen million, you will have a remote hint of a conception of how much misery a man who wages aggressive war can cause, and you will begin to understand why I should not be proud of being descended from Chingiz Khan, or any other aggressive barbarian, whatever century or nation he may belong to."

"But what about Hsien Lu, sir?"

"My dear boy, do you not see the essential difference between aggression and self-defence? I have a high regard for the character of a soldier—not that Hsien Lu is a very shining example of that character, perhaps—but none at all for the character of a bully and a thief. A man has a right and a duty to defend his home and his country from attack: if his country is attacked he must defend it, and if he defends it well he is worthy of the highest praise. But if, on the other hand, he sets out to conquer other people—and he will always choose what he considers a weaker nation— then, for all I can see, he instantly degrades himself to the level of a destructive pest, a kind of vermin that should be destroyed as quickly as possible."

"I entirely agree with you," said Sullivan. "Aggressive war is the great crime of the world."

"You're right. And in my opinion much too much fuss is made about bravery," said Ross, who was as brave as a lion himself. "A man without it is precious little use; but a man may have any amount of it and still be a mean, base creature, a gangster or a half-witted, illiterate barbarian."

"Like Chingiz Khan," said Sullivan, with a smile. "That settles your hero's hash, Derrick. Now you had better go below—cut along to bed, I mean—or you will never be up in time."

The road led on and on, climbing very gradually until they were on a high plateau, and the air was hard and keen.

"We are coming into my own country," said Chingiz, sniffing the wind.

Every day or so they passed one of the Great Khan's

151

relays, and often they camped in them for the night. The sides of the road were littered with the white bones of horses and camels, and sometimes the picked skeletons of forgotten men, bones that had accumulated through the centuries until now a traveller could hardly go a mile without a grim reminder of his mortality. It was a striking proof of the road's antiquity and of the great numbers it once had carried. If there had been much vegetation, the bones would hardly have been seen, but there was almost none. Now and then a few patches of low thorn bushes broke the monotony of the even plateau, but there was never a tree to be seen at all, and, as Olaf remarked, a man would be hard put to it to hang himself there.

It was a strange, deserted world. Sometimes they saw great herds of wild horses, turning and wheeling like cavalry regiments at a distance, but they never approached, any more than the rare steppe-antelopes. They rode day after day without seeing a single trace of a man, and it almost seemed that the rest of humanity had perished, leaving them in a deserted world. Smoke on the horizon or the track of camels that had passed recently became an event.

Derrick, as the Professor had promised, embarked on the delights of Greek as they rode steadily along in the early morning, and twice a day, under the supervision of Ross, he shot the sun and worked out their precise position, as if they were navigating a ship; he was also unable to escape his mathematics, but in spite of that he spent most of his time with the Mongols. He knew his chestnut pony very well by now, and by dint of hard riding all day and every day, he could almost hold his own with Chingiz as a horseman. He dressed as a Mongol, for their clothes were far and away the most practical for their own country, and he grew to fit the deep Mongol saddle and to feel entirely at home in boots with felt soles several inches thick—the only boots that would really be comfortable in the strange Mongol stirrups. He now habitually greased his face as they did against the biting wind, and he rolled in his walk without having to think of it. He acquired a taste for koumiss, and although he still found it hard to repress a shudder, he could eat horse-flesh with the best of them. What was more important, he grew, by continual practice, to speak Mongol with such fluency that he no longer had to think of the words. His Mongol was very far from correct, but it came easily, and it improved every day.

On and on they went, day after day. The grass of the plain became more and more sparse: it no longer covered the ground, and between the tussocks lay sand that deadened the footfall of their beasts and swirled up to fill their eyes and throats in the wind of the afternoon. But for the stones that marked its sides, the road would often have been lost under the sand-drifts: they had entered the Gobi, and the whitened bones showed far more often.

Derrick, plotting their position on the map, added one more red dot to the thin line of them, a line that marked their passage and that was now wriggling slowly onwards into the heart of the great desert. Each day's travel was but a tiny advance on the map, but the days had mounted up, and already the red dots extended for hundreds of miles behind them to the Great Wall of China. Before them on the map stretched a much longer pencilled line that showed the route that they intended to follow: here and there small arrows pointed to the places where the Professor hoped to work, to disinter his ancient fragments and to investigate the possibilities of further excavation for a later full-scale expedition from his university, that was to be equipped with much more money, many experts and a large number of workmen for the digging.

Only once, as they crossed the worst part of the Gobi, did they see any human beings. In the middle of the day a caravan of Tibetans met them, travelling slowly towards China with their yaks and ponies. Some months later they would reach the western Chinese towns, where they would exchange their goods for tea, spend the worst of the winter, and return, after nearly a year's absence, to their high, cold homes behind the Kunlun mountains. The travellers stopped to take stock of one another and to exchange the news of the road. Derrick looked curiously at them, and at the great mastiffs which walked at the heels of the black, heavily laden yaks. In many ways the Tibetans resembled the Mongols—most of them spoke some Mongol, too—but they were taller men. In some ways their manners were alike, and it seemed to him that the main difference was that the Tibetans were not horsemen, as the Mongols were, and that they were much more concerned with their religion. They were Buddhists of a sort, and every one of them had charms, amulets and prayer wheels stowed somewhere in the greasy clothes which swaddled them about.

They were not lovely objects, the Tibetans, and they smelt very strongly indeed; but they were friendly and hospitable, and as Derrick sat by their fire, drinking the thick Tibetan tea, full of butter and other curious things, he felt a strange thrill, for there was a certain mystery about these men from the most remote of all the countries in the world, something that set them apart from other men.

Chang did not care for the Tibetans, or their mastiffs. These were very big dogs, half wild and uncontrollably savage. After Chang had had a set-to with three of them, Derrick tied him up out of harm's way until the morning, when he awoke to find the Tibetans already gone. They had left in the dark, and but for the smouldering fire of dried yak-dung they might have been a dream.

The worst of the desert passed under their feet, and they came to the Green Tomb: here they found the thin grass again. The country was just a little less blasted and sterile, and there was enough grazing for wild asses and a few shy antelopes. It was here that they made their first big detour, a long southward curve to the bed of a dried-up lake, where men had once lived in the distant past, although it seemed incredible. The

Professor found his site, and he set them all to digging, all except the Mongols, who would have nothing whatever to do with what they considered women's work.

It was hard and tedious work, and nobody but the Professor and Li Han cared very much for the results of the long hours of digging: there was nothing but a small heap of dusty, unrecognisable clay objects and bits of broken pot. The Professor was pleased, however, and labelled them all. "This," he said, holding up a particularly brutish fragment, "may well have been a quern."

"A quern," cried Li Han, rapturously. "Oh, sir!"

The Professor wrapped it up with care, and they moved off to the next place, three days' march away. The second site was a repetition of the first: a few barely traceable remnants of wall, dust flying in the cold wind, and at the end of the work a small collection of reddish potsherds and one villainous little broken lamp of primitive design. But this time Olaf did at least find a piece of jade, which excited them all. But when he ran to show it, the Professor gave it a cursory glance and said, "No. I am afraid it has nothing to do with the site. It is quite modern, a hundred years old at the most. Probably some wandering hunter took shelter here and dropped it." Olaf's face fell. "But at least," continued the Professor, not wishing to disappoint him, "it might bring you luck. The characters on it form a charm." Olaf brightened, breathed heavily on the jade, polished it on his sleeve and put it away in an inner pocket.

"Ay reckon a man ban a fool who throws away luck on a long voyage," he said. Olaf persisted in regarding the expedition as a voyage, although they were by now well over a thousand miles from the nearest ocean.

"It is strange how they have taken to green jade these days," said the Professor, over supper. "They used to despise it. In the older graves you will find nothing but mutton-fat jade. Take the most famous of all the Chinese collections, the Wu Ti, for example: there is not a single piece of green jade to be found in it. Or, at least, so they tell me. I have never seen it, of course, nor any other European. But the Chinese scholars who have seen the Wu Ti collection assure me that it is quite unrivalled, even in China. What a curse these strong nationalistic feelings are: I am sure that Wu Ti and I would get along wonderfully together, if only he would admit any foreigner to his house. Dear me, I would give a great deal to see that collection."

"Then why didn't you ask Hsien Lu to show it to you?" asked Ross. "It was in Shun Chi's loot, you know."

The Professor dropped his bowl of rice and stared at Ross without a word for some minutes. "Do you mean to say," he exclaimed at last, "that Shun Chi possessed the Wu Ti collection?"

"Why, yes," said Sullivan. "He looted it when he took Chang Fu. Wu Ti had moved it there for safety,

157

and hanged himself when he heard the news. It was the first thing that Hsien Lu looked for in the lorry behind Shun Chi's tank."

The Professor could not get over it. "That priceless jade was being jerked and banged about over mountain roads in that lorry," he said, "and exposed to the danger of bombs and bullets. Good heavens above. And I was within a few feet of it. And then I was in the same city with it, and on excellent terms with its new owner, and I never knew. How bitterly disappointing."

"I would have mentioned it," said Ross, apologetically, "but it never crossed my mind until this minute."

"I am very sorry, too," said Sullivan. "I ought to have told you. But I did not think you were interested in jade particularly."

"Not interested in jade!" exclaimed the Professor, throwing up his hands. "It is my . . . well, well," he said, in a calmer tone, "it cannot be helped. And, after all, I have my Han bronzes, which are reward enough for all our pains and trouble. Let us not think about it any more." He smiled round the table to show that he was not at all downcast.

"I could kick myself," said Ross. "I am very sorry. But I wonder that Hsien Lu did not think of it himself."

"But then," said the Professor, "if he had shown me the collection, I should certainly have been unable to conceal my admiration, and he would have felt obliged to offer it to me. Of course, I would never have accepted—its market value is truly incalculable—but it would have raised an awkward, disagreeable situation. No, it is all for the best, no doubt. And now let us dismiss the matter from our minds. Let me see, our march tomorrow should take us to this point on the map, should it not?"

It was three days after this that they came across a deep, rocky gully cut out by a stream that had dried up generations ago, and they had considerable difficulty in getting the camels across. When it came to the turn of the camel that carried the Han bronzes, Professor Ayrton skipped about like a cat on hot bricks. "Gently, now," he cried, as Olaf thumped the camel from behind, while Hulagu pulled in front. "Be very careful, if you please. Take care, the pack will slip! Drive the animal from the other side. No, no, Olaf; this way. Beware of the slope. Look out, look out! Hold it, quick. Derrick, run!" But before Derrick could get there, he heard a slithering noise and then a series of bumps.

"There," cried the Professor, wringing his hands, "the pack has slipped. Oh, you clumsy fellow." With these strong words the Professor sped nimbly down the gully after his bronzes.

The strong cases and the careful packing had saved them from injury, but the cuckoo-clock and the brass Buddhas were lying all abroad. The clock gave a last strangled crow as they reached it, and then became dumb for ever. The Buddhas, being heavier, had reached the very bottom of the ravine, and one of them had broken against a spur of rock.

"Look," cried Derrick, scrambling down, "there is something inside."

He knelt by the fragments of the image and picked up several objects, each wrapped over and over again with silk: it was obvious that they had been hidden in the hollow brass.

The others gathered round, and the Professor unwrapped one of the silken envelopes: it came off in a long ribbon. "They took good care of it, whatever it is," he said, unwinding steadily. Under the silk there was a piece of cotton wadding. He removed it, and there in his hand was a small tablet of mutton-fat jade covered with an inscription. The Professor gazed at it for a full minute without saying a word.

"What is it, Professor?" asked Sullivan. "It looks pretty good to a layman."

"Pretty good! Why, my dear sir, this is the finest piece of jade of the Chou dynasty that I have ever set my eyes upon." He gasped, incapable of expressing his emotion, and hurriedly began to unwrap the next package on the ground. The others joined in, and presently a triple line of superb pieces of jade stood before him. Sullivan lugged one of the other Buddhas over on to its side: underneath there was a cunningly hidden panel; he prised it open, and from the cavity slid dozens of heavily padded bundles. The third Buddha contained as many more. Soon the ravine was littered with silk wrappings and pieces of wadding, and the ranks of jade in front of the Professor had swollen threefold.

"It is the Wu Ti collection," said the Professor, in an incredulous voice, "or else I am dreaming." He sat on a rock and wiped his spectacles. "How dull of me!" he exclaimed, after a pause during which he carefully dusted each piece with his handkerchief. "How blind I was. When that most excellent Hsien Lu gave me those hideous brass images, had said that I would find that they had a certain inner worth —those were his very words—and I never . . . Well, well. Of course, he knew that I would refuse them as a present, so he chose this ingenious way of making me take them."

"It certainly was very handsome of him," remarked Sullivan.

"And I insulted his taste by thinking that he admired those horrible images. How glad I am that I shall be able to take photographs and detailed notes upon them before I give them back."

"If you give them back you will hurt his feelings beyond all measure," said Ross, decidedly.

"You could not possibly do that," said Sullivan. "It would be like grinding his face in the mud. He gave you this collection because you were a scholar, and could appreciate it, as well as because you had done him a great service."

"And he knows very well," said Ross, "that a valuable collection like that is in great danger of being lost, broken or dispersed in times like these. He would certainly like them to be in a place of safety—after all they have been looted twice already."

"Do you really think so?" asked the Professor, his face lighting up.

"Don't you agree with me, Sullivan?" asked Ross, and Derrick could have sworn that he saw a wink pass between them, although their faces were very grave.

"Of course I do," replied Sullivan. "I would have mentioned that point about the collection being in safety now, only I thought it was obvious."

"Well," said the Professor, with an uncontrollable smile creasing his wrinkled face, "that is a very sound argument, a very good argument indeed. I do not know that I have ever heard a better argument—so well expressed, so forcible." But he still, seemed to be wavering, and Derrick said, "Do you remember how they chucked things into that lorry, sir? And how nearly Shun Chi blew the whole thing up when he dispersed himself all over the landscape? That might happen again."

"Good heavens, yes," cried the Professor, clutching at the nearest piece with a protective hand. "What an appalling thought. The collection must certainly be guarded from such barbarous mishandling in the future. You are a very intelligent fellow, Derrick, probably the most intelligent boy of your age I have ever seen. I am very much afraid that it begins to look as if I shall be obliged to accept this princely —nay, more than princely—this imperial gift. Li Han, my good friend, be so good as to pass me the silk and cotton wrappings. And to think," he said, carefully enveloping a small jade toad, "that I so grossly injured the worthy Hsien Lu by considering him, in the recesses of my mind, as a speechless clock."

"Speechless clock," cried Li Han, "is most poetical and philosophical image."

"What does it mean?" asked Derrick.

"My poor boy," said the Professor kindly, "before you visit your mother's country you really must remind me to give you a little course in Americanisms. You will be quite lost if you do not understand widely accepted figures of speech of this nature. Speechless clock is a term on the lips of every free-born star or stripe: it is the most current of usages. Am I not correct, Sullivan?"

"Well, Professor, I rather believe that it is a little more usual to say dumb cluck."

"Oh, come," said the Professor, "are we not making a distinction without a difference. Speechless and dumb are synonymous, are they not? And of the two speechless is to be preferred, seeing that it more nearly approaches the Greek —and the locution is obviously a play on the Greek *alogos*, with its double meaning of speechless and without reason. As for your suggestion of cluck, I am afraid that it must be rejected out of hand. We use the onomatopoeic word cluck for the noise made by the domestic hen when she is pleased: at this moment I would cluck myself, were I a domestic hen. But if we qualify cluck by an adjective that implies soundlessness, we fall into an absurdity. No: clock is the word, Sullivan. Early clocks, as no doubt you are aware, told the time solely by the ringing of a bell—indeed, you have retained the custom on board ship—and the very word itself is derived from the late Latin *cloca,* meaning a little bell. Now a clock, therefore, that is speechless, is the very type and example of a useless, stupid thing, and thus we have the exceptional force and bite of this valuable expression. I am sure, my dear sir," he said, looking benevolently at Sullivan over his spectacles, "that after a moment's reflection you will discard your meaningless corruption—the perversion of an untutored Redskin, no doubt, that you must have heard in your impressionable childhood—and that in future, if ever you have occasion to reprove your shipmates, you will refer to them as speechless clocks."

Eight

"IF the latitude were marked as clearly on the earth as it is on the map," said Sullivan, "this would be an easy journey. We would just have put our noses down on the fortieth parallel at Peking, and we would never have lifted them until we reached the neighbourhood of Samarcand. But as it is—well, can you see the fortieth parallel anywhere, Derrick?"

"No, sir," said Derrick, "I rather think the Mongols must have stolen it."

They were in the middle of a bed of giant reeds, and although they could not see it, there was a wide stretch of open water before them. They had left the main party some way to the north while Sullivan tried to

164

find a shorter way through the swamps of Ulan Nor: he had passed this way once with the father of the Mongols, but that was some years ago, and the way through the vast marshy depression, devoid of land-marks, was difficult to find. From the steppe all they had been able to see was a vast fringe of reeds, with winding arms of white water leading through it, and beyond, mud-banks and the surface of the enormous lake. But now that they were in the reeds they could see nothing at all.

Derrick knew that his uncle was a few feet ahead of him, but he could see nothing of him, and if he had not known that Sullivan was steering their course by com-pass he would have felt lost indeed.

"We should not have very much farther to go now," said Sullivan: his voice was more distant now, farther over to the right, and Derrick pushed strongly through the reeds towards the sound. He was knee-deep in evil-smelling mud, and he knew that if he broke through the tangle of submerged roots he would sink down and never be seen again. It was disagreeable knowledge, and he struggled through as quickly as he could. But before he could reach his uncle there was a sudden prodigious roar, a noise higher than thunder, yet not unlike it: then a second later the sky was dark-ened, and he heard his uncle shouting, "Do you see that?"

Derrick stared up, and there, above the high reeds, were countless thousands of duck, close-packed and rising quickly through the air, which trembled under the beating of their wings. He watched them for a moment, and then scrambled through to join his uncle, who was standing in the ooze on the water's edge. As Derrick broke through the reeds still another great raft of duck lifted from the farther end of the water, lashing the surface and then sweeping up into the wind to gain height. The first multitude passed over the lake again, still rising and weaving in a close-knit skein, and the second joined it: soon they vanished like a cloud, and on the chill waters of the lake there was nothing but a few floating feathers and a single unmoved diving-bird, something like a grebe, that continued to bob about near the farther shore.

"Well, here we are," said Sullivan. "This is the right place, all right: do you see that stake standing in the water there? Old Hulagu Khan's brother planted it there to guide me years ago, and it is still standing. But I am afraid that the kachak yol—that is what they called this route—is no use to us. We would never get the camels across that in a month of Sundays. It was not so bad when I came this way last: that stake was on dry ground then. The swamp has been filling up. It's a pity: it would have saved us five days at least."

"We shall have to go round the north of the swamp, then?"

"Yes. Even if we could get the camels through this, there's worse beyond. No: it's a nuisance, but it was worth trying, and at least we have got this compensa-tion—we'll have a few hours of the best duck-

166

shooting in the world before we go back and join the others."

They forced their way back through the reeds, a long, long path with very heavy going, and returned to the place where they had left the horses and Chang by the black felt tent, the yurt, in which they were to sleep.

Derrick was awake well before the dawn, but his uncle was up before him, already sorting out the ammunition and filling his belt by the light of a small Mongol lamp—their electric torches had given out long before—whose flame hardly flickered, in spite of the wind that was bowing in the wall of the yurt, for the felt let in no air at all. It was a cold night outside, and the hoar-frost showed under the waning moon: the sky was clear, but a strong wind blew from the northeast, and Derrick was glad to be moving.

"We must get there before the moon goes down," said Sullivan, as they set off, "or I shall not be able to find the place I have in mind."

Chang raced in the faint moon-shadow of Derrick's pony as they rode swiftly over the silvery steppe: they went gently downhill all the way towards the remote, whitened fringe of reeds that hid the lake. Presently the ground became boggy underfoot, and the horses slowed down: Sullivan swung over to the right, aiming for a slight rise in the ground where a few ghostly alders stood bowed against the wind. The horses picked their way with care, but soon their riders' high boots were splashed with mud. The trees, the only trees they had seen for weeks and weeks, grew nearer, and suddenly the ground was firm again.

"We'll leave them here," said Sullivan, dismounting and strapping his blankets well over the horse's back, "and we'll go the rest of the way by foot." They tethered the horses and plunged into the reeds. Almost at once they were sheltered from the wind: it sang through the tops of the reeds like a half-gale in the rigging of a ship, but Derrick, well below the top, was soon warmed through and through as he pushed along behind his uncle's back. He welcomed the warmth, for it had been perishingly cold on the steppe, as it always was at night, even in the height of the summer, but very soon he began to feel that he was warm enough. His boots were heavy and clogged with mud, and he panted with the effort of keeping up with the strong, broad back in front of him: he thrust on and on through the reeds, as hot and sticky now as if he had been running under the noon-day sun. Just when he was beginning to feel that he could not carry his gun any farther, and that he would have to stop and take off his boiling boots, he saw the gleam of water through the thinning reeds ahead: in another moment they were through, and Sullivan already had out his long knife.

"Hurry up," he said. "There are no duck down yet, and we have got time to make ourselves a butt." He began cutting the reeds in great swathes and laying the bundles criss-cross on the mud: Derrick imitated him, and he was glad to do so, for in a moment the wind had whipped away his heat, now that he was out of the shelter. Using the thinner reeds for rope, they lashed the reeds in bundles to form walls, and in a little while they had a dry and wind-proof little pen. Sullivan planted a few tall reeds round it to screen it from view and then crept in, sat on a bundle of reeds and lit his pipe. It had been getting darker fast as the moon dipped down, and the flare of his match showed all round the butt. "There we are," he said, in a contented voice, "all set up with an hour to spare. They will start flighting a little while before the dawn, and if this wind does not change they will all come up the lake from over there, right across the butt. I hope that animal of yours will be able to retrieve. I suppose you didn't think to bring any food with you, did you?"

"No, I didn't think of it," said Derrick. He had not thought about food at all in the hurry and excitement of getting away, but now it occurred to him that he was ravenously hungry.

"Well, it's a good thing that somebody thinks of these things," said Sullivan, feeling in the bottom of his game-bag and bringing out a parcel. "There. That's cold roast sand-grouse: an emperor could not ask for a better breakfast."

They ate in silence for some time, and now that he was thoroughly satisfied, warm and comfortable, with his feet buried under Chang, who served as a foot-muff; Derrick began to wonder how he could ask his uncle a question that had been worrying him for some time. Ever since the three of them, the Professor, Ross and Sullivan, had talked to him so strongly about the wrongfulness of war, Derrick had been thinking about what Hsien Lu had told him— about Ross and Sullivan having been pirates in the China Seas. If they had been pirates, Derrick thought (and he knew very well that there were hundreds of pirates on the China coast, some of them with European skippers), then they had no right to talk in that way: unless, of course, it was just a grown-up manner of speech which did not mean anything. Yet it seemed impossible that they should have spoken so sincerely, if *they* really did not think as the Professor did. And, on the other hand, if they had agreed with him so heartily without believing it . . . it was difficult to know what to think. But then, of course, Hsien Lu might have been mistaken.

It was a difficult question to ask. He looked across the butt: all he could see was the intermittent glow of his uncle's pipe as he drew on it. Suddenly he blurted out, "Uncle Terry, were you ever a pirate?"

"A pirate?" asked Sullivan, taking his pipe out of his mouth and ramming the bowl with his thumb. "A pirate? Yes. Certainly I have been a pirate, and pretty nearly everything else on the high seas. I was a stowaway once, too."

"When was that, Uncle Terry?" asked Derrick, with his heart sinking: he meant, when had his uncle been a pirate.

"A stowaway? Well, it must have been when I was five, or maybe six—before we left Ireland, anyhow. I stowed away aboard a steamer in Queenstown. They didn't find me for twelve hours and more."

"Had you got far?"

"Not very. You see, it was a ferry going to and fro across the harbour. Some wicked old swab had told me that they were bound for the South Seas. I was determined to lie doggo until they had gone too far to put back, and then, thought I, they would be obliged to take me along as a cabin-boy. I had told my sister— your mother, of course, but she was a little girl then— and she had given me a jar of treacle, by way of provisions for the voyage. But they took it away from me in place of my fare for having crossed the harbour eight times without paying. I regretted that jar of treacle, and perhaps it was that sorrow that kept me from going to sea, except as a passenger, until I was a man, years and years later. And even then I did not go of my own free will."

"What happened?"

"Well, it's a long story. I was in a waterfront bar. I had gone down there to see how the simple sailormen enjoyed themselves when they were ashore: I think I expected them to sing shanties and to dance the hornpipe, or something like that, but all I found was a few Blue-noses and a melancholy Dane, a great whale of a man who was sitting at the same table as I was. He told me that he was off a barquentine in the harbour— a lovely vessel: I had already seen her and thought how nice it would be to go for a picnic up the coast in her in the summer—and that he was looking for some of his crew who had deserted. I remember saying that I wondered how anybody could desert such a fine-looking ship: then we had a few drinks together, and I began to feel rather queer. I remember how they stood looking at me in a curious way, and how the man at the bar nodded to the Dane. Then, when I woke up, there was a foul taste in my mouth, and I found that I was lying in a dark bunk. It was heaving underneath me, which was scarcely odd, because we were at sea, two days out of port. They had put a knock-out drop in my drink, and they had shanghaied me, being several men short of a full crew. They had been unable to sign on any of the sailors on shore, as it was known that the ship was bound round the Horn to Chile for nitrate, and that she had a bucko mate aboard, so they had picked up what men they could as best they could.

"Presently a man came below and had a look at me. He was the big Dane I had been talking with, but now he did not seem nearly so pleasant as he had on shore. Instead of wishing me a good morning and asking after my head, which was aching as though there were a wedge driven into it somewhere, he said, 'Get up on deck, you.' Well, I was young and foolish in those days, and I told him that I did not like his manners or his face, or anything about him at all. He murmured, 'Fractious, eh?' and pulled me out of the bunk by the scruff of my neck. I took a crack at his jaw, and the next second I was flat on my back, wondering what had hit me. I got up, and let him have a good one on the end of his nose just before he laid me out again.

Then he picked me up and threw me bodily on deck. 'Throw me a bucket of water over this swab,' he said, 'and put him to work.' 'I'm an American citizen,' I said, feeling good and sore, but not getting up—I was learning wisdom fast—'and you can't do this to me.' 'Throw me a bucket of water over the American citizen,' he said, 'and show him how to heave on a rope.'

"Well, I got two buckets over my head, one for being a swab and the other for being an American citizen, and they damped my ardour for the moment. They put a rope into my hand, and I heaved as tame as Mary's little lamb. But after a while I began to feel better, and when I had got some duff into me and had managed to keep it down, I said to this fellow—his name was Lars Gunnar, and he was second mate— 'You can't do this to me,' I said, 'I am an American citizen.' When he had knocked me down again he picked me up and leaned me against the rails and addressed me in these words, 'Listen,' he said, 'you poor bum, you're a citizen of this ship now, and a hundred brass-bound consuls won't keep you alive if you don't work.' He was quite right. Every time I got in the least uppish or made a landlubber's mistake right up in the to'garn-stuns'ls, way up in the air miles above the deck, Lars Gunnar would beat me up; and if it was not him, it would be the master or the first mate. I was never a very timid fellow, but they knew how to keep their footing on a heaving deck, and how to crack a man with a belaying-pin, and I did not: anyhow, each one was as big as the side of a house, and I got weary of skinning my knuckles on their heads with no effect at all. They were terribly short-handed, and they drove their crew like blacks, but, even so, we were too late to slip round the Horn easily, and we beat to and fro for what seemed like years. It was a very bad passage, and two of the men were lost overboard, but somehow I survived, and by the time we dropped anchor in Antofagasta roads I had learnt a wonderful lot about being a sailor.

"Now they sound tough, from what I have said, and they were tough: but they were not a bad lot of men at all. If you worked hard—and I did, when I understood how badly it was needed coming round the Horn—they treated you very well. They had shanghaied me because they felt that their ship's need was more important than my comfort, and they beat me up so that I should be some use to the ship, not out of any personal spite against me—it was just like hammering a horseshoe into the right shape, no ill-will in it at all.

"By the time we reached Chile I had come to the conclusion that I liked the sea. I had started out a weedy, lanky young chap, but at the end of this voyage, and it was a very long one, I had filled out and put on weight. When we were ashore in Antofagasta I beat the daylights out of Lars Gunnar and helped him back to the ship more dead than alive. They were still short-handed, for they had been able to pick up nothing more than a decrepit old Portuguese in Antofagasta, and they were desperate about their return passage. Lars and the Old Man asked me as civilly as they could—and to see them being civil was a wonderful sight, like two polar-bears trying to behave as if they were on a Sunday-school outing — to ship back with them, as a favour. Well, I had no people to worry about: there was only my sister, and I wrote to her to say that I was going on a voyage to see the world—I knew she would not worry in the least, as she was used to my comings and goings, and I signed on with them. It was a wonderful voyage, down to Australia with nitrates, and then with grain to Helsinki, where we paid off. I crossed the Atlantic again in a Cunarder, as a passenger this time, and very queer it felt; but when I got home everything seemed dull and flat. I fooled around on shore for some time, and then I took to studying navigation and so on and got my ticket. Some of my relatives said that it was a waste of an expensive classical education to be a nasty, low, common sailorman, but my sister thought it was fine, and so did your great-uncle Simon, who in spite of being a professor of pastoral theology was quite a rich man.

"He was a dear old gentleman, and although he knew nothing about the sea at all, except that he rather suspected it was the sharp end of a ship that went first, he left me enough to buy my own schooner after I had risen to the dizzy height of a master-mariner's certificate." He suddenly stopped and cocked his head, listening intently. "No, they won't be moving yet," he said, after a minute. "What was I talking about? Oh, yes, I was telling—by the way, do you know whether your horrible dog can retrieve in water?"

"Chang will do whatever he is told," said Derrick. "He is a very intelligent dog."

Chang, hearing his name, stood up and waved his tail.

"If he is," said Sullivan, "he conceals it very well." He knocked out his pipe, packed it carefully and re-lit it. For some time he was silent: then he began again, "Yes. I had my own schooner. I had been a good many voyages in steam, but it was not the same thing. There is nothing like sail; nothing like it at all. I knocked about all over the place in her, chiefly in the South Seas—pearling and copra—but I was going to tell you how I became a pirate, and that started in South America, in the Republic of Rococo. I had got mixed up with one of their revolutions, but if I were to tell you all about that the dawn flighting would be over before I had begun. The long and the short of it was that my friend, Porfirio Broll, came out on top: he wasn't a bad chap at all; we used to call him Little Brolly at college, and I believe he really did have some sound notions about liberty. Anyway, he was President, and he made me a full-blown admiral. Now that was very kind, and it would have been kinder still if Rococo had ever got around to building a navy, but it had not. I pointed this out to Porfirio, and he gave me the choice of being Postmaster-General, Ambassador to Luxemburg or Minister without portfolio: I said that we would call it quits if he would give me the

176

right to work a guano island that I had sighted off the coast. He jumped at the idea, and gave me a nine-hundred-and-ninety-nine-year lease of the island, all written out on a fine piece of parchment and covered with seals.

"As soon as I had got my lease I set sail for my island. It was only a couple of sheer rocks stuck in the sea a hundred miles from anywhere, and nothing lived on it but sea-birds. There was no anchorage to speak of, and there was no water, but the guano had never been touched, and it lay twenty feet thick all over the island—it is the droppings of gulls, you know, and the best fertiliser in the world. It was a very valuable find indeed, and I was in a fair way to make my fortune. I put some convicts ashore—Porfirio had provided me with his predecessor's cabinet—and left them to provide a cargo against my return while I went off to arrange about selling the stuff. The first cargo was all ready according to plan, and I began to work out how many voyages it would need before I could buy Long Island and the county Mayo, where we came from.

"But the next time I went back to the island for a fresh cargo I found a ship lying there, and all my convicts busy loading her up to the Plimsoll line with my guano. In Rococo Porfirio had got in the way of a bullet, and he had stopped being a president the moment he had begun on his new career as a corpse and a national martyr. There was a new president— they can't rest easy without one in those parts—and he had leased the island to a group of businessmen in El

Liberador. All this seemed very unjust to me, so I waited until their ship was laden, and then in my capacity as Lord High Admiral of Rococo I confiscated ship, cargo and all. It is true that I did it in the dead of night, in rather an unofficial way, but it was foolish of them to get so annoyed. They called me a wrong-doer and a man of wrath and all sorts of unkind things, including a pirate, until I persuaded them to stop with a belaying-pin: I put them ashore on the Spanish main and told them to consult a lawyer. They would find one, I said, by marching through the jungle for a month or two towards the north: but I assured them that it was hardly worth the trouble and expense, because I had a perfectly good and legal lease, which could not be upset by their President, who was only an upstart rebel.

"Some time later I heard that they had got home, and that the rebel government had proclaimed me a pirate. They had even offered a reward to anyone who should catch me, and they had ordered the entire navy of Rococo, which consisted of the Presidential pleasure-launch and one confiscated dinghy without a bottom, to search for me on the high seas. I wrote to them and said that my nine hundred and ninety-nine years was not up yet, but that when it was, I would resign the islands to the next comer: I thought that was fair enough. But the new company fitted out another vessel, stuck guns all over it, and came back to my island. I lay hull down on the horizon, watching them from my cross-trees, and when they had loaded her and fixed her hatches I confiscated her again. It was rather more boisterous, but I had a mixed crew of Solomon Islanders and Irishmen, and we overcame their objections.

"When the company heard about this, they were hopping mad: they hired a tough skipper with his own crew to get the guano. I had heard a good deal about this man. They called him the Hellbender, and they said he used railroad ties for toothpicks.

"He came to my island a good while before I was expecting him, and half my men were ashore when he hove up out of the mist. I had to cut and run for it, leaving the cargo ready on the little wharf we had made. I slipped round behind the island, got my men off in the night, and then came round to try conclusions with him. But the current was setting very strong, and the wind was against me, so I was delayed longer than I could have wished, and by the time I had worked round the island I could only see his tops'ls over the rim of the sea to the west. That made me think a bit, for nobody but a first-rate sailor could have picked up my guano and turned around so quickly. I cracked on everything we had, and by the evening he ran into a calm, so that I could see his vessel clearly in the distance. She was a tops'l schooner, with lovely lines, and she was being very well handled. My ship, the one I had then, was a good sort of a ship in her way, comfortable and beamy, but she would not come as close to the wind as he could, being in ballast; and with a weedy bottom too, having been so long at sea, we were as slow as a dead porpoise compared with him. Presently he got the wind again, and it was our turn for the calm: he went away straight into the eye of the breeze, and we were left there without a sail drawing.

"The next day we never saw him at all, nor the next, and I had to resign myself to the loss of that cargo. But it galled me. It galled me very much, and the more I thought of it, the more it galled me. It was my island: I had discovered it and I had first worked it, and I dare say that an international court, working on the broad principles of equity, would have upheld my lease. Anyway, I was determined to uphold it, and I set a man ashore to tell me when the tops'l schooner next set out.

"When I got the signal I kept her just in sight, and then I doubled back to the mainland. I hid the ship up a lonely creek, and we marched overland to the mouth of the river—El Liberador is some way up the Rococo river, you know, and they have a tug to bring vessels up the narrow part to the city. I had kept her in sight until she had started loading, so I knew we would not have long to wait. Sure enough, three tides later, the tug came down. We stopped her in mid-stream and invited her crew to take their ease under hatches for a while.

"Then, when the tide began to flow, the tops'l schooner came in over the bar. It was pitch-black night when we went down into the estuary and hailed her. They never suspected a thing, and threw us a line:

we got the tow aboard and made all fast. Then, very gently, and stopping every now and then as if we were having trouble with our engines, we edged her round and towed her out across the bar. I had arranged to have the shore-lights doused—a few dollars can work wonders there—and I reckoned that a man who did not know the river very well would never know that he had been turned about. But we had not got very far before a great voice came bawling through the night, telling us to heave to. We did not reply, and presently we heard them working on the hawser. I flashed the searchlight on to them, and said that I would shoot the first man who touched the tow: that stopped them for a bit, but then a bullet came whipping across and smashed the searchlight. I rigged up another, but by that time they had brought a hatch up for'ard as a shield, and they were busy casting off the tow, so we boarded them.

"They were a tougher crew than I had expected, but we were fairly evenly matched. There was no light for shooting, which was a good thing, or we should have destroyed one another entirely, like the Kilkenny cats. It was their skipper who gave us the most trouble. He rushed up and down the deck with a capstan-bar in each hand, laying about him like a man threshing beans in a hurry—only the beans were my men, and by the time the moon rose they were getting a little discouraged. I got at him once or twice, but each time we were pushed apart by other swabs getting in the way: at last I did reach

181

him, and we set to very briskly. He had either broken his capstan-bars or thrown them away by this time, and we went to it with our fists, hammer and tongs. He was a heavier man, I found, and he packed a terrible punch, but I had a longer reach, and I spoilt his face for him. But banging his face did not seem to do much good, and when he got in close he paid it back with interest. He had me up against the rails and thumped away at my ribs like a steam-engine. I knew I could not hold out much longer, so I grabbed him by the neck and flung myself backwards over the rails into the sea, still holding him. I had learnt to swim before I could walk, and I felt that maybe I could deal with him better in the water. I lay there for a moment, getting back my breath, and he floundered about like a grampus, blowing and bellowing. He went under once or twice, and as far as I could judge he was more concerned with keeping afloat than looking out for me. I came up behind him and gripped his head. He threshed about like mad, and I had a pretty business keeping free of him, but when I had ducked him a good many times and had filled him up with sea-water he began to weaken. Then I whispered in his ear, 'You're for the sharks in five minutes if you don't give in, my man.' He said, 'I'll see you hanged first, you dirty pirate,' and he turned to bite my hand. So I began to drown him in good earnest—mark over."

Sullivan reached for his gun. There was the sound of

wings high overhead, and they listened tensely. The noise circled above them and came lower. Suddenly his gun leapt to his shoulder: two orange flames stabbed the darkness, and from out on the lake came two heavy splashes, one after the other, and a threshing in the water.

Sullivan waited for a moment, with his gun poised, to see whether the duck would circle again, but they swung wide and high.

"Now let's see whether your animal can do his stuff," he said.

"Fetch, Chang," said Derrick, pointing to the lake. Chang hurled himself in, and they heard him splashing in the distance.

"I really believe there's some good in the old flea-bag," said Sullivan. "It sounds as though he were trying to bring them both."

"Fetch them, Chang," called Derrick, hoping desperately that his uncle was right. Chang barked in answer, and they heard them surging towards them. He reappeared, dripping and charmed with himself: there was a large stick in his mouth.

"That will be very useful for cooking the birds, no doubt," said Sullivan.

"Ducks, Chang. Go and fetch the ducks. Birds on the water." For half a moment Derrick thought of flapping his arms and going quack, quack to help Chang understand. The dog looked worried, and offered the stick again. "No, not that," said Derrick, scarlet in the face. "Fetch the ducks, Chang. Ducks, there's a good dog." Chang was very willing to please, and he plunged in again, but Derrick was almost certain that he would only bring back another stick.

"Don't blame him," said Sullivan. "You can't expect beauty as well as intelligence. We'll try and shoot them so that they fall over the land next time. They were widgeon, by the sound of them."

Chang swam back. In his mouth, beautifully held by one wing, there was a fine teal.

"Good dog," cried Sullivan, giving him a piece of meat. "Why, that's strange, this is a teal."

"Perhaps there was just one teal among the widgeon," said Derrick, trying to conceal his triumph, and it appeared that he was right, for the next bird that Chang brought in was a widgeon, a lovely drake, with a sulphur-yellow crest.

"How did you manage to hit them, Uncle Terry?" asked Derrick, smoothing the widgeon's feathers. "I never saw them at all."

"Nor did I," replied Sullivan. "You can't wait to see them in this light. You have to shoot at the sound. It'll be better in half an hour. These were probably the first birds to get moving."

They stood in silence for a while, listening for the duck. "Did you drown the man?" asked Derrick eventually.

"What man? Oh, Ross. No, I didn't drown him, but I let him get thoroughly waterlogged, and then I towed him back to his schooner. By that time I found my crew had licked his —they were not much

184

good without their skipper—and they hauled us aboard. At first I was afraid that I had overdone it: he looked too much like a corpse altogether. But when we had up-ended him and let the ocean out of him he came to. But he was very sick for a long while, and I had to nurse him carefully—it was touch and go with him for weeks. I ran his schooner up the coast and tied up alongside my ship for a while. I found that he had no great liking for his job, or for his employers, who had never paid him and never would, for by the time we had transferred the cargo we had news that there had been another revolution in Rococo. Well, to cut it short, we took a liking to one another, and we decided to ship together. I sold my cargo, ship and lease to a big American company, who could deal with the legal side of the matter better than I could, and we sailed for the Friendly Islands after copra. That sounds like mallard. They're coming our way. Now you take the birds on the right, and shoot well ahead."

The sound of the wings came down as the duck planed in to pitch on the lake. The four shots cracked out, and there were two splashes in the water. Chang stood tense and expectant.

"You want to shoot well ahead as they are crossing," said Sullivan, reloading. "Wait for it, now, they are circling again." He knocked another bird out of the flight, but before Chang could bring it in there were more duck overhead, Muscovy duck this time, and from then on they stood there as the dawn came grey around them, shooting so often that the barrels of their guns were warm.

"I think that will do," said Sullivan at last, surveying the pile of birds in the butt.

"There's another flight coming in," said Derrick, eagerly. "Well, get one more brace if you like," said Sullivan, "but we'll finish then."

"Will that be the end of the flighting?"

"No. They'll go on for quite a long time still, but we have got all we can eat. You don't want to kill for the sake of killing, do you?"

"No, I suppose not," said Derrick, rather regretfully, as he watched the duck skim in and rise as they saw the movement in the butt.

"I'm glad you don't," said Sullivan. "I hate these big shoots where you kill a hundred brace or more just for the fun of it. Shooting for the pot is another matter."

In the thin, cold light they made their way back through the reeds with their game-bags heavy on their backs, and when they had mounted again and had ridden a mile or so, Derrick said, "So you never were a pirate in the China Seas."

"What's biting you?" asked Sullivan, looking round at him curiously. "You're very full of questions this morning, young fellow."

"Oh, it was only something that Hsien Lu said," said Derrick, going red, "and I thought that if it was true, then what you said about war—well, I mean, piracy is a kind of war, isn't it?"

186

"Oh, that's the trouble. I see. Yes, real piracy is almost exactly the same as aggressive war, and it has got some of the same phoney glamour when you hear about it at a distance. Well, you can set your mind at rest about that. I have done some pretty queer things in my time: I did a good many things when I was young that I would not do now, but I never hung out the black flag in earnest. I think I know what Hsien Lu was talking about. You know that there are plenty of genuine pirates in the South China Sea? Some of them are ordinary merchant junks that will turn pirate if they find a weaker junk in the offing—sort of half-time pirates —and some are the real article. But both kinds like to get hold of a white captain if they can—I don't mean the coast-wise pirates, the ones you hear most about, but the gentlemen who work on the high seas. That was what we had in mind when we cast around in Wang Tso for the leaders of the Benign Chrysanthemum. We had had a brush with the pirate junk belonging to the Fraternal Lotuses in which they had killed our bo'sun, a Kanaka who had been with us for years—we were very fond of him, and we thought our best way of dealing with the situation was to blow the Fraternal Lotuses out of the water. Perhaps what we ought to have done was to have lodged a complaint in the proper quarters, but I never knew any good coming of that in China, particularly in those days. So what we did was this: we told a good friend of ours, Suleiman ibn Yakoub, that he had bought the *Wan-*

derer—we had the *Wanderer* by then—and we hung about Wang Tso looking down-at-heel and miserable and poor, as like two master-mariners on the beach and out of a job as we could, until we got in touch with the old lady who ran the pirate organisation called the Benign Chrysanthemum. We knew that if we could get into her confidence we would learn about the hide-out of the Fraternal Lotuses: and I may say that we had a long score to settle with the Fraternal swabs, quite apart from the bo'sun. She took us on, and after she had tried us out with a few legitimate voyages, all above-board, she began to come round to thinking that perhaps we would do as full-blown Benign Chrysanthemums: but she did not want to hurry about it, and as we did not want to linger in those waters for very long, we thought the best thing to do was to impress her with some pretty hearty doings. All that we had been able to learn was about the society called the Everlasting Wrong: they were long-shore pirates, and they did not interest us very much, but they were a thorough-going pest to peaceful coast-wise ships, and we thought they would be as well out of the way as not, especially as they would serve our turn. So when there was a very big feast going on in their harbour Ross and I went and blew the bottoms out of their junks—it would be a long story to tell you all about it, but in fact it was quite simple, and it impressed the old lady immensely. It was rather irregular, of course, because the two societies were supposed to be at peace, but they were rivals in their trade, you see, and old Yang Kwei-fei—that was our old lady's name—was really as pleased as Punch. She suddenly conceived the idea that trade would be much better all round if she had no rivals at all, and she told us all she knew about the Fraternal Lotuses, and in a week the Lotuses had withered to the extent of having to work for their living, which was something that no Fraternal Lotus had done for generations. That was what Hsien Lu had heard about, no doubt; and if he said that we were pirates, he certainly thought that he was telling the truth, because in the days before we had dealt with the Lotuses we stalked about boasting about how we had sunk this ship and that ship, murdering every man jack aboard, and drowning the women and children and so on, like the biggest villains unhung. I am sure he thought it was a compliment when he said it, but I am afraid I must admit that we were never quite such great men as Hsien Lu believed. We never even made anyone walk the plank, and to tell the truth, I don't think that I should enjoy the entertainment very much—I haven't really got the makings of a really good bloodthirsty pirate. If some swab starts knocking my ship around, I'll sink him if I can, but I am such a mild-natured creature that I have to be hit first before I begin to get sore—not cast in the heroic mould, as you might say." He had been gazing at the horizon for some time, and now he reined in and shaded his eyes with his hand. "What do you make of that?" he asked.

Derrick made out a single horseman on the skyline. "It is not one of our people," he said.

"No," said Sullivan. "It looks to me more like a Kazak, from his lance. It is strange to see one here. We are a long way from their country."

Nine

THROUGH the bleak lands beyond the great marshes the column pursued its steady road. Day after day they went straight over the high steppe or the half-desert where the cold sand blew perpetually over the dun earth: they no longer dug in the minor sites that the Professor had marked, and although he said that there were still three or four places where they must certainly stop, he said it without conviction. He was in a ferment about the jade, and his chief wish was to get it safely back to the museum: he carried the pick of the collection about his person, and the rest he confided to Li Han, who sewed the pieces into his quilted cotton clothes and walked about as though he were treading on eggs. The Professor had already begun a rough catalogue of the jades, and every night the lamp burnt until after midnight in his yurt. He said, "Our aim must now be to reach Samarcand as early as possible: fortunately, the worst of our journey is over, and we have only the Takla Makan to traverse or to circumvent, and then, I understand, the rest of the road is comparatively simple."

"Only the Takla Makan!" exclaimed Sullivan,

thinking of that howling desert. "Only the Takla Makan." But seeing the Professor's anxious face he added, "Yes, you are quite right. Once we have got that behind us, the rest should not be too difficult."

When he was alone with Ross he said, "Are they still there?"

"I saw them at break of day," said Ross, "but I have not seen them since. It may be that we are wrong— growing over-anxious and seeing boggles behind every door, like bairns."

"I hope so," replied Sullivan, scanning the horizon. Ever since they had left the swamps he had had the impression that they were being followed. Sometimes it was a group of horsemen who kept so far away that they might have been antelopes or the tall wild asses of the steppe, and sometimes it was a single rider; but Sullivan and Ross had powerful glasses, and the form that might have been a distant antelope to a naked eye showed up as a Tartar in the binoculars, a Tartar with the head-dress and the lance of a Kazak.

Yet when some days later they met with the immense herds of the Churungdzai and camped for the night with the tribesmen, they heard nothing of the Kazaks; they felt that their suspicions had been mistaken, and they were glad that they had not mentioned them to the others. The Churungdzai were a tribe related to the Kokonor horde: they were as friendly as could be, and they gave news of Hulagu Khan. He was a week's journey to the north, on the edge of the Takla Makan, and they thought that he might come south to

191

cut their route near the place called the Kirgiz Tomb.

It took them nearly the whole of the next day to pass through the innumerable herds of the Churungdzai, although they were but a tenth part of the tribe's wealth, but by the evening they were alone on the steppe again, and in the days that followed, the old, calm routine settled down as though there had been no change.

Derrick had traded some ammunition for a hawking eagle with one of the Churungdzai, and with the great bird on his arm he rode out with Chingiz to see what they could find for the pot. The eagle was big enough to strike down an antelope, and Derrick, at intervals of working out the problem in trigonometry that Ross had set him for his morning's task, had thought that he had seen some on the far edge of the sky.

"You must ride with your right arm across your saddle-bow," said Chingiz, and Derrick quickly realised that he was right. He had been trying to imitate the Mongol's way of carrying his falcon with his arm free at his side, and each time that his arm had moved under the much greater weight of the eagle, the huge talons had gripped his muscles through the thick glove that he wore as the hooded eagle stirred to keep its balance.

They had gone almost out of sight of their caravan, and Derrick was riding more easily, when they heard the drumming of horse's hooves: it was Sullivan, coming up fast to join them.

"I thought I would come and see how your new purchase behaves," he said, drawing alongside. "Is it any good, Chingiz?"

"I hope so," said Chingiz, looking at the eagle with his beady eyes narrowed still further. "But it is very small."

"Small!" cried Derrick, thinking of the steely grip of those talons, and how they had gripped him to the bone when the bird was merely sitting there, with no intention of doing harm. "Small! What do you think we are going to hunt? Elephants?"

"My father has an eagle twice that size," said Chingiz, stroking his little peregrine.

"Yes," said Sullivan, "but your father is a Khan, and drinks the milk of white mares. Naturally he has a larger eagle than anybody else."

"And my ancestor," said Chingiz, who was not altogether pleased about Derrick's eagle, "had one four times the size of my father's."

"That must have been difficult to carry," observed Derrick.

"Not for my ancestor," replied Chingiz, firmly. "He had two on each arm."

Derrick was about to say something, but he checked himself. He had learnt by now that if he pulled Chingiz's leg the results were likely to be rapid and bloody.

"Did your ancestor ever have any trouble with the Kazaks?" asked Sullivan.

"No," said Chingiz. "He built a tower of ten thousand Kazak skulls—Maiman Kazaks, they were—and then he never had any trouble with them at all."

"Ten thousand?" asked Derrick.

"Yes," said Chingiz, "ten thousand. You will see them when we come to the rocky country soon: they are still there, at the place called the Kazak Tomb."

Sullivan nodded. He had seen it.

Suddenly Chingiz shouted, "Loose, loose, loose!" While they had been talking an antelope had sprung up out of a single patch of shade, and now it was flying towards the horizon. Derrick tore at the jesses, the leather thongs that held the eagle to his arm, but he was unhandy with his left hand, and his pony was too excited to stand.

"Cast off," cried Sullivan. "Look alive, boy."

Chang barked, the pony shied, and it was minutes before Derrick had the eagle in the air. By this time the antelope was no more than a swiftly-moving mist of flying sand.

The eagle towered, its huge wings making a bar of shadow over them, and circled high, with its wing-tips flaring in the wind. It seemed to take some time to make up its mind, and they could see its head turned from side to side as it scanned the plain; but then, with no perceptible movement of its wings, it began to travel down the sky, faster and faster, as if it were sliding down an oiled groove. They galloped at full stretch below it, with their reins loose and their horses racing at the height of their speed, but it left them as if they were standing still. On and on it went, growing smaller in the distance; then Derrick saw it mount again and stoop.

Chingiz was up first, but the eagle had already lifted, and it was floating easily in the sky. "Call him," Chingiz shouted to Derrick, and when Derrick had called the eagle without effect, the Mongol cried, "Lure him, lure him as fast as you can."

Derrick unslung the lure from his saddle, a stuffed piece of felt on a short length of rope, and he whirled it in the air, calling still. The eagle looked, dropped twenty feet, hesitated and rose again.

"He sees something," said Chingiz. "We must follow." He stopped for a moment to hoist the little antelope across his saddle-bow—the eagle had broken its back with one gripe of its claws—and they rode slowly after the towering eagle, calling and luring, but in vain.

They were so busy watching the bird that they did not see the men until they were quite near them. They were two, one mounted and watching the eagle, and the other looking at his horse's hoof. They were fully armed, with slung rifles, curved swords hanging at the left side of their saddles, and in his right hand the mounted man held a lance.

Sullivan motioned Chingiz and Derrick to a halt and rode slowly forward.

"Peace be with you," he said.

"And on you be peace," replied the mounted man.

At this moment the eagle came down to Derrick's arm, and he was too busy hooding it to catch what was being said. But when the bird was quietly on his arm again he heard the mounted man say, "Are you in the company of the idolaters?"

"We are people of the Book also," answered Sullivan.

Derrick noticed that the dismounted man had his rifle unslung, and for a second he thought there was going to be trouble, but Sullivan swung his horse about, and saying over his shoulder, "A good journey and peace, in the Name of God," he rode back to them.

The Tartar's deep reply, "In the Name of God, peace and a good journey," came over the sand, and each group rode away from the other.

Sullivan went on silently for some time, and although Derrick looked questioningly at him he said nothing until they were nearly up to the column.

"They were Kazaks," he said in an off-hand tone. "They are Mohammedans, you know. They are probably on a journey. Can you tell what horde they belong to, Chingiz?"

"They were not Kirei Kazaks," said Chingiz, "nor Uwak. They might have been from the Altai, though that is far away. But they were Kazaks, and they must have had my father's permission to be here.

"And yet," said Chingiz, as they rode up to the halted column, "if they were going on a journey, it is strange that they had no led horses. The Kazaks always lead two or three if they are far from home."

Derrick thought it strange, too, but the camp was just forming, and as they hurried to the kitchen tent to deliver the antelope to Li Han, he forgot all about it.

Li Han was doling out a measure of rice to Timur, a lame, one-eyed, dog-faced Mongol to whom he had delegated nearly all the work of cooking for the past few weeks.

"Come on, Li Han, you've got to do this yourself," cried Derrick, bringing in the antelope. Timur was an expert in loading camels, but his one idea of cooking was thin, rubbery strips of flesh, as nearly raw as possible.

"That's right," said Olaf, suddenly appearing from behind a mound of provisions. "You turn sea-cook again for a day, Li Han."

Li Han sniffed, and turned to light the fire. The Professor had more and more entrusted him with duties as far from those of a sea-cook as could be imagined. For a long time now he had copied Chinese inscriptions and had arranged the Professor's notes, taking endless pains and writing with beautiful neatness: he had thrown himself into it heart and soul, and all day long, as they rode, he was to be seen gazing into a book, in order, as he said, "to fit himself for service and society of august philosophical sage". But all this, though it pleased the Professor, pleased nobody else. Both Derrick and Olaf regretted the days when Li Han would turn out a succulent dish at a moment's notice. They reminded one another of the meals aboard the *Wanderer*, wonderful meals that came in rapid succession from the galley stove; and that evening, when the keen air and the long day's march had given them a needle-sharp appetite, they looked forward eagerly to something very good indeed from the antelope.

But as they sat round the fire, Li Han appeared from the Professor's tent, carrying a fresh sheaf of papers: he pointed to the iron pot and sat on a box, frowning over the written sheets. Olaf helped himself and stirred moodily in his dish: it contained an evil mess prepared by Timur by way of an experiment. The antelope was still untouched. Li Han sipped at his tea-bowl, staring thoughtfully into the distance.

"You going to eat any of this duff, eh?" growled Olaf.

"By no means," replied Li Han. "Have already partaken of egg with learned Professor."

"Humph. Ay reckon you ought to try some of this stuff. What you say, Derrick, eh?"

"It is horrible duff," said Derrick, offering a little to Chang, who refused it apologetically. "Why don't you cook us some decent chop, Li Han?"

"When engaged in learned pursuits, cannot bend mind to menial tasks."

"Don't you like to eat good food yourself?"

"For disciple of philosopher, preserved egg suffices. I no longer worship belly, as in former days of besotted ignorance."

"You ban getting too high-hat," said Olaf, angrily. "Who are you calling besotted ignorance, anyway? You mouldy son of a half-baked weevil, if you was in the *Wanderer*'s galley right now, Ay reckon we would wipe the dishes with you, eh, Derrick?"

"Abusive language invariable mark of cultural backward person," said Li Han.

198

"Relax, Li Han, and turn us out something we can eat. Look, there's a nice clear fire, and there's that antelope all ready at hand," said Derrick, persuasively.

"Regret am otherwise engaged. Also, certain personal remarks add touch of obnoxious compulsion. Shall remain in vindictive immobility."

There was a short silence, in which Olaf came to a slow boil. "Skavensk!" he cried, suddenly throwing down his bowl and leaping to his feet. "Lookit here, you cook-boy, you cook us a meal right now, or Ay ban going to tie you up in a knot like you've never seen before."

"Steady, Olaf. You can't beat him up: he's too small."

"Well, is he going to sit there like a heathen image just because he's small, eh? Too high-hat, he is, see? Besotted ignorance, eh? You heard what he said? Ay sure got a mind to turn him inside out. Maybe he'd look better that way."

Derrick whistled softly, and Chang thrust his muzzle against his knee. "Listen, Chang," he said. "You grab a hold of Li Han and make mincemeat out of him. Seize him, Chang! Break him and tear him then. Bring me his liver and lights, Chang." Chang rumbled like thunder in his throat, waving his tail.

Li Han started up. "Physical violence is mark of barbarian mind," he said apprehensively. "I will dissociate self from distasteful brawlery."

"High-hat, eh?" cried Olaf. "You dissociate yourself from that!" Olaf swung the iron pot in a high arc. Li

Han dodged, but too late. The mess came down squelch on top of his head and the pot slammed down over his ears. At this moment Chang joined in, leaping delightedly for the seat of Li Han's trousers and roaring like a bloodhound.

Li Han sprawled into the fire, sprang out, spinning like a teetotum, and shrieked curses in a high-pitched yell. Derrick tripped him up and sat on his stomach. "You'd better pull the pot off, Olaf," he said, "it might be hot."

"Ay reckon we ought to leave it on for ever," said Olaf. "That ban a fine high hat, eh?" Olaf had rarely made a joke of his own, and now he was so pleased with it that he could hardly stand for laughing.

When he could stop he pulled once or twice at the pot, but it was immovable. Muffled bellows came from Li Han. "Crack it, Olaf," said Derrick.

"That won't never crack. It's iron, see?"

By now the bellowing from inside had assumed a pleading tone.

"No. Ay reckon there's nothing but a winch will ever unship this pot," said Olaf. "Or maybe a monkey wrench," he added thoughtfully.

"I'll hold him by the shoulders and you pull," said Derrick. "I think he's drowning."

"Drowning a thousand miles from the nearest creek!" exclaimed Olaf. "Cor stone the crows, that ban funny." He howled with laughter, but he grasped the pot again and heaved. But suddenly he changed his mind, rapped smartly on the sounding iron and hailed Li Han within, "Ahoy, Li Han. Will you cook if we let you out?"

"Yes, yes. Me cookee top-chop one-time. Let out, plis," came the muffled voice, and Olaf heaved again. They pulled, grunting. Li Han shrieked like a stuck pig. Suddenly the pot came off with a loud plop: Olaf fell backwards into the fire, and Chang, charmed with the game, pinned Li Han to the ground, baying wildly.

Between them they made such an appalling din that they never heard the approaching thunder of the Mongols. The camp was filled with Kokonor tribesmen before Derrick could get up for laughing.

As they came in Hulagu and his brothers ran from the horse-lines, where they had been doctoring a sick mare. The leading tribesmen leapt from their horses, saluted Hulagu and spoke rapidly for a few moments. Hulagu ran to Sullivan's yurt: in a minute he was out again, running for his horse, and before the dust of his going had settled down he was out of sight, together with his brother Kubilai and the other tribesmen.

Chingiz stood staring after them, fingering the dagger at his belt. "What's the matter?" asked Derrick.

"The Altai Kazaks have come down from the north," replied Chingiz, with a savage grin. "They have come for their revenge for the tower of skulls, and they have joined with the Uruchang horde. They are raiding our yurts and killing whatever they can find. They have driven some of our herds into the Takla Makan, and they think they can destroy us, because my father is away. We are going to try to lead some of them into an ambush beyond the Kazak Tomb."

Sullivan came quickly out of his tent and passed down the lines, giving his orders quietly and distinctly. An indescribable bustle filled the camp for half an hour, and then, out of the apparent confusion, a well-armed, well-mounted and well-prepared troop rode westward after Hulagu. Chingiz rode on Sullivan's right hand to show the way, and once again Derrick was impressed by the way in which the Mongol seemed to carry a compass and a chart in his head. He was never at a loss, although the bare steppe seemed always the same, and as they rode fast through the gathering night he said that they were coming near to a single rock that stood out of the plain, and that there they were to stop. Hardly had he spoken when out of the dusk loomed the rock, straight ahead of them: he said that in the light of the dawn they would see broken country beyond, and that was to be their goal for the hour of the rising of the sun.

They lit no fire, for no light was to be seen, but they sat in a circle as though a fire had been there, and they ate their horse-flesh cold.

"This is very instructive," said the Professor, as he wiped his lips. "As I understand it, the tribes beyond the Altai have been pushing the Kazaks to the south, and now the Kazaks in their turn are attacking our friends: it is surely a repetition of those great waves of barbarians who came one after the other to destroy the Roman Empire. And there are many other instances which will occur to you. One sees the evidence of these successive invasions so clearly in the excavation of any archaeological site, but to see the whole thing in present action is to have history brought to life in the most vivid manner—more vivid even than the most pronounced differentiation of the culture strata at, let us say, Beauplan's classic excavation at Chrysopolis."

"I am sure you are right," said Sullivan, "but speaking as a layman, I must say that for my part it is a demonstration that I could do without. Living history has an awkward way of separating you from your head, and I would rather reach Samarcand all in one piece. For the moment I could wish that history would keep in its proper place—between the covers of a history book."

By the time the eastern sky began to lighten they were in the saddle again, making their way towards a region of abrupt rocks and twisted ravines, a great stretch of country that seemed to have been torn apart by an almighty earthquake in the past.

Li Han took a gloomy view of the whole affair: he was riding behind, between Derrick and Olaf who kept near to him to pick him up when he fell, for although they had now traversed hundreds and hundreds of miles of Northern China, Inner and Outer Mongolia and Sinkiang on horseback, so that even Olaf could navigate his mare efficiently, Li Han had never become more than a most indifferent rider, and he was apt to pitch off on one side or the other whenever they went faster than a walk. "Surely," he gasped, clutching again at his horse's mane, "surely peaceful negotiations will suffice? Soothing remarks and well-turned compliments will assuage the barbarians: or if not, a small present, accompanied by promises of more, will turn their wrath."

"These guys ban tough eggs," said Olaf. "They ain't out for no parlour-conversation. Ay reckon the best kind of present ban one ounce of lead, right between the eyes, see?"

"But suppose the barbarians should shoot first, with two ounces of lead? Or leap upon us with horrible cries?" Li Han shuddered. "But doubtless," he added, to comfort himself, "philosophic Professor will dissuade both sides from actual blows at the last moment by honeyed words and sage-like example."

"Not at all, Li Han," cried Professor Ayrton, who had caught these last words, "I am all for blows in this emergency. If these invading Kazaks try to come between me and the Wu Ti jade, I shall endeavour to deal out the shrewdest and most painful blows that I can manage, with no honeyed words at all. You must remember the precept of Chih Hsu, 'In a sudden encounter with a tiger, a double-edged sword of proved temper is of a greater material value than the polished manners of Chang-An.'" He raised his voice, and speaking to Ross and Sullivan, he said, "I feel quite like the warhorse in Job. Have we much farther to go?"

"A fair distance yet. Did you say a warhorse, Professor?"

"Yes. 'He saith among the trumpets Ha, ha; and he smelleth the battle afar off, the thunder of the captains, and the shouting.' I believe you people have corrupted me by your example: why, when I return to the museum, they will call me the Scourge of Bloomsbury."

"The Professor says that he feels like a warhorse," said Derrick to Chingiz.

"Hum. Well, perhaps his learning will be of some use to us with spells and incantations."

"Don't look now, Professor," said Ross, quietly, "but I think your principles are slipping."

"My principles? Oh, yes: I apprehend your meaning. But, my dear sir, do you not appreciate the difference between attack and defence? Here are we, in the middle of our good friends' country, and we find them being annoyed, harassed and put to serious inconvenience by a pack of invading ruffians. Are we not to show our displeasure? Furthermore, Sullivan assured me that the Kazaks will undoubtedly associate us with the Kokonor horde, and that if they are not discouraged by firm action on our parts, they will certainly molest us, even to the point of taking away our belongings. And thirdly as the Kazaks are Mohammedans, and there is an element of religious fanaticism in their attack, they may, if victorious, go so far as to destroy the Wu Ti jades, many of which, I am glad to say, are graven images, and anathema to these bigots. All these things being considered, therefore—loyalty to our friends, a due regard for our own safety, and the preservation of these artistic treasures—I feel wholly justified in crying 'Forward, with the greatest convenient speed, and smite them hip and thigh.' "

Chingiz pushed his horse up to Sullivan, and when the Professor had finished, he pointed. "There is the Kazak Tomb," he said. On a high rock before them there was a low, crumbling mound: once it had reached up in a steep-sided pyramid; the centuries had brought it down, but as they came nearer they could still see that the whole erection had been made of hundreds upon hundreds of skulls.

"We will add to that before dawn," said Chingiz, "either with their heads or our own."

Beyond the Kazak Tomb the way grew harder. On either hand the broken, weathered rocks leaned over their path: they rode in single file, picking their way with care. From the shadow of a great boulder came a single man, a Kokonor Mongol who was waiting for them. Down through a steep canyon he led them, and there the shadow of the night lingered still: they tethered their horses in a place where there was a thin sprinkling of grass, and began to climb. They came up into the light over a difficult shoulder of moving shale, and as the first red glow of the sunrise appeared they reached the skyline.

They were at the top of a cliff that overlooked a narrow valley, almost a ravine, with sheer sides: the valley led out into the distant plain, in the open country far beyond; but anyone who tried to pass through the tumbled ridge by this valley would find themselves brought up short by the perpendicular cliff at the hither end of it. The plan was that the Kazaks should be lured up this ravine to its very end, and that there they should be caught by rifle-fire from the heights.

They strung themselves out along the sides, finding good hiding-places among the boulders. They would have several hours to wait, but alit was impossible to say for certain when Hulagu and his men would lead their pursuers into the trap, they must remain hidden, silent and motionless for the whole of the long wait. When they had been there an hour Chang barked. "Put a strap round that dog's muzzle," snapped Sullivan. Some minutes later there came a soft whistle, to which Chingiz replied, and they saw another group of Mongols creeping among the rocks on the other side, taking up places opposite to them.

The hours passed slowly, very slowly, and the sun crept up the sky. A wind blew up from the farther steppe: it increased in strength, and as it howled and whistled through the rocks and down the narrow gully, it became very difficult to listen for the sounds they hoped to hear.

Derrick was changing from one cramped position to another when he saw the heads of the three men to his left all whip round at the same moment; they were listening intently down the length of the ravine. He froze motionless, and he heard the crackle of many rifles, far away and whipped from them by the wind.

Sullivan nodded and winked his eye: at the same instant Derrick became aware of the Professor's lanky form stretched out behind him and creeping towards Sullivan.

"Forgive me, Sullivan," whispered the Professor, "if this is an inopportune moment—I should have thought of it before, but it slipped my mind. What I wished to say was that although I am conversant with the general principles underlying the use of firearms, I have never actually—"

"Get down," hissed Ross, pulling the Professor off the skyline. "Here they come."

Derrick flung himself flat and rammed home his bolt: he heard the same sharp, metallic sound to his right and his left. From where he lay he had a perfect view of the whole of the gulley, and he saw Kubilai and Hulagu with some twenty of their men coming into sight at the far end. Behind them came the Kazaks. It was difficult to see how many there were, because of the number of spare horses that galloped with them, but they were many; and as they raced nearer Derrick saw among them a white horse whose rider carried a lance with a yak's tail flying like a pennant.

"That is the son of the Altai Khan," murmured Chingiz, staring down his sights.

"Quiet," whispered Sullivan. "Wait for it, wait for it."

Now Hulagu and his men put on a great burst of speed: as they passed the silent watchers, Hulagu

208

took the reins in his teeth, turned in his saddle and fired back. He scanned the rocks anxiously, and raced by.

The Kazak lances swept nearer and nearer, and above the wind came the thundering of their horses' hooves. "Just a little closer," whispered Sullivan, cuddling the stock into his shoulder, "and you're for it."

A shot rang out behind them. The bullet spat rock six inches from Derrick's heels, and the Professor said, "Dear me, it went off."

The Kazaks pulled up in a cloud of dust. Ross and Chingiz fired together and two men fell. There was confusion in the ravine, some pushing on and some turning back. Sullivan waited a moment and then fired six shots so fast that it sounded like a burst of machine-gun fire. On the other side the Mongols opened up, and Hulagu's men from the foot of the cliff kept up a rapid fire.

"One," said Olaf, calmly reloading. Li Han aimed at the white horse and fired at last: he struck an escaping man fifty yards in the rear.

In the van of the Kazaks the yak's tail banner tossed and waved. There was a piercing shout from below and the banner rushed forward, with fifty men behind it, charging for the dismounted men at the foot of the cliff. In a moment they had swept by the withering fire from the heights, and they were engaged in a battle at hand to hand, so close that the men above could not fire without hitting their own friends.

The Kokonor men were outnumbered more than two

to one: the sheer cliff was behind them, and they could not fly.

"Professor, stay here with Derrick and Chingiz. Pick off the Kazaks down the valley," said Sullivan, as he lowered himself over the side. Ross was already going down before him, and Olaf followed fast. On the far side the Kokonor Mongols were also climbing down. One fell, and rolled the whole length of the steep slope to a Kazak lance.

Ross was the first down, but Sullivan out-paced him to the fight. Two horsemen came at him, and running he missed his shot, but he leapt aside from the nearer lance and sprang for the horse's head. He wrenched horse and rider to the ground, and the second man came down in the threshing legs. The Kazaks bounded free and came for him again, but before they could strike he hurled his rifle at them. He was within their guard, and in each hand he held a Kazak by the neck. With a crack like a rifle-shot he smashed their heads together: the helmets rang and fell, and the Tartars dropped senseless from his hands.

Sullivan gave a bellow like an angry bull and dashed into the fight. A horseman, wheeling, cut the shoulder off his coat: as the horse reared Sullivan gripped the rider by the leg and jerked him down. The Kazak fought like a wild-cat: Sullivan raised him, hurled him down on the rocks and then flung his body into the knot of swordsmen surrounding Hulagu. He followed right behind the hurled body, roaring and striking right and left.

The battle was more even now. Ross, using his rifle as a club, was over on the right, taking the Tartars from behind: Olaf was by his side, with a boulder in each great hand that converted his fists into two deadly maces. A rush of horsemen from the farther end was checked by the men above: the Professor had the hang of his weapon now, and now even Li Han could hardly miss. Only four men got through.

In the middle of a ring of Kazaks Sullivan fought like a man possessed. He had no weapons, but he held a man by his feet, and whirling him round he drove the Kazaks before him. They scattered, and he threw the body with all his force, knocking three of them down. From one of the fallen men he snatched a sword, and for a moment he stood alone. It was a long blade, heavy and straight: he shifted it in his hand. It was a brave man who came against him, Attay Bogra, the son of the Altai Khan. The blades leapt in the sunlight, hissing against each other, hissing and clashing so that the noise was like the noise in a smithy when two men hammer on the iron. They went to and fro, and men fell back from either side of them. The red wound from a half-parried blow sprang open on Sullivan's forearm, and the blood flowed fast. He gave back a step, but as he stepped the Tartar lunged, slipped in a pool of blood and almost fell. He straightened, saw Sullivan's sword whip up in both hands to the height above him, and flung up his sword against the blow, but in vain: the sword flashed down, a blinding arc of light, and through helmet, skull and bone the sword bit to the ground. The Tartar fell, clean cut in two. There was a great cry, and a moment of sudden panic among the Kazaks. At this instant the Kokonor Mongols from the farther cliff reached the bottom—they had had a longer and a steeper climb, but now they flew into the fight.

Sullivan wiped the blood from his eyes and glanced around to find the thickest of the fray. There was none. The Kazaks were already horsed, and the survivors were racing down the gulley.

Ten

A T the edge of the Takla Makan they met the old Khan of Kokonor. He was a little man with a straggling white beard and streaming white moustaches that flew out on each side of his helmet. Derrick thought he looked a curious figure to lead the fiercest horde in Mongolia, and he was surprised at the deference with which Ross and Sullivan greeted him. They dismounted before he did, and walked across the sand to shake his hand: the old Khan was ill at ease out of the saddle, and he waddled on his bowed legs as he advanced to meet them.

Everyone stood well aside in silence while the three talked. After a little while they parted: the Khan shook hands again, nodded to his sons, and was gone in a cloud of dust.

"Was that funny little man the Khan Hulagu?" asked Derrick.

His uncle was thinking of other things: he looked worried, and his face was dark. But after a moment he forced a smile and said, "That funny little man, as you call him, is the Khan. He has probably killed more men than you have ever spoken to in your life, merely in guarding his own lands: what he could do if he went on the loose, I hesitate to think. I wouldn't call him a funny little man if I were you."

Sullivan and Ross walked on to where the Professor stood: they drew him aside out of earshot, and Sullivan said, "I am afraid we have bad news. We cannot go on by the road we planned, and we cannot go back. The Kazaks have cut the roads to the Gobi, and they have defeated the Khan's men north of the Takla Makan. He is very short of men just now, until he can get his scattered horde together, but he will give us a dozen men for a month to take us south of the Takla Makan to the Kirghiz country. We will be safe there. It is a quicker road than the one we proposed before, but it will give you no archaeology at all—it will be hard riding all the way."

"I am all for speed at this juncture," said the Professor, "and I feel that I would rather get the jade home than make any number of diggings, however exciting they might be. But will it be necessary to deprive this worthy man of so many of his followers?"

"If you want to carry your head home as well as your jade," said Ross, "you will thank your stars that the Khan has made the offer. I wish that he could let us have ten times as many. Ever since this clumsy lubber Sullivan killed the Altai Khan's son there has been a blood-feud between us and them, and they'll be after us like a pack of wolves."

"Yes. That is the case," said Sullivan, shaking his head. "And that is not the only danger. The old Khan does not know exactly what has happened in the north, and there is the possibility—the very faint possibility, mind—that the Kazaks might come down through the middle of the Takla Makan and cut our road before we can get through." He drew a rough oval in the sand. "Here are we," he said, pointing to the narrow end of the egg, "and we have got to hurry along the southern edge. If they should come down thus"—he drew a line through the middle of the egg—"and hit this southern edge by the Kunlun mountains before we have passed the point where they reach our path, why, then things might be very bad."

"Yes," said the Professor, gravely. "I quite see that."

"But," said Ross, "although they might be very bad, they would not be hopeless. There are some places where it is possible to get up through the Kunlun into Tibet—but we hardly need worry our heads about that. The chances of the Kazaks coming down through the desert are really very slight. Our chief aim must be to get along as fast as ever we can, and I think we should talk from our saddles, rather than wandering about like lambs waiting for the butcher."

They stripped the column down to its bare necessities. Bale after bale they left standing in the sand, food, books and the Professor's rubber bath: they changed all the camel-loads that could not be left behind on to horses, and by the light of the crescent moon alone they rode hard for the south. Yet fast though they went, the Mongols were not satisfied: they pushed on and on until Derrick slept in his saddle, and Li Han had to have his feet tied under his horse's belly to keep him on. Twice young Hulagu made wide sweeping detours through stony patches of the desert, keeping the horses trotting throughout the night, although they were so tired that they could hardly stand: but in spite of all their care, on the third day they saw dust on the horizon behind them, and by noon through the binoculars they could see that below the dust rode a troop of Kazaks. It was that same evening that on the southern sky there appeared a long, low cloud that never moved. It was the Kunlun mountains, and as the sun set they could see the snow of the distant peaks glow red.

Day after day they travelled swiftly to the south, keeping to the edge of the desert for the rare wells and the grass for their horses; and day after day the Kazaks followed them. It was hard on the men, but it was harder on the horses: they carried very little corn, and the grass the horses could find was not enough to keep even those hardy beasts going at that killing pace. The mares that they brought with them for their milk dried up, and then one horse after another dropped behind. Fortunately they had many spare horses, in the Tartar fashion, and they hoped that under the mountains they would find better pasture.

When they first appeared, the Kazaks were more numerous than the flying expedition, but Hulagu had hopes of reducing their numbers: not only had they fewer spare horses, being so far from home, but they did not know the springs so well, and every night, once it was certain that they were discovered, the Kokonor men fired the grass so that there would be none for the pursuers, for during the first ten days of their flight the wind was in their faces, and the fire, when it spread, ran back towards the Kazaks.

Hulagu was right. In time the Kazaks dwindled in number to such a degree that the expedition was no longer hopelessly outnumbered, and after they had made sure of that by repeated counts, they slowed their pace to a speed that would not kill their horses— a speed that they could keep up for a month on end. The Kazaks did the same: by pressing hard they could now have caught up with the expedition, but they hung back, waiting like wolves for some disaster, some well that would fail, or for some one of the hundred mischances that could befall to happen and deliver their prey to them unarmed.

The column no longer rode in a compact line: there were the baggage horses in the centre, with the poorest riders; then a rear-guard of the Kokonor Mongols, with either Ross or Sullivan; and far in front three or four of the best horses. Chingiz and Derrick were usually sent out in front, being the lightest of the

216

party, and the least likely to tire their horses; and all day as they rode they scanned the horizon to the north and west.

Every day as they rode south the Kunlun range rose higher in the sky, a vast series of mountains like a wall, rising abruptly from the plain: from less than half-way up they were covered with snow, and innumerable higher, more snowy, peaks showed behind them. Behind that monstrous wall was Tibet, but it seemed impossible that any man should get up there, or live if he ever succeeded in his climb.

At last they began to turn right-handed to the west. The sun set in their eyes now, and now they were in the more fertile tract of country that led between the desert and the great rampart of mountains that floated above the clouds on their left, a long, thin stretch of country that would lead them to safety in the Kirghiz land.

They were in the foothills now, high, rolling, down-like slopes with grass that gave their horses heart and strength, and they were so near the mountains that they filled half the sky, towering up and up so that they had to lean back to see the tops. The days went by, so many of them that Derrick lost count of the days of the week, and they came at last to the place called Tchirek Chagu. Several of the Mongols had been here, for it was a meeting-place for those who had come down through the desert to the southern trail, and here sometimes in the earlier part of the year a few Tibetans would come down and trade. They rode with redoubled caution here, looking out far ahead; but when it was passed even Ross, who was the most cautious in saying hopeful words, said that he thought there was no longer any danger from the north. Several times they thought of turning to deal with the danger from the east, but whenever they stopped, the Kazaks stopped too. It would need several days to bring them to action, so the expedition went on, more slowly now, and almost at their ease.

They were riding along the most spectacular part of the southern trail, with the edge of the Takla Makan in sight on their right, and on their left the mountain wall rising sheer and black in the noblest precipice in the world, when one of the Mongols who had been there before pointed out the Gingbadze pass and the lamasery.

It seemed impossible that the small downward nick in the towering heights should be a pass, but as Derrick followed the pointing finger he could make out a minute square object just under it.

"That," said the Mongol, "is the lamasery of Gingbadze, and the lamas who lived there made those steps that lead up to the pass." Derrick looked harder still, and he made out a thin line running up the precipice, a continuous line of steps cut out of the living rock.

"So that is Gingbadze," said the Professor. "I have often heard of it, but I never expected to see it."

"Why did they cut the steps, sir?" asked Derrick.

"For the pilgrims," replied the Professor. "They used to go up there in great numbers to the shrine of

Sidhartha's tooth in the days before the Red-Hats ruined the monastery."

"Red-Hats, sir?"

"Another sort of lama—Tibetan monks, you know. A vicious, war-like set of men, from all I hear, whatever their theories may be. I should very much like to go up there. Sullivan, do you think we could go up to Gingbadze? The Kazaks were not seen today, I believe—and even if they are still behind us, they do not seem inclined to molest us anymore."

"No, they do seem to be falling back now: but consider, Professor, we should have to leave the horses at the foot of the pass, and if the Kazaks were to come up, where should we be then?"

"You are quite right, of course. How foolish of me. Still, on a happier occasion, it would be very agreeable to go up."

They rode on, and that evening they camped in long grass, the most comfortable beds they had had for weeks: the grass was already in seed, and the horses ate themselves fat. In the morning they rode out at their leisure. There was still no sign of the Kazaks behind, but wishing to see farther back Derrick and Chingiz went up a knoll that gave them a clear view for a full day's march and more behind them. The morning air was clear and sharp, but for a long while they saw nothing on their trail.

"There they are," cried Chingiz, suddenly. He pointed, and Derrick saw a movement in the distance, far away, but still much nearer than he had been looking.

"Yes, they are still there," he said, shrugging his shoulders. He was just about to go down again when the cry of a bird along the mountainside made him look round. He could not see the bird, but as he searched for it his eye caught a gleam from far away, something that sent back the rays of the rising sun. The gleam winked, twinkled, and was gone: yet he thought he could make out something moving far down there, between the desert and the hill. He called Chingiz, and they stared together. "It may be a mirage," said Derrick —they had seen plenty, in the Gobi and in the Takla Makan —but Chingiz shook his head. "We cannot risk its being a mirage," he said, and they hurried back to Sullivan. Sullivan looked doubtful. "It hardly can be anything," he said, "but you had better take the glasses and look again. Keep well out of sight."

They rode quickly to the knoll again, and raising only their heads above the skyline they searched the country with the glasses. Derrick caught the gleam again, a little line of flashes, and focused the glasses nearer. For a moment he could not make it out: the reflection seemed to be attached to nothing. Then the distant horseman topped the rise, and Derrick understood. All he had seen before was the row of lance-heads winking in the sun: the Kazaks had been hidden by the rising ground. The first came over the brow and into full view, then the second, then the third. He counted them: fifty, sixty, eighty-seven men. He handed the glasses to Chingiz, who gave one look and raced back.

"Dear me, what is the matter?" asked the Professor, as Sullivan called in the outriders and swung the column round.

"It's Kazaks before and Kazaks behind," said Sullivan. "There's the desert to the north and the mountains to the south. You'll see Gingbadze yet, Professor."

He seemed in a high good humour, and for the moment the Professor did not understand. "Why should we see Gingbadze?" he asked. "Only yesterday you gave some excellent reason for not going there."

"They have cut the road before us," cried Sullivan, urging his horse to a gallop. "We have got to reach the Gingbadze steps before nightfall, or we shall be between two fires."

They raced through the morning and the afternoon, never drawing rein for a moment, and continually watching the skyline before them for the Kazaks who had followed, them so long. If the Kazaks from the east made a stand—and they were still too numerous to be brushed aside—the delay and the noise of battle would bring the western Kazaks up at full speed, and that would be the end.

Mile after mile sped by under their horses' hooves, and at last they saw the great rampart of the Gingbadze wall appear. Still there was no sign of the Kazaks from the east.

At last the lamasery came in sight, vanishing and appearing through the drifting clouds high above them on the right, and at last they saw the Kazaks, a straggling band of men strung out over the plain.

"Now for it," said Sullivan, as he saw the Kazaks drawing together in a compact body. He could make out no more than seven or eight riders, with a few led horses. The Kazaks stood firm, and one of them fired his rifle in the air—a signal, obviously, to bring up the slower men behind.

"Ross," he said, when they were within extreme rifle-range, "you are a better shot than I am. See what you can do."

Ross nodded, swung out of the column and dismounted. He unslung his rifle, the rifle he called the Messenger of Bad News, and rubbed its foresight on his sleeve: he lay down tranquilly on the grass and drew a bead on the midmost Tartar. But as his finger was curled round the trigger the Kazaks wheeled and fled from the advancing column. The dust obscured them, but Ross shifted his aim to the outside man on the left and fired. The Kazak threw up his arms and almost fell; but he gripped his horse's neck and rode on, bowed low and drooping in his saddle.

Ross galloped after the column and rejoined them as they halted at the foot of the precipice. Already they were stripping the baggage-horses, loading the essentials into packs—warm clothes, food and ammunition—and one of the oldest Mongols was hastily scrawling a map on a piece of sheepskin for Sullivan.

Olaf was high up the steps, keeping watch. From

time to time he reported that the eastern Kazaks were still going, and that those from the west were not yet in sight.

"No, Professor, you cannot take the Han bronzes," said Sullivan firmly, folding away the map. "You can carry them well up the steps, and then you must bury them. Another expedition can fetch them away. After all, they have waited two thousand years—they can wait a little longer. And you had better do the same with the jade."

"I will bury the bronze, if you insist," said the Professor, "but I will not be parted from the jade. It is quite light. I can easily carry it."

"All right, all right," said Sullivan, tugging at a strap, "but whatever you do, do it quickly. Olaf, do you see anything to the west?"

"Nothing, Cap'n. Unless that little cloud is their dust. The sun will last another hour."

"Hurry, hurry!" cried Sullivan, and they bent to their task.

In the twilight they were ready. Chingiz and two Mongols were to stay with them—the Khan's orders had been exact, and these men were not to leave them until they were on the Kirghiz steppe—and Hulagu, Kubilai and the tribesmen were to break out to the north through the desert. They could travel faster alone, and they hoped to rejoin their own horde, which would be gathering for the war at the Kodha well, before the Kazaks could reach them.

"Horsemen in the west," cried Olaf from above.

"It is time," said Hulagu. "Let the wise man give us a wind from the north, and we are safe."

"He will do his best," said Sullivan. They shook hands, and with a few words of parting they were gone.

For a moment the expedition watched them, and then began the climb. The steps were ancient and weather-worn, but they were as sound as the day they were first cut, for they were part of the hard rock itself. The rise was close on a yard with each step, and often the tread was narrow: it was a laborious climb, and after the first hundred they were sweating, though the air was cold.

At every hundredth step, wherever the rock formation made it possible, there was a broad platform for resting, but Sullivan drove them on and on. Derrick began counting the steps as he toiled up, but after a thousand he gave up.

In the gathering darkness they mounted, always up and up, and at last Sullivan said that they could take a rest.

"We are still within their range," he said, "but this platform lies so far back that it gives us cover."

"I suppose," said the Professor, panting under his load, "that there is the possibility of their pursuing us still."

"No, none at all," replied Sullivan, peering over the edge. "Wherever a horse can go you are not safe from a Mongol. But they will not go where they cannot ride. Besides, they would never come up here, even if they could get their horses up, for fear of the devils. These men here would not be with us if they did not believe you were a powerful magician: even as it is, they are not at all happy, and the others who are somewhere down there below us are glad not to be in their places. I cannot see them," he added, sweeping the plain with his glasses. The others joined him, but down there all was blank.

"They are probably riding slowly not to make any dust," said Ross. "But it looks as though the Professor had done his business very well." He pointed to the northern horizon, and there they saw the familiar shape of a dust-storm looming over the desert.

"That will cover their tracks before the morning," said Sullivan. "They were relying on you for a wind, Professor."

The Professor violently disclaimed any magic powers, but Chingiz and the two Mongols looked at him with marked respect, whatever he might say. He felt so strongly about it that he made Derrick translate his words to Chingiz.

"The Professor says that he has no control over the winds," said Derrick. "He says it is all nonsense and superstition. He says you mustn't believe what they say about him."

"All the best magicians say that," said Chingiz. "It is part of their magic."

They slept that night on a platform three hundred steps higher up, and in the morning they awoke in a vague world of cloud. There was white cloud below them and above, and when the morning breeze tore them, they could see nothing but the frightful precipice plunging down into vacancy, and black rocks dripping in the wet. The steps were slippery, and the temperature had dropped nearly to the freezing-point. Ross was shivering with fever, but he climbed silently with the others.

They mounted blindly: they could not see twenty yards above them, nor twenty yards below. The whole world seemed to be confined within the narrow walls of the cloud: the desert below might never have existed, nor the pass above. They followed the endless steps as they rose, zigzagging to and fro across the mountain wall: sometimes the precipice was less sheer, and then in the water-worn gullies the steps gave place to a hacked-out path. This was a great relief, but the paths were short and few, and nearly always it was the perpetual upward climb.

At noon they came quite suddenly out of the cloud, and there far above them they saw the lamasery. Beyond that there were the peaks, black and white against the pure blue of the sky: below them rolled the impenetrable clouds, layer after layer of them, stretching out as far as the eye could see. They were nearing the snow-line, but still the mountain towered over them: it seemed to be just as high as it had been when they started.

"Is this going on for ever?" wondered Derrick, hitching his pack up on his shoulders. He had barked his shins several times on the high steps, there was a blister forming on his heel, and he was sore all over from the weight of his load and the gruelling climb. Chang whined in sympathy, and Derrick grasped his thick fur to help him up the awkward rise.

The only one who was enjoying himself was Professor Ayrton. He had always spent his holidays in the mountains, and he was much more at home on a steep slope than in the saddle of a horse. Furthermore, the light had revealed the presence of rock-carvings, ruined shrines and inscriptions all the way up the pilgrims' way to the lamasery, and the combination of mountaineering and ancient inscriptions rejoiced the Professor's heart. The carvings were quite recent—a mere thousand years or so—but they made the Professor's day. Often, as they mounted, he would ask Olaf to make a back, and he would scramble up to inspect the deep-cut writing, still clear after all the centuries. But at last, when they were just below the snow, Olaf struck.

"Ay don't care if it's double-Dutch," he said, "and anyway, Ay reckon it only says 'Do not spit' or maybe 'Ole's Beer is Best'. But even if it was poetry, Ay reckon the son of a sea-cook would of wrote it at a proper level if he wanted it read," and he stumped obstinately away.

"I wonder that he should speak so petulantly," said the Professor to Derrick, "he is usually such an obliging fellow. How could he suppose that it was an advertisement? It reads, 'The thrice-born bearer of enlightenment. . . .' " But Derrick trudged on without waiting for the end.

They were none of them as cheerful as the Professor. Sullivan was moody and thoughtful: he was in a new country, not sure of his bearings and worried. Ross, habitually silent, was more taciturn than ever, for his fever was rising, and the lance-wound in his thigh was hurting cruelly. He had received it in the battle of the ravine, but he had not mentioned it, and he had thought it was healing well; but now it throbbed and ached so that every step was a torment.

Slowly the lamasery crept nearer, and by the evening they were at its gates. The roof had fallen long ago, but they found shelter enough and a few low shrubs to make a fire. The next morning saw them up and over the pass. Before them lay a great valley, sloping gradually upwards towards the south and reaching a great height at its farther end. In the extra-ordinarily keen and transparent air they could see the whole length of it, dazzling white, without a living thing.

"It is a good thing that we are carrying enough food," said Sullivan, looking at his rough map. "We must go the whole length of this valley, and then at the far end we shall find a branch leading down to the west. We take that and come to a pass that leads down to the village of Hukutu. There is a glacier about half-way down, but once we are across that we drop to Hukutu, and there we should be able to get food, yaks and a guide." He checked the loads of food, and said,

228

"Yes, I think we should have enough if we press on. Professor, you have buried your bronzes? Good, then we must get moving."

Twice, as they made their journey along the southern valley, they saw ibexes, but neither time could they get a shot, and they had no time, with their limited rations, to spend half a day in stalking a group of them that they saw on the ridge to their left. The travelling was not too hard, once they had got used to the unaccustomed exercise of walking with heavy loads—an exercise which called muscles into play that were quite unused on horseback—and going along the southern valley they made good time. But when they came to the western branch they met a bitter wind that pierced them through and through, a more biting, cutting wind than the icy blast of the steppe. All the time they were climbing higher and higher, and in the rarefied atmosphere their ears and their noses bled; they soon became exhausted, and they grumbled almost to the point of mutiny as Sullivan urged them on. The bitter wind that never stopped cut the heart out of them, and the sun, while it heated them too much whenever they found shelter from the wind, served most of the time only to send a blinding glare from the snow below them and on either side.

The glacier proved very difficult: it was hatched all over with profound crevasses, and without ropes or proper boots they were often on the brink of disaster. Had it not been for the Professor's knowledge of the

229

high mountain they would never have crossed it; but they reached the top, and there they rested. It had been painfully slow, nearly a whole day for a pitifully short distance, but it had been shockingly arduous, and they felt that they deserved their rest.

"We had better camp just under the steep slope, and keep that to warm us up in the morning, don't you think, Ross?" There was no reply, and he looked round. Ross was not there. They called and shouted, but there was no answer.

They found him at last, half-way down the glacier, creeping on his hands and knees along the edge of a crevasse, still trying to find a way across. It was a narrow crevasse, but he could not see to jump it: he was completely snow-blind, and he was very ill.

Now that they knew the way up the glacier it was easier, and they brought him up to the top before nightfall: their packs stood at the foot of a steep slope of old, hard snow; it seemed a wretched place for a sick man to spend the night, but he was at the end of his strength, and they could not go on.

"Ay got an idea," cried Olaf, pointing to one of the Mongols' swords. The Mongol gave it up, with a wondering stare, and Olaf began to cut great blocks from the hard snow. "We done this when Ay was a whaler," he explained, arranging them in a circle. "It ban a snow house." He raised the circle while the others cut and carried snow, raised it layer by layer, each layer forming a narrower circle until the whole thing was a dome. He cut the door, pommelled the arch that he had made, gave it a kick or two to make sure that it held, and crept in. They heard him thumping the inside, and then he called, "All ship-shape, Cap'n. Sling him in."

They helped Ross in through the low arch and laid him on their sheepskin coats. There was room for them all, huddled close and sitting round the wall, and soon the place began to warm. To be out of the wind was already a huge advantage, and to be warm as well was bliss, in spite of the drops that fell from the roof. Ross started to feel very much better: he ate a strip of horseflesh, and shortly after fell into a profound sleep.

In the morning he still could not see anything at all, but he insisted that he was perfectly fit otherwise, and that he could carry his pack. They all felt wonderfully refreshed for a night's sleep in comparative warmth, and they faced the climb to the pass with renewed strength. Sullivan bent the end of the Mongol's sword over at right angles, and the Professor went ahead, cutting steps in the packed snow: Olaf led Ross, and slowly they mounted to the pass.

"At the top we should reach our highest point," said Sullivan, "and I think we ought to see straight down to Hukutu, or at least into its valley."

Up and up they went. The wind died at noon, and they came up out of the deep shadow of the ridge into the hot sun as they reached the pass.

But there was nothing there. No village below them, no valley: not even a descent. There was only an unending waste of snow and rock that rose, after a short plateau, on and on as far as they could see. It was heart-breaking: they stopped all together, without a word.

"What is the matter?" asked Ross, as he stood, holding on to Olaf's shoulder.

"It is not important," replied Sullivan, after a moment's pause. "It is just that I underestimated the distance a little. I misread the map, and said that we were at the pass before we had really reached it. It is some way farther on."

He took a compass bearing, and said cheerfully, "We will make for that ridge, and then I dare say we shall see our valley."

But no one believed him. They had all seen the map, and it clearly showed the pass and the fall to the valley as being just beyond the head of the glacier. Either Atakin, the Mongol who had drawn the map, had forgotten the way, or they had climbed on the wrong side of the glacier. Before them lay the enormous stretch of country between the Kunlun range and the Himalaya, hundreds of miles of it, with a cold death in every single mile. They had been so certain of the map that they had eaten well in the snow house, and in the morning they had used almost all their fuel. Food and fuel sacks were nearly empty.

Derrick felt a kick behind that shot him a yard forward. "Don't mooch along with a dismal face, boy," said his uncle, walking along to the head of the line and whistling as he went. But his whistling could not restore the expedition's heart. They had made a great effort, and now, some of them at least, felt so hopeless

232

that they trudged slowly, unwillingly, without any spirit left. It was not that each of them was not a brave man in his own place, at sea or on the dusty steppe, but here they were dealing with enemies they did not understand, the altitude had given each of them the mountain-sickness to some degree, and for the Mongols there was the added fear of their inherited beliefs.

Olaf resisted well enough, but it was the Professor who behaved the best of all. He was as nearly sure as Sullivan that the map had been mistaken, and he knew perfectly well that if they did not find Hukutu or some other human habitation in the next few days they would be in a very serious position, for there was no going back; but he exclaimed on the excellence of the snow-crust and the pleasure of walking on it, he even made Li Han run, and he encouraged them all by singing a discordant Tyrolean song. And it was he who discovered the hidden valley that lay on their right just before the midday halt: it was a narrow cleft between two snowy slopes, and as its end ran parallel to their route it had escaped the notice of the others. Even when he pointed it out, they scarcely saw it, for the white of its near side merged so perfectly with the white of its far side that it was nearly invisible.

"While the banquet is being prepared," he said, "I think I will just go over and look down that little valley." He had already left the line to explore several others, and they watched him apathetically while Li Han unpacked the meagre store of food. They were squatting there when a shadow passed over the snow, and two choughs landed a little distance from them.

"Who would have expected to find them up here?" exclaimed Sullivan, shooting them both. "They were extraordinarily tame," he said, bringing them back. "I hope they will taste better than they look."

They were still eating and discussing the birds when the Professor rejoined them: he sat down and ate his three pieces of meat, and when they were getting up again Derrick asked him if he had seen anything in the valley.

"Why, yes," he said, in a conversational tone, "I looked down on a village that I take to be Hukutu. It is remarkable in that there appears to be no lamasery there, whereas I had—"

"You saw Hukutu!" exclaimed Derrick. "Where? Is it far?"

"—whereas I had been led to suppose," continued the Professor, "that there was hardly an inhabited place in Tibet without its monastery. It is directly below us, as you always maintained, Sullivan. I should say that it is about seven thousand feet lower than we are, but I fear that the descent may present some difficulties."

With twice the speed of their morning's march they hurried to the narrow valley. Here the snow lay loose and drifted, and they plunged in knee-deep. It was sweltering work under the noon-day sun, trapped as it was between the narrow walls, but their fresh hope— doubly strong after such a disappointment—carried them through in the Professor's tracks, and very soon they were staring down a dark precipice that dropped a sheer two thousand feet, ice-coated here and there with ice that trickled now in the sun, but which would freeze again that night. Below the precipice there stretched the snow, but no longer unending snow, for it stopped five thousand feet below them, and then came a brown bar of naked earth, cut by streams that shone white in the distance. Below the brownness there was green, the green of pastures, and then the whole sweep of the broad valley, a river, a few dark patches that might be trees and even the tiny squares of fields, as small as postage stamps from that vertiginous height.

"Where is Hukutu?" asked Sullivan.

"You will have to lean out and look down to the left to see it," replied the Professor, "but for heaven's sake do not go too near the edge. This is only a snow cornice, and it might give."

Sullivan lay down and began to creep out, but the Mongols, who understood only the Professor's pointing finger, walked boldly to the edge and peered out.

"Take care," cried the Professor, and as he spoke the jutting out rim of snow gave way. The two Mongols vanished with a cry and Chingiz hurled himself on his back, but half his body was over the edge and his hands clawed in vain for a split second in the snow for a hold. Derrick hurled himself forward, flat on his stomach, and grabbed Chingiz's right hand as it went. There was a low, moan from below, and Derrick felt the grip of the fingers slacken in his own: he held with all his force, gritting his teeth, and in a moment he felt Chingiz's left hand come up and grasp him by the wrist.

Sullivan had Derrick by the feet. "Have you got him?" he cried.

"Yes. But pull me back. The snow is giving under me." He felt himself slide back, and then the edge of the snow, wind-blown out from the precipice and overhanging it, gave way. A piece stretching from his chin to his stomach fell. He saw it hit Chingiz, who gave a grunt, and then Sullivan had pulled him farther back.

"Hold on," called Sullivan. "Olaf's coming alongside of you."

Olaf edged himself rapidly against Derrick's side: his long arms reached down to Chingiz's elbows, raised him, took him by the neck and brought him up.

Derrick crawled backwards on to the firm snow and saw Chingiz sitting with his back to a rock. His face looked terribly strange and drawn, but he smiled.

"This will hurt," said Sullivan, picking him up and laying him on his back. "His arm went backwards as he fell," he said to Derrick, "and he was hanging by it with his shoulder dislocated."

He put his foot under Chingiz's armpit, took his hand and pulled. The Mongol kept his face expressionless: he got up, moved his arm and nodded. "Thank you," he said, and walked carefully towards the edge again.

They all peered down the shocking drop, but there was no sign of the two tribesmen. There was a tumble of huge boulders, flecked with snow, that hid their bodies: there was no sort of hope at all.

"They were good men," said Chingiz, getting up at last.

The others said the same, and they moved slowly back into the narrow valley. There was one thought in all their minds, but no one uttered it: the Mongols had been carrying the food and the fuel.

"What do you suggest, Professor?" asked Sullivan. "We have got to get down there somehow. Two more nights up here would kill Ross, and I don't think we'd last much longer ourselves without food. And I think it's coming on to blow."

"Ice is what I am afraid of," said the Professor. "We have been very lucky in meeting so little so far. Ice . . ." he paused. A distant thunder away to their left mounted, surged into a roar that made the still air tremble, and died away. "Ice and that," he said.

"What was it?"

"An avalanche. A still, warm day like this will bring them on wherever the snow hangs steep. In a way it would be better if the temperature were to drop—it might be better, I mean, if the wind were to start again, however unpleasant it might be for us."

They stood thinking, and on the face of the valley opposite to them, a mile away at the most, there was a puff of powdery snow, then the deep rumble, and the side of the mountain appeared to shift. A vast expanse of snow moved slowly, and then with enormously increasing speed, rushing down the slope, breaking into an almighty rolling wave under a cloud of spray-like powder-snow it hurled itself down into the floor of the valley. They could hardly hear themselves speak under the roaring thunder. Behind them, an ice-pinnacle, quivering in the vibration, fell with a metallic crash.

"One starts another," observed the Professor. "It is undoubtedly of the first importance to get down out of these narrow and steep-sided valleys. But the question is, how? I need not waste time pointing out that if we had ropes and crampons it would be much easier. No." He stroked his chin. "I am of the opinion," he said slowly, "that the best thing is for us to build a shelter for Ross and that unfortunate young Chingiz, who must be suffering agonies, and to leave them with Derrick, while we separate and explore this ridge in each direction. The path certainly exists: I have no doubt of that. The trouble is to find it."

"From the map it should be to the west-nor'-west."

"Then if you will go along the ridge in that direction, I will go in the other. I suggest that we meet at the camp at sunset."

But when they met again, they had found nothing: nowhere was there a fault in the sheer plunging cliff, nowhere a hint of a path. The shadow of the night fell across the valley, and instantly the cold began again. With the setting of the sun the wind that Sullivan had prophesied sprang up, and although they were in the shelter their breath froze on their faces.

In the morning they looked out into driving snow. It looked like the end, but in an hour or two it stopped, and the Professor, Sullivan, Olaf and Li Han went out. It was beyond all words frustrating to be within sight of salvation and yet to find no way down, but although they searched all day they found nothing but one valley far to the west that might, if it were followed, and if it turned to the left, lead below the snow. At least it did slope down, and they moved the camp to there. Sullivan shot another chough, and they cooked it over a fire made from fragments of a lacquered box that Li Han carried in his pack.

They were all very silent, but at the end of their brief meal Olaf said, with a laugh, "Ay reckon Ay was right when Ay stowed away all that duff with Hsien Lu."

Sullivan said nothing, but Derrick saw him look thoughtfully at Chang.

In the morning they drank the snow-water that they had melted overnight, and they went on: Chingiz could not carry a pack, and now Ross could hardly walk. The valley did descend, sometimes so sharply that the climbing down was hard, and Sullivan and Olaf had to carry Ross; but it twisted and wound, and in spite of their compass bearings they could no longer be sure that it would ever join the valley of Hukutu. That valley seemed so distant now: Derrick remembered it with an effort as he tried to distract his mind from the awful gnawing hunger that worked in his stomach like a living thing and made him shiver all the time, whether he was in the sun or not; he remembered how they had looked down into it, and how strange it had been to see that down there it was summer.

He was walking steadily behind Olaf, slowly but steadily, chewing on his leather belt. Suddenly he bumped into Olaf's back, for Olaf had stopped.

Olaf stood still, staring down and to the left. He put his hands up to his mouth, drew a deep breath and hailed with all the force of his lungs. "Ahoy!" he roared, and from the rocks the echo came back, "Ahoy!" But after the echo had died, there came from far over the snows an answering hail, quavering and long-drawn, the call of a Tibetan.

Eleven

THEY had staggered into Hukutu more dead than alive, but they left it fit, strong and fat, with four Tibetan guides and a little train of yaks. Only the Professor was not well: after having survived the bitter days above the precipice, the hunger and the wicked cold, he came down with dysentery after two days in the village. All of them had it, more or less, except Chingiz, who was salted from birth against such ills, but all of them, save the Professor, got over it quite soon: he remained weak, thin and pale, and when they left he rode the only pony that the place could provide. Ross's fever yielded to the vile grey brew that the old woman who ruled the village forced down his throat, and his sight came back. By the time they left he was as strong and formidable as ever.

Several times on the way over the mountains Sullivan had cursed the weight of gold in his money-belt; he had even been tempted to throw it away as an encumbrance that might lose him his life; but now he was glad of it. A handful of the mixed coins—sovereigns, twenty-dollar pieces, louis d'or and even gold mohurs—bought all that the village could afford to sell. It was not much, for the Tibetans there had little more than their bare subsistence, but there was food and warmer clothing—Tibetan furs and mountain boots —as well as yaks and the solitary pony, which would suffice to carry them westwards to Tanglha-Tso, where they could buy more provisions.

They set out as soon as the Professor could ride, for they had three high passes to cross before they reached Tanglha-Tso, and an unknown number beyond that point to the distant pass that would let them down to the Mongols' land beyond the Takla Makan. Every day counted, for it was already harvest-time, and soon the early Tibetan winter would come on and close the passes; it would close them with impassable walls of snow, and guard them with the howling tempests of wind that no man could survive. Go they must, and quickly, for not only might the passes close, but if they lingered there would be trouble: they knew very well that Tibet was a forbidden land, and if once the authorities, knowing of their presence, caught up with them, there was no telling what would happen. The best that they could hope for was interminable delay. They pressed on, therefore, and although they were kept to no greater speed than the mild walking pace of the yaks, who would not and could not be hurried, yet they covered a surprising distance in their first week.

They had been lucky in finding two men in Hukutu who had enough Mongol to understand something of what they said, and one of them, Ngandze, was a widely travelled, intelligent man. He knew the country intimately as far as Tanglha-Tso, and he spent hours with Sullivan drawing a map: they chose their route with great care to avoid the bigger lamaseries, and in one place they decided on a detour of no less than twenty miles over bad country to avoid a monastery of the militant Red-Hat lamas, for an encounter with them would be dangerous to a high degree.

The days went by peacefully, one after another: they travelled through long, empty valleys, with plenty of fuel and game, roe-deer, maral, thars and a few birds like white quail. Their shooting did not please the Tibetans, who were devout Buddhists, and killed nothing whatsoever; but this did not prevent them from coming, one by one, around the pot when Li Han was cooking one of his excellent stews.

Once they were on the march the Professor recovered his health, and he plunged with characteristic enthusiasm into the compiling of a list of Tibetan words: he was still weak, and now Li Han carried all the jade sewn into his padded clothes or into a long cummerbund which he wrapped about his middle and never took off—an inner sash that gave him the girth of a mandarin and made him waddle like a duck —but the Professor stated that he felt very like a war-horse, or at least like a convalescent war-horse; and a little while after the others had been trying to persuade him to ride and not to walk so much, with his own hands he shot a snow-leopard. They had risen for days to the last high pass before Tanglha-Tso, and they were just descending again towards the snow-line when a thar dashed across their path, leaping madly over the rocks: immediately behind it came a snow-leopard, gaining on it fast in huge bounds. The Professor, who was in front, whipped up his rifle and fired. The snow-leopard seemed to check in mid-air. It fell awkwardly on its side, staining the snow with scarlet blood. It gave a great coughing roar and came straight for them. The Professor was fumbling at his spectacles: he had knocked them sideways as he fired, and the others could not shoot without hitting him. But five yards from the Professor's maddened pony the leopard fell, rolled, twitched and lay still. Chingiz, racing through the line of plunging, panicking yaks, put a bullet between it eyes for good measure, but the great beast was already dead. Chingiz ran forward to take its whiskers for a charm, and the others gathered round it. Lying there on the snow it looked unbelievably large, with its thick yellowish fur and its long, deep-furred tail.

"Big, big, big," cried Ngandze in admiration, stretching out his hands: he bent, cut off an ear and ate it with every appearance of appetite.

"What an extraordinarily bold creature," said the Professor, who was still a little flustered.

"They are very bold," said Sullivan. "I suppose it is because so few of them are killed."

"Professor," murmured Ross in his ear, "you were not aiming at the thar, were you?"

"I cannot deny it," replied the Professor, with a blush, "but they were very close together, you know, and I assure you that I did fire on purpose."

Down they went, below the snow-line again and to the high pastures where the yaks were grazing by the small summer settlements of the herdsmen, down to the racing, ice-cold river and the hardy trees, and after three days more they saw the village of Tanglha-Tso, dominated by its high, white-walled monastery. It looked like a morning's ride, but in that high, clear air they knew very well by now that distances were deceptive, and it did not surprise them to find that three days elapsed before they reached the little, dirty, huddled village.

This was the first inhabited lamasery that Derrick had seen, and he asked his uncle whether he could go up and look into it: he also asked whether it was not dangerous for them to stay there.

"Didn't you say, Uncle, that we were going to avoid lamaseries?" he asked finally.

"If I had asked my Uncle Paddy half so many questions," said Sullivan, "he would have kicked me from Connaught to the city of Cork, and if I had asked my Uncle Murtaghbut I am a quiet, civil-tempered man and mild to a fault. In the first place, if we were to go through Tibet without passing any villages with monasteries, we would have to have wings and feed on the air, like birds of Paradise. In the second place, this is not a Red-Hat monastery: it is a small place, of no great importance, and from what I hear the abbot is a good, gentle creature. And in the third place, if I catch you peering about that lamasery, I'll have the hide off you with a rope's end. We must not offend their religious ideas in any way at all, and until you know their habits there's no telling what may upset them. The Professor is going up with the Tibetans to pay his respects: he doesn't want the whole ship's company hanging around and gaping like a lot of stuck pigs."

In the evening the Professor came back. "I cannot tell you how charmed I am with this place," he said. "Nothing could have exceeded the friendliness of my reception. The abbot was delighted with our little offering, and he sends you each a scarf. It was extraordinarily fortunate that we arrived today, or I should have been deprived of the pleasure of his conversation: he and all his monks are to go on a pilgrimage to the Gompa Potala early tomorrow morning."

"Did you say conversation, Professor?" asked Ross. "You must have done very well with your Tibetan vocabulary."

"That was the most delightful thing about it: the abbot speaks Chinese. He spent years in Peking with the Teshoo Lama many years ago—he is an old man— and he is more fluent than I am myself. He told me a great many fascinating things, and he was kind enough to say that he bitterly regretted the necessity for his journey tomorrow. He is writing a book on the ceremonies peculiar to this part of Tibet, and he gave me a detailed account of the progress of his manuscript."

"Did he tell you anything about our route?" asked Sullivan.

"Yes. But first I must give you a glimpse of the worthy abbot's character. He astonished me by taking me for a Chinese."

"It is hardly so very astonishing, Professor," said Sullivan. "With your tinted glasses and in your present robes, I think you could very well pass for a Chinese of the taller kind, particularly among people who are not accustomed to Europeans."

"Well, be that as it may, my command of the language is hardly that of a native of the country, and when I attempted to disabuse him, he would not listen to me. With what I at first took for an unexpected discourtesy he interrupted me, and repeated emphatically that I had come from China. I agreed, but before I could go on, he said, 'For all practical purposes, those who come from China are Chinese.' He then added that it would be a great pity if he or his monks were to spread it abroad that foreigners had illegally come into the land and were travelling about it without permission; whereas if it were known that a Chinese scholar was moving from point to point in a peaceable manner, no notice would be taken: the Chinese, you know, have a vague suzerainty over Tibet. I understood his meaning in time, and I thought it not improper to acquiesce in the innocent deception. I am afraid that I went so far as to describe you all as barbarian porters for whose almost-human good behaviour I could vouch. 'Oh, as for the outlandish slaves,' says he, 'nobody will take any notice of them, so long as you govern them strictly.' "

"Almost human, sir?" said Derrick.

"I thought it necessary to flatter you, my boy," said the Professor kindly, "And seeing that I had already committed myself to deception, I felt that I might as well go on to the limit of credibility."

"I hope," said Sullivan gravely, "that it has not strained the abbot's power of belief beyond all repair. But we must comfort ourselves with the reflection that he has never seen Derrick. But tell me, Professor, what did he say about our route?"

"He was very encouraging, except for one matter; and he gave me a highly detailed map. Here it is . . ." The Professor felt in his robes. "Bless me," he exclaimed after a minute, "I must have left it behind."

"Perhaps sitting upon?" suggested Li Han deferentially.

"Why, how very extraordinary," said the Professor, rising, "so I was. Well, here we are, you see, just by

the mouth of this benign scarlet dragon. It is not, perhaps, quite as clear as your charts, but he assured me
that it is accurate. No, one should hold the north to the
right, thus." They leant over the map: it was beautifully decorated with phoenixes, dragons of different
colours, and fiends, and at first it conveyed very little;
but when they got used to the curious shifting scale
and the various symbols, it made thoroughly good
sense.

"This is an absolute treasure," said Sullivan, with
keen approval. "But what was the discouraging point
he spoke about?"

"The Red-Hats," replied the Professor. "He advised
us at all costs to avoid their. villages, and he has
marked all the places where they are likely to be
met—here, you see, and here. But there are two places
where we cannot avoid them without a very long
detour, and a third where it is impossible to get by
without climbing a ridge that must, from his description, closely resemble the precipice that we all
remember so well—only this one is higher, and the
entirety of it is perpetually coated with ice. He suggested that we should so arrange our journey that we
pass by this place at night by the light of the moon."

"That is a very sensible idea," said Ross. "I think
your abbot must be a decent sort of a body."

"He is the most swollen of guys, I assure you," said
the Professor. "It is the world's pity that we cannot
stay here a week—that is, if he were staying too—in
order to become better acquainted. But, of course, we

must not forget that the highest passes, here and here on the map, and here, are likely to close very early. The abbot kindly said that he would continually pray for a late winter for us."

"But what about this valley?" said Sullivan, who had been studying the map intently. "It is surely far more direct, and it cuts off the worst Red-Hat place."

"Oh, yes. I had meant to ask him about that. He has, as you see, drawn his pen across the end of it—the map is very old, by the way, and he has made several alterations and additions to it here and there—and I was just about to ask him why he did so when we were interrupted."

"I suppose it must be blocked by an impassible ice-fall, or something of that nature," said Sullivan. "Yet it might be worth exploring: it is so very much more direct."

He returned to this subject in the morning. "Do you think, Professor," he said, "that you could send a note up to the abbot asking him about that valley?"

"But I am afraid that he is already gone. Did you not hear the horns and the gongs at the first light this morning?"

"Yes. I couldn't very well avoid hearing them. But Li Han could ride after him. They won't be going very fast. And that would have the advantage of giving the other monks the impression that this is really a Chinese affair—he could be the overseer of the barbarian slaves."

"Of course. We could send a note. I had not thought

of that. Now wait a moment: how had I better phrase it?"

Li Han hurried after the lamas with the note and a supplementary present, and before noon he came back with the answer.

"What does he say?" asked Sullivan eagerly.

"Well," said the Professor, looking thoughtfully at the paper. "I am by no means sure. I am very much afraid that the dear man's knowledge of Chinese is largely confined to the spoken language. As you know, one can speak Chinese perfectly without being able to write a single word or read one solitary character—that is the case with Derrick, for example, and the vast mass of the Chinese peasantry. Indeed, it is said that the proportion of illiteracy——"

"But the message, Professor?" urged Sullivan gently.

"Yes. The message. Let us be business-like. Now the beginning is clear enough—a conventional greeting—and so is the end, which is a conventional blessing. But the middle contains a number of unrelated characters of which I can make out this one, which means impossible, and this, which resembles the character for 'kwei'—that is, 'devils or fiends'. Or perhaps I should say malignant demons. Then we have 'pu hsing', which means 'it would not work' or, to use a colloquialism, 'no go.' Then the character for impossible, with an emphatic reduplication."

"Oh, well," said Sullivan, "the general meaning is clear enough. It does not very much matter: now that

250

we know exactly where the Red-Hats are, I dare say that by using a little common sense we shall be able to get by them."

They had been very pleased with Tanglha-Tso when they reached it, but when, at the end of many days they were still there, they began to detest the place. They were in a fever to get on: every day counted, and yet they could not get away. Every day there were excuses—the yaks were still on the summer pastures far away, the barley had not yet been threshed, they could not yet spare any men for guides. They were conscious of sour looks as they walked about the village, and they began to find that their few words of Tibetan were no longer understood. Their guides from Hukutu had gone back, and these people disclaimed any knowledge at all of Mongol. Then one day two of their yaks disappeared: nobody seemed to be responsible or interested. They made gestures that appeared to mean that the yaks had run off on their own. The next day a third was gone.

"What the devil is the matter with these people?" cried Sullivan, in exasperation. "If only the abbot were here, he would set about them, I'm sure."

"I've a good mind to bang their silly heads together," growled Ross, who had spent most of the morning offering little drawings of yaks, loads of food and other necessities to the few men who would pay any attention. One had taken the paper and put it in his prayer-wheel, in case it might do any good, but the others had been uncomprehending and uninterested.

"I have offered them money," said Sullivan, banging his fist into his palm, "and they just stare at it and walk away. Flaming death!" he cried, "I shall start to get angry soon."

"I do not think that this is a case where physical violence would serve our purpose," said the Professor. "But I believe I have a clue to the trouble. It cannot have escaped your notice that Tibetan society has a matriarchal structure. The old woman in whose house we live is the virtual ruler of Tanglha-Tso—she is also, by the way, the abbot's aunt, and in secular matters he goes in awe of her. The same applied at Hukutu. Now the Tibetan woman is not only a matriarch: she is also polyandrous."

"Polly Andrews!" exclaimed Olaf.

"I mean she has several husbands. The old woman has four. Ngandze was his wife's second husband, and thus occupied the position of a second wife in China."

"Four husbands! Ay reckon she ban a wicked old beezle—"

"Olaf, pipe down," cried Sullivan. "Please go on, Professor, and tell us more about Auntie."

"Well, we have these two essential facts, matriarchy and polyandry. Now let us suppose that one of these women has taken it into her head to acquire one of us as a spare husband, would not that account for the delay, the black looks of the men and the general change of attitude? We must remember that these men are as much subjected to their wives as wives are to

252

their husbands in other countries that are more civilised—in the United States, for example," he said, bowing to Sullivan. "Does not my theory square with the facts? We have calculated delay, in order to detain the object of the woman's passion. We have black looks from the men, either because they resent the intrusion of a stranger or because they had hoped to be chosen in his place. Furthermore, all this has taken place since the departure of the abbot, who would be the only other governing influence in the village. Does it not all point to a clearly defined intent on the part of the old lady whose name I have not yet caught, but whom, for the sake of argument, we will term Auntie?"

"Good Lord above," exclaimed Ross with a groan, "I'm afraid you're right."

"Who is the man?" cried Sullivan, glaring round. "I'll wring his—you don't think she has picked on me, Professor, do you?" he asked, turning suddenly pale.

"No," said the Professor. "I have been watching closely, and incredible as it may seem, I believe it is Olaf."

"I never," roared Olaf, starting up.

"You have been monkeying about with Auntie," cried Sullivan, advancing upon him.

"No, no," said the Professor, waving his hand, "I do not think any fault is to be attributed to Olaf. The choice appears to be entirely one-sided. Though upon my word," he said, lowering his spectacles and gazing at Olaf over them, "I find it difficult to credit that a young woman . . . However, I am still not wholly convinced. We must watch them narrowly, cautiously, you understand, so that they will not notice, during this party to which it appears that we are invited this afternoon."

"Have they really picked upon Olaf?" asked Derrick, in a wondering voice.

"Some resemblance to heathen idol," said Li Han, "or perhaps local fabulous monster."

"You quit that," said Olaf, going redder still. "My face ban okay, see? Ay reckon it ban a natural choice. But Auntie . . . aw, shucks."

"It is not Auntie who is the prime mover, in my opinion," said the Professor. "It is rather that stout young matron whose name, I think, is Ayuz, Auntie's daughter. But that, if anything, makes the choice even more extraordinary."

"I would believe anything of people who put butter in their tea," said Sullivan. After a minute of hard thought he said, "What are we to do? In a case of this kind it's like being without a compass or a chart. If you're right, and I fear you are, these infernal women will never let us get on the road until they have their way. I've had something to do with women, and they're all the same: they always get you down in the end."

"The first thing to do is to make sure of our suspicions," said the Professor, "and then perhaps we can think of some plan to confound the sirens."

A few hours later they were sitting in the largest

room in Tanglha-Tso, facing the formidable old woman they called Auntie. Behind her stood three of her four husbands, meek men, all of them, and at her side stood the. young, stout woman whom Olaf now called Polly Andrews: her hair was more thickly buttered than usual, and she wore a towering scarlet hat. In the background there were all the villagers who could squeeze in: the air was thick with smoke and heat.

"That girl ban nuts," muttered Olaf. The words were hardly out of his mouth before Polly stepped forward and pinned a silver brooch, studded with turquoises, on to Olaf's coat. He went as red as a beetroot. He sprang up, saying, "Why, thank you, marm," and crashed his head against the ceiling. He sat down again, rubbing his head and muttering, "Aw, shucks."

Polly went back to stand by the old woman, and she gazed unceasingly at Olaf while the old woman poured out a flood of words, mostly directed at the Professor, but some at Olaf, who sat there with an impassive countenance, wishing, above all things, to prove his innocence to the others.

Presently tea came in, and a jar of a sticky, greenish substance, very dark. They were all given bowls of buttered tea, but Olaf alone had something from the jar. Polly squatted by him and fed it to him from a spoon. He absorbed it without any expression whatever, but Derrick, squeezed firmly against him by the villagers, felt him tremble. From time to time Polly stroked Olaf's golden hair and murmured loving words.

There was no doubt left in their minds at all, and they watched with profound misgiving.

When the tea was being carried away, the holder of the tea-pot did not move quickly enough to please Polly: she lifted her long coat and swung her boot forward in a kick that shot the attendant far out into the darkness.

"That young person has a will of her own," remarked the Professor.

"Lifted him a yard," muttered Olaf, nervously wiping his brow. "What ban Ay let in for?"

The old woman's flow of words became slower, more emphatic. There were several scraps of Mongol in it: she clearly meant to be understood.

The Professor replied, and the room was silent, listening intently. He broke off, consulted his list of words, and went on.

The old woman began again, and all the eyes in the room, whether they could understand or not, turned to her. Then the Professor spoke, and all the eyes swung back again. He said a long sentence. There was a gasp of horror from the Tibetans. He repeated it, pointing up towards the monastery, and they gasped again, gazing at Olaf and drawing away from him. The old woman started a long harangue, pointing at Olaf with one hand and waving a prayer-wheel with the other. The whole room stared at Olaf, edging still farther away. While they were doing this, the Professor pretended to consult his book, and behind it whispered rapidly to Sullivan, "Olaf must go mad when I strike the table. Let him shriek, and then knock him down. Pass it on." The whisper ran down the line while the old woman was still speaking, but it did not reach Derrick, who was the other side of Olaf, and who was therefore petrified when, after the Professor had pronounced another sentence that made the Tibetans gasp and recoil so that the weaker members were crushed against the wall and cried out in agony, and had held up a charm with one hand while he banged the table with the other, Olaf suddenly rose in a weird, hunched attitude, drew his face into an appallingly contorted mask and began to shriek like a steam-whistle, "Hoo, hooo, hoooo." At the same time he began to lurch madly from side to side and grasped at Derrick's throat with hands like crooked claws. At this moment Ross and Sullivan hurled themselves upon Olaf, flung him to the earth and began to belabour him with their fists. But they could not master him: with wild heaves he flailed about, still pouring forth his hideous and deafening scream until the Professor stepped up to him, and holding the charm over him said, in a chanting voice, "Oh thou able seaman, hold thy tongue. Go limp, therefore, and look as meek and peaceable as thou conveniently mayest."

Olaf relaxed, an expression of imbecile benignity over-spread his weathered features, and he lay still.

But the horror and alarm—to which Derrick's unfeigned astonishment had added—was too great for

257

the Tibetans. They rushed madly into the night, and only the old woman and Polly, with one person who was too paralysed with fear, remained. The old woman was trembling, but she would not run: Polly, as pale as she could very well go, gestured faintly towards Olaf and whispered something. The Professor bent over Olaf, whispered, "Foam a little," and unpinned the turquoise brooch. Olaf foamed like a whirlpool and twitched horribly. Polly took her brooch and vanished.

"I think it would be advisable if Olaf were now to crawl on his hands and knees through the street to our yaks," said the Professor, sitting down. "Dear me, what an exhausting conversation."

"How did you do it, Professor?" asked Sullivan, with admiration.

"I had in mind a passage in a book of travels by the Buddhist monk Yen Tzu, who was in these regions during the last days of the T'ang dynasty. I was by no means sure of my ability to convey the anecdote, but they seem to have caught the gist, though with heaven knows what distortions, because I have only the most general notion of the meaning of some of the words I employed. However, the story that I intended to convey was this: Yen Tzu, on one of his journeys, met a Siberian person who had captured a semi-human monster in the desert and had taken him to an abbot famous for his piety to have him entirely humanised— it appears that he was a serviceable monster. But the abbot had only been partially successful: with the waning of each moon —and I happened to notice that the moon was very small last night—the power of the charm diminished, and the monster returned to his habit of eating human flesh, female human flesh. He could only be subdued by a jade charm, and then only when it was held by his owner. This was the tale I adopted, using the convenient departure of our good friend the abbot as a circumstantial detail, and as far as I can see they understood and believed the greater part of it. At all events, I venture to prophecy that none of them will willingly encounter Olaf as he crawls about the streets, particularly if he continues to snort in that disagreeable fashion."

From outside came the sound of Olaf's progress as he shuffled industriously round and round the narrow streets, grunting as he went, and scratching horribly at each door to strike terror and dismay into the silent and cowering inhabitants.

"I am really sorry to have added to the burden of superstition that weighs on these unfortunate people," said the Professor, in another tone. "It would have been inexcusable if our need had not been so pressing: but I shall leave a letter, in the simplest Chinese that I can devise, to explain the situation to the abbot on his return, and I trust that he will be able to undo at least some of the mischief."

"It was a wonderful feat, Professor," said Sullivan. "Now I understand why you were drawing crescents and full moons on the table. But I hope we have not overdone it. I am quite sure that they will not want to keep Olaf in their bosoms any longer, but if they get so frightened that they won't trade with us or lend us guides, then we shall be in a pretty fix."

"I do not anticipate that," replied the Professor. "Auntie is a very strong-minded woman, not at all unlike a Mrs. Williams, the wife of one of my colleagues. But perhaps it would be as well to restrain Olaf's zeal at present. Derrick, will you take a chain and lead him to the yaks? He will have to spend the night out, poor fellow; but it is all in the common cause. And by the way, ask him to be so good as to provide himself with a short tail, will you? I mentioned, in passing, that he had one, in the course of my remarks. Perhaps he had better let it show a little in the morning—but discreetly, you understand?"

Sullivan's fears were baseless. In the first light of the morning the village notables, all strong-minded females, gathered outside the house with their attendant husbands and a train of yaks. All the difficulties that had plagued them for so many days suddenly vanished: the barley was found to be threshed, men could be spared, food was abundant, the missing yaks were found, the Professor's Tibetan was understood and several men remembered scraps of Mongol or Chinese.

Before the sun was well up the expedition was on its way again. The black looks of the men were gone, replaced by an anxious friendliness: they pressed little gifts on all the members of the party except Olaf, whom they regarded with unfeigned horror. He was obliged to walk forty yards behind the others, and whenever he approached nearer, the Tibetan guides thundered on a gong that they carried with them for the purpose, and blew on shrill-voiced horns, waving their prayer-wheels at the same time. He was obliged to be fed at a great distance from the fire, and after some days of this he became very melancholy and low in his spirits. He complained of the inconvenience of his tail, but when the Professor assured him that he would be reinstated as a human being when the new moon appeared he grew less despondent, and watched the waning moon with the keenest attention.

Their route led on and on, always to the west: it was never a marked road, except where it entered the villages, but the Tibetans followed it as though it had a pavement on either side. Up and down they went, sometimes ploughing knee-deep through the snow at fifteen thousand feet and more, sometimes panting in the heat of an enclosed valley roasting in the sun. They had game in abundance, and they dried many pounds of lean meat against emergencies to come. As the days went by they shortened Olaf's tail inch by inch, and when the new moon showed a silvery sickle over the gleaming mountains that hemmed them in, he was allowed to put it away altogether. The Tibetans, with some misgivings, admitted him to the fireside again; but they would never sit near him if they could avoid it.

They had one bad snowstorm that caught them in one of the high passes and delayed them for two days.

Olaf built one of his snow houses, but the Tibetans would have none of his monstrous practices, and huddled motionless against their shaggy beasts, who stood, quite unconcerned, while the snow covered them.

It was after this storm that they first met a great herd of yaks being brought down from the summer pastures: the next day they met two more, and they understood the herdsmen to say the early winter was coming on apace. "We must hurry," said Sullivan, with a round, seafaring oath, as he tried to urge his stolid yak to a speed greater than a crawl. "If only those half-witted omadhauns had let us go, we would be a hundred miles farther on by now."

But the yaks would not be hurried: they kept to their invariable sluggish plod whatever happened, and if they were vexed with pulling, pushing or with blows they would dig all four feet in, close their large eyes and become absolutely immovable. Only when they smelt a snow-leopard —which was not rare when they were just above the snowline—would they run, and then, as often as not, they ran in the wrong direction.

But they were patient, incredibly hardy and enduring creatures, and wonderfully sure-footed. Only once did one ever fall, and that was at the ford of the river a little before the first Red-Hat monastery. The river was swollen, the load was badly tied, and the yak went down: nothing was lost except, by great bad luck, one single heavy little box that contained most of what ammunition they had not abandoned in their dreadful days above Hukutu. They dived for it in the freezing water, but it was at the bottom of a whirlpool, and they had to give it up. They were reduced now to a very few rounds apiece, and Sullivan gave the order that no one was to shoot except Ross, who could be relied upon never to waste a single shot.

They got by the first dangerous strip of country, however, with no difficulty at all, and although a week later at the second they saw what they took to be a party of lamas in the distance, they had no unpleasant encounters. The weather was holding up, and they were making good distance every day.

Their detour to pass the second lamasery had been arranged, by two forced marches, to coincide with the full moon, and it was wholly successful: they rejoined their road exactly where they meant, and followed a winding river—still clear and unfrozen—as they pushed on to Thyondze. But once the full moon began to wane, Olaf became an object of horror to the guides. He was made to keep a great way off, and this time, as the road was clear along the riverside, he elected to walk in front. Sometimes Derrick and Chingiz walked with him for company, although the Tibetans often urged them not to take the risk, and on the first day that they struck their road again, all three of them had been walking well ahead of the main party when Derrick remembered that he had left the barley-cakes and the dried meat that they were to eat at midday. He ran back to his yak. Sullivan was saying to the Professor, "We shall not be able to pass the third Red-Hat lamasery at Thyondze with the full moon: but I am not sure that it would not be better altogether to get by on a darker night. They tell me that there is a road so clear that we cannot miss it, and it turns so sharply to the left that we shall be out of sight of the monastery well before dawn—hullo, what's that?" He broke off and pointed to the river. Bobbing down towards them on the broad and rapid stream there was something floating: it came nearer, and they saw that it was a tall felt hat, a red Tibetan hat.

"I hope some poor fellow has not fallen in," said the Professor.

Sullivan was already running along the bank up the stream. He turned a corner where the rocks cut out the view and saw Olaf and Chingiz coming back. In a few moments he had reached them, and Olaf said, "Ay didn't mean no harm, Cap'n, but this guy wouldn't let us pass, and the other guy fetched me a bang with his stick. It was on that bridge along for'ard," he said, pointing to a rough log crossing on the river.

It appeared that they had meant to cross the river and that on the bridge they had met two men. The first, a tall man with a sword, had started to shout at them in a loud, hectoring voice and had barred their way. Olaf had listened for a while, and had then tried to edge past. The tall man had drawn his sword, the shorter one had hit Olaf with his staff, and Chingiz had whipped his keen dagger through the tall man's ribs.

The tall man had fallen into the water, and the second had run off.

"Well, it's no good swearing now," said Sullivan, running back to the yaks. "Professor," he said quietly, "I'm afraid we have killed a Red-Hat lama. We shall have to get out of this as quickly as we possibly can. Their monastery is some way behind us, and we may be able to get past Thyondze before they catch us up. If not, we must take the valley that the abbot marked as closed. Please find out all you can about it from the guides."

"As I remember from the map," said the Professor, "we should see the opening of that valley on our left quite soon."

"Yes. It is behind that mountain there. I am going forward to reconnoitre, and I will ask Ross to drop back as a rear-guard. In the meantime, please keep everything moving as fast as possible—no halts for food, no pitching camp tonight. I will take Olaf with me: he will only upset the Tibetans here. If anything happens, fire three shots, but only if it is absolutely necessary. We have not a round to spare."

He vanished up the river at a long, loping run, accompanied by Olaf. The Professor walked up and down the line, urging the sluggards along and talking to the Tibetans. He had received the news with the utmost steadiness: he had changed a great deal since their first encounter with Shun Chi.

For a long time nothing happened, but in the afternoon they heard, faintly in the distance, the blaring of horns and the throbbing of a drum. Then, in the evening, they saw a file of men scrambling along the high ridge to their right: they were moving with incredible rapidity over the rocks towards Thyondze.

Sullivan came back in the moonlight, exhausted but with good news. "I have seen the valley," he said, "and it is not closed at all. The mouth of it runs down into this one, and there is a stream in it; it is so clear that we shall be able to strike it even in the night. There appears to be a fair-sized glacier half-way up, but from what I could see through my glasses it should not be too difficult. I could not see the pass —it was shut out by a spur running down from the left—but I could see three days' march up it, and it looked all right to me. We shall have to take it: the men you saw on the ridge are certainly going to warn the monks at Thyondze, and if we go on we shall be caught between the two of them, exactly as it was down in the Takla Makan. What have you learnt from the Tibetans?"

"I am sorry to say that they seem absolutely horrified by the suggestion. It was a long time before I could make them understand, but I succeeded in the end. They kept making gestures of the utmost refusal and one of them eventually whispered to me the word nahjedli, or nahjetli: he seemed unwilling even to say it, and he kept his hand over his mouth. Then, apparently as an explanation, he went over to a large patch of snow and made a hand-print in it, with another several yards away. I wish I could understand what he meant: the irritating thing is that I am almost sure that

I have heard, or perhaps read, a word not unlike it. Nahjedli, nahjedli: what can it be?" He bowed his head in thought. "My memory is not what it was," he said.

"Would it mean devils, or something of that sort? You know how superstitious they are."

"That is probably it. Yet there are several other words that they use more commonly—I employed them myself, back at Tanglha-Tso. Nahjedli, nahjedli: or was it two words, nah jedli, or nah yeti?"

As he repeated the words in a meditative voice, the Tibetans approached. They were carrying their personal belongings. The leader came to the front: he was obviously in a state of terror. He said something in a low and trembling voice, pointing up towards the valley and then back down the river: then he threw down the gold coins that they had been paid, and turned about. In another moment the four of them were running at full speed down the river.

Twelve

"THIS is not so bad," said Sullivan, heaping wood on to the fire. The leaping flames glowed pink far over the snow beyond them and lit up the low dark forms of the yaks in their shelter under the rocks.

"No, indeed," said the Professor. "It is a very much pleasanter end to the day than I ever expected."

They were all in high spirits. Not more than ten hours before they had been lying behind a rough bar-

267

ricade of piled rocks in the mouth of the valley, awaiting the attack of the lamas. The Red-Hats from Thyondze had come down very much faster than they had expected, and the party had not had time to reach a good, defensible position high up the valley before they were forced to turn and fight. They all knew that they were in a bad position, exposed from the front, and what was worse, exposed to outflanking parties on either side. There were at least two hundred lamas there, and while a hundred came at them in front, fifty could advance at each side of the broad valley and take them in the rear. They had only six rounds each. The Professor and Li Han had only two apiece, to be used only in the closest fighting, and although Ross had a pocketful, they could not possibly account for half the lamas, even if every shot found its mark.

They waited and waited. The forces of the Red-Hats grew at the valley's mouth, not two hundred yards from them, as fresh contingents poured in from lower down the river. The blaring of the ram's horns increased, and the drums thundered; but the attack never came. An ineffectual shower of arrows struck the ground well in front of the barricade, and one solitary musket sent its ball trundling over the stones behind them, and then burst at its second discharge. The main body of the lamas never moved, and although the beleaguered expedition watched anxiously, no flanking parties were sent out. The banners waved, and the chief men moved about down there, but not a single one advanced into the valley.

After some hours, Sullivan gave the order for the others to withdraw, while he and Ross stayed at the barricade to cover their retreat. At the sight of the movement, the lamas raised a great cry, and the sound of a huge gong filled the air: there was another flight of arrows, but that was all. The lamas did not go away: they just stayed there, and presently Ross and Sullivan left the barricade.

All the way along the straight stretch of the rising valley they had kept a close watch on the lamas through their glasses, but never did they move.

Now the party was encamped in a comfortable, sheltered part of the valley's bed, a little to one side of the stream from the glacier: the valley was narrower here, but the towering ridges on either hand were much too far away for an out-flanking party to roll stones down upon them, and indeed, those mighty ridges were so steep and craggy that no enemies could possibly reach them in anything under several days, if at all. Before them lay a clear, unimpeded view of their way up the valley: no one could approach them unseen, and as Sullivan had waited until the others, with the yaks, had retreated for a good half-day's march, he felt confident that their pursuers, if they came on at all, could not reach them until well after sunrise: therefore it was safe enough to have the fire.

"It is very strange," he said, leaning forward to warm his hands, "they had us on toast, and yet they let us get away. They must have had very little stomach for the fight: we could have picked off their leaders easily as they stood there, but I am glad we did not, now. It might have gingered them up."

"Perhaps they did not want to fight because they are monks," suggested Derrick.

"No," said the Professor. "I have read and heard a good deal about the Red-Hats. I am afraid they do not wear swords for nothing."

"But they are religious men, aren't they, sir?"

"Yes. In their way they are," replied the Professor. "But when you get to school—it seems to be a long time coming, and I must admit that our road to Samarcand and thus to school has taken some turnings that I did not foresee—you will no doubt learn some history, and then you will see that religious men, or men who call themselves religious, have never been averse to cutting off the heads of those who disagree with them, or burning them alive, either. It is always the same terribly sad story, over and over again. With us it is Catholic and Protestant—first one oppressing the other with horrible cruelty, and then the oppressed taking over in his turn and using exactly the same beastly methods on the oppressor. With the Mohammedans you have the extreme, bloody-minded puritans, and then on the other hand the open-minded Sufi. And even with the Buddhist, who profess to follow the kindest, mildest teaching of non-violence, you find these fierce, intolerant, iconoclastic, barbarous . . . words fail me to describe the turpitude of religiosity run mad. And it is always the same, however pure the teaching." He shook his head sadly, and after a pause he went on, "No, I should account for their backwardness by supposing that the place has some local sanctity."

"But would not that mean that they are taken in by their own superstition, Professor?" asked Sullivan. "Surely the Red-Hats are more likely to impose on others than to be imposed upon."

"Don't be so sure of that," said Ross. "I remember that voodoo priest in the Antilles who went nearly mad with fear when he heard that another of his kidney had put the evil eye on him. Don't you remember him, Sullivan?"

"Yes, I do. I dare say you're right, and the lamas have gone on so long that in the end they have deceived themselves—they certainly deceived the good old abbot of Tanglha-Tso. But now that I come to think of that voodoo fellow, he had some reason for his blue funk: he swelled up and died just before we had those new cat's-heads fitted. But of course, that was not a typical case. He probably ate something poisonous."

They were in a very strong position: an outcropping stratum had laid a litter of vast boulders which made a natural fortification for them, but nevertheless they kept watch all through the night. The middle watch fell to Derrick and the Professor. They were very quiet, not only for fear of waking the others, but also because they were tired: they had had very little sleep the night before—it had been their longest forced march, leading them just in time to the foot of the

271

valley—and the going that day had been hard, quite apart from the tension of the expected battle. The stillness of the valley, too, kept them from talking much. It was a windless night for once, and even the stream flowed so evenly just there that it made no sound. It was a strange silence, somehow unlike the silence of the high snows; a heavy, brooding silence—a positive thing, not a mere absence of sound.

At length the Professor began to tell Derrick something of his own life at school, long ago: Derrick, listening to his deep, quiet voice and staring into the embers of the fire, began to nod off. He fought against the sleep that kept engulfing him like a warm wave, and from time to time he glanced over his shoulder with a curious, disagreeable but unreasonable feeling that the silence was somehow wrong. But still saying to himself, "I must not go to sleep: I must not," he slipped away into a doze, and from that into a deep, dreamless sleep.

He awoke suddenly, instantly alert. The moon was up, lighting the whole valley, and the yaks were stirring, grunting and straining at their head-ropes. The Professor was asleep, with his spectacles fallen to the end of his nose and his rifle drooping from his arm. The fire had died very low. Derrick had an absolute certainty that there was something behind him: the Tibetans' horror of the valley came strongly into his mind, but with a powerful effort he forced himself to whip round. There was nothing. But as he turned again he thought he saw something move in the shadow of the rocks behind the Professor: he felt the hair prickling on the back of his neck. "If there had been anything, Chang would have barked," he said to himself, and reassured he pushed a half-burnt branch into the fire before going to see to the yaks. At that moment Sullivan got up. "Eight bells," he said, stretching. Then he noticed the Professor. "Hey, what kind of a watch is this?" he cried, prodding him with his toe. He was about to make some caustic remark about sleeping on duty when his eye caught something in the snow a little way behind Derrick. He stared fixedly at it, and Derrick turned, following his gaze. Clear in the moonlight there was a footprint in the snow. One single footprint, monstrously large, and shaped like a man's hand, an enormous hand with a shortened thumb.

They stared at one another, and Derrick saw in his uncle's face a look that he had never seen there before. In a moment the look was gone, and Sullivan walked over to the print. He called to Ross, who was already awake: the two men looked at the print, looked at each other and nodded. "That's what it is, all right," said Ross.

The Professor joined them. "It is not at all unlike the mark that—why, how stupid of me. I remember perfectly now. Of course, that was the word the man was saying, nahjedli, the Abominable Snowman. In the southern dialects it is yeti, as I remember reading . . ." Sullivan nudged him violently, and at the same moment Olaf cried, "Hey, what ban the matter with this dog?"

Chang lay at the edge of the firelight, crouched in a

strange, unnatural position. Derrick ran over to him and raised his head, "He's trembling all over," he said. "Is he having a fit?"

"No," replied Sullivan, looking at him. "He's all right. He's just scared."

"But he's not afraid of anything," cried Derrick. "There's nothing alive that could frighten . . ." His voice trailed away into silence, and for a long minute nobody spoke.

"Well, you turn in," said Sullivan at last, with an effort. "We'll take over the watch."

They did as they were told, but Derrick for one had little sleep that night. He lay quiet, however, comforting Chang, and when the moon had gone half-way down the sky, he heard his uncle murmur to Ross, "I wish Ayrton hadn't blurted that out in front of the others."

"Aye," said Ross. And after a long pause, Derrick heard his deep voice ask, "What have you heard about them, Sullivan?"

"Oh, the usual thing—huge, man-like creatures, white and hairless, who live in the high snows. Always mentioned in an undertone, as if there were something too horrible about them to mention—running in enormous leaps—chewing up snow-leopards like rabbits—smashing rocks with their teeth—nobody ever seeing one and living to tell the tale all that sort of stuff, nine-tenths of it nonsense."

"Yes. But I'll bet you five pounds the Red-Hats won't set foot in this valley."

"That's all to the good. Still I wish the sun would come up."

The sun did rise at last, and it brought another windless day. Ross and Sullivan set themselves to cheer the party up. "We'll have a really good breakfast," said Sullivan, piling up the fire with branches from underneath the boulders. "We might as well profit by this fuel: I don't expect we shall find much more wood until we're over the pass and down again."

"How long will that be?" asked the Professor, sipping his tea.

"With good luck and no snow, I should say a fortnight. Eat hearty, everyone: we'll make a long day's march and get clean out of this place."

There was a feeling of unnaturalness and constraint hanging over them all: even Chingiz had somehow got the idea that was in each one's mind, and Chang kept in very close to Derrick's heel. But after they had been marching for an hour or two everything seemed much easier; it was as if they had left an evil, but half-forgotten dream behind. Only Olaf dampened the spirits of the party a little by telling a long, pointless and lugubrious story about a northern werewolf until Sullivan told him to go and climb a tall pillar of rock on the side of the valley to see if there was any sign of the lamas.

There was none, and they stopped at noon in an open, flat space for their midday meal. It was on the most open southern side, and although they were above the snow-line, and had been for many miles, the snow had not lain here, and there was herbage for the yaks. The valley was somewhat less shut in at this point, and the queer silence that had persisted all day seemed less oppressive here.

"You know, Sullivan," said the Professor, putting down his knife, "I have a curious feeling, a not wholly agreeable feeling, that something is watching us. Do you know that impression that one has when one is in a train, and without looking up, one knows that the person opposite is staring at one? A sense of ill-defined discomfort. I have exactly that feeling now."

"Oh, it's just imagination. Have some more tea?"

"No, thank you," said the Professor, rather stiffly. "I am not a particularly imaginative man, and I am convinced that there is something watching us from those rocks over there."

"An animal, maybe," said Ross, frowning heavily.

"No, I think not. It has been observed, and I have remarked it myself, that whereas animals are particularly sensible of a man looking at them, men, on the other hand, are not commonly aware of the gaze of animals."

Sullivan leaned over and said something to the Professor in what Derrick thought was French. The Professor started, and said, "Oh. Oh, quite. Yes, I quite understand. Foolish of me," and began to drink his tea vigorously.

Sullivan said, "I think I shall just have a stroll around before we go on." He picked up his rifle and clicked a round into the breach. As he turned away there was a rushing noise in the air, the fire shot in all directions, and the rock that had scattered it bounced clean over Olaf's head.

They leapt up, gripping their weapons. Tensely they stood, waiting. Nothing appeared. There was no sound but the tossing and snorting of the yaks. Slowly they relaxed, and Ross went over to the rock: he picked it up with both hands: it was the size of a man's head, and rounded.

"Come on, Olaf," cried Sullivan, "we're going over to those rocks. Ross, you cover us."

Olaf swallowed painfully, he hesitated for a moment, then said, "Aye, aye, Cap'n," in a hoarse, savage voice and ran after Sullivan. They went fast over the rising ground to a piled litter of ice-worn rocks. Sullivan paused, looking quickly from side to side. "This is where it came from," he said, pointing to a heap of great smooth pebbles. They went on cautiously. Suddenly Olaf pointed. A huge print showed deep in the clean snow, a print like that of a hand with shortened thumb: the big Swede looked down at it without a word, and the cold sweat ran down his face.

Sullivan looked up the slope: ten yards away there was another print, and ten yards beyond that a third. The line went straight to the sheer wall of the valley, and there, at the bare, unclimbable rock, it ceased. He looked from side to side —no sign of a living thing. He looked up; the cliff soared three thousand feet. He looked back to where the yaks stood a black group in the sun: they were two hundred yards from the heap of rounded stones.

They turned back, and reaching the others, Sullivan said, "There's a good deal of loose stuff up on the cliff. Falling from that height it can easily bounce as far as here." He spoke in an artificially cheerful voice, but he deceived nobody.

However, they were soon on the march again, a long, black train strung out along the floor of the silent valley, and they all found that it was far better when they were moving. Nobody referred to the subject of all their thoughts until Chingiz, who was marching behind Derrick, caught his eye as he looked round over his shoulder for the twentieth time, nervously scanning the rocks and the slopes of snow: Chingiz smiled, and said, "You are afraid, I think."

At any other time Derrick would have resented the remark promptly, but this time it was said without any offence, almost as if Chingiz had said, "It is going to snow, it seems." Derrick nodded, and plodded on. He wondered at the imperturbability of Chingiz: the Mongol was superstitious enough for three; Derrick remembered the awful fuss and outcry that he and his brothers had made when Derrick, coming into their yurt for the first time, had stepped on the threshold: that was apparently the place where ghosts lived, and it was never to be touched, however awkward it might be to leap into the low tent in a crouching hop to avoid it when one was carrying two saddles and a heavy pack. And he remembered the extreme anxiety with which Chingiz had burnt the shoulder-blades of a ram, in order to foretell the kind of journey that they would have from the fire-cracked bones. But now he alone of the party was unmoved, either by the queer silence or by the haunting, oppressive threat that surrounded them, unseen, on all sides. Derrick looked up at the sky: the clouds were racing across the top of the lofty ridges, straight across them from left to right; up there it was blowing a full gale, but down in the valley-bed not a breath stirred.

"I would be afraid if I were you," said Chingiz, after a while. "But I have a charm and a spell against all devils of every kind. I wear it round my neck. A Buryat gave it to my grandfather: he had it from a Kalmuk, and the Kalmuk had it from a shaman of the north. It is the little finger of a crucified Russian, and there is something else there, something without a name. I will give you a piece tonight."

Derrick envied Chingiz the strength of his belief, but he remembered his father, and how for years and years he had tried to persuade his Chinese converts not to worship their ancestors, not to light crackers to prevent the sky-dragon from swallowing the sun during an eclipse, not to make secret sacrifices to the earth-dragon and not to carry charms, and he refused the gift. He knew that if he said it was against his religion Chingiz would not mind at all; but he refused against his own desire: it would have been a comfort to have had some armour, however heathenish.

They reached the glacier, and although it was difficult to get on to it, once they had brought the yaks up through the boulders and broken ice, they found that it was easier than they had expected. It was not the glacier, at any rate, that had caused the old abbot to mark the valley as impassable. Two men went ahead to work out the route among the séracs and the crevasses, but there were few that offered any great difficulty, and they made surprisingly good speed until the sun went down. They pitched camp in the most open place they could find: it had no shelter, but it gave an uninterrupted view of the glacier for three or four hundred yards in each direction. There had been no incident all the day since noon, but as they were making the fire Ross stared fixedly at the far side of the valley through his glasses.

"Do you see an animal?" asked the Professor.

"No," said Ross, "it was just a falling piece of ice."

"It is a curious thing," observed the Professor, "but we have seen no animals all through this valley. I do not usually watch for them, but today I made a point of looking about me as we came along, and I did not see a single bird or beast anywhere. Surely that is most uncommon?"

"Oh, no," said Sullivan, "we are getting too high for them now."

"You must be mistaken," said the Professor. "I remember thars much higher than this, and there was that group of wild yaks beyond the village where they so kindly gave us that horrible beer—I forget its name—and then there are always birds far above the snow-line."

Sullivan opened his mouth, but closed it again without making a reply and went on with his work.

That night they slept much better, with no alarms; but in the morning they found the tracks again, rounder this time, and three-toed, in the light powdering of snow that had blown off the high ridges in the night. Some were almost in the camp, and some led off to the edge of a wide, uncrossable crevasse in the ice, a crevasse so deep that when Derrick kicked a lump of frozen snow into it he never heard it land.

It had turned very much colder in the night: they woke up with their breath frozen on the fur of their hoods, and when Li Han incautiously seized the iron pot to melt the snow for tea it stuck to his hand. It took the skin clean off like a searing burn, and after a minute or two it began to hurt so much that Li Han howled aloud: the echoes came back strangely, one long after the others, and that last one sounded more like hellish laughter than the echo of his cry.

It was bitterly cold, and the sky was dark. It looked like dirty weather coming, but for the moment the valley was still as silent as ever it had been: it was so silent that they could hear the deep, faint, remote grinding of the ice in its incredibly slow journey down the slope, a sound quite unlike the loud surface-cracks or the echoing fall of the ice-pinnacles on the farther side.

"Today," said Sullivan, consulting the map, "we

281

shall turn that long projecting spur up there. The whole valley turns with it, but I think the main glacier comes from the high valley on the right up there, flowing into this one from the north. Unless I am very much mistaken, we shall get across this glacier before the snow comes on, and with luck we shall find no ice up there on the left. We shall find wind though. That valley runs straight into it. Now here—" he said, holding out the map. There was a crash as a viciously jagged lump of ice slashed through the map and hit the fire. They were up in a second, standing in a ring, facing outwards. But it was the same as before: there was no movement anywhere, no sound but the stamping of the yaks and the sizzle of the ice as it put out the fire.

"It does not matter," said Sullivan at last, wiping the blood off his injured hand. "I have the whole thing clearly in my mind, and I can copy it exactly."

They did not waste time in following the single pair of tracks that they discovered later, but reloaded their beasts and set off across the ice. It was a long time before anyone spoke, and then it was only brief orders about getting the yaks round a bad moraine. Towards midday they came to a very broad and difficult crevasse. It had a few snow bridges over it, but although they held the men the yaks refused to go on to them.

"They probably know best," said Ross, and he set to work making a bridge at the narrowest place from the two long timbers that they had brought against such an emergency. This delayed them a long time, for even when the bridge was laid and paved with blocks of ice the yaks were very unwilling to approach it. They had to be dragged and pushed and pulled, one after another.

"Thank Heaven we do not have to do this over fresh snow," said Sullivan, looking anxiously up into the lead-coloured sky as the last yak crossed.

There were more crevasses after this, and getting across the glacier was like tacking into the wind—ten miles run for one mile gained—for they had to work out a zig-zag course to find the crossing places. It was not before the late afternoon that they reached the huge left-hand turn of the valley, and there they met the wind. It was as bad as any that they had ever yet encountered: it had no snow in it yet, but it carried ice-crystals so sharp that they drew blood, and the cold was so intense that every breath was like a stabbing pain.

"At least we have no ice," shouted Sullivan, above the wind. He pointed up the left-hand valley—sheer black rock and hard white snow, but no glacier-ice—and then back to the right-hand branch of the valley they were leaving, where the glacier came down in an appalling ice-fall that they never could have passed.

Their new valley came fully into view as they struggled round the spur: it was narrower by far, and its bed was littered with enormous rocks. When they could see at all for the driving ice-crystals they saw that there was another bend in it about five miles farther up: it looked difficult, but not at all impossible.

"We will get to that clear space in about two hours," shouted Sullivan. But he had reckoned without the yaks. Their thick coats were heavy and matted with the flying ice, they were growing obstinate and very tired. Soon it was evident that they could go no farther, and as the light was already failing, although the day was not yet done, Sullivan decided to pitch camp when they came to a fairly sheltered hollow among the rocks.

It was not a good place at all, but once the yaks had stopped under the lee of a square-faced rock, nothing would make them budge, and although once he had thoroughly realised how difficult the hollow was to guard, Sullivan wanted to go on, he was forced to remain. The trouble was not so much lack of shelter—indeed, they were as well covered from the wind as they could be—but the fact that anything approaching them could keep out of sight to the very edge of the hollow.

"We'll have to make the best of it," said Ross, as the first eddy of snow swirled round the boulders. "If you can stick it out on that rock over there, I will take this on the left, and Olaf can be in that cleft below us. That should give us a fair view, once the moon is up."

That was clearly the best idea, and they followed it. There was the saucer of the camp, then about fifteen yards above it the great square boulder from which the yaks would not move, and then, beyond the circle containing the camp and the yaks, there were the three guard-points, with Sullivan on the left, Ross on the right and Olaf down at the apex of the triangle, toward the glacier.

They wedged themselves into positions as comfortable as they could manage, with as little of their bodies exposed to the wind as possible. The night darkened, the tearing wind increased and piled up drifts of snow on their leeward sides. But although the moon was not yet up, there was a faint glow from the whiteness all around them, and so far the snow was not driving too thickly: they could see a little way, and they were all men accustomed to keeping their watches in the night. It was the wind that hampered them most; in the howling, tearing, unceasing racket they could scarcely hear a hail from one to another, although each could let out a roar like a fog-horn if it were necessary.

The cold hours crept by, and at last the moon rose behind the mountains: they could not see it from where they were, but it threw a faint radiance into the sky. The wind slackened, but the intense cold did not: Sullivan felt his hands, deep under their fur gloves, growing numb. The cold crept in and in from the hole that he had made for his trigger-finger, and which was protected only by two thin layers of silk. To ward off the dreaded frostbite he got up, pushing the snow away, and stamped his frozen boots and swung his arms. A dim shape loomed up in the falling snow before him. He hailed, "Ahoy, Ross!" and at once the form vanished to the right, while from the left he heard the answering hail.

Ross appeared, running. "Did you see anything?" he shouted.

"Think so. Not sure," answered Sullivan. They groped their way over the boulders down to Olaf, and found him squatting in the snow. He flung up his rifle as he saw them.

"All right, Olaf," roared Sullivan. "Have you seen anything?"

At this moment the moon showed through a break in the driving cloud above the ridge, and they saw Olaf's face, crusted with rime and snow: his pale eyes were glaring beyond them: he kept his rifle up, and they flung themselves down as the tongue of flame shot between their heads. Sullivan whipped round as he fell. He was on one knee in a flash, and he fired with the rifle half-way to his shoulder. Above the wind they heard an inhuman shriek. Olaf pushed between them and rushed towards the camp.

"What was it?" shouted Ross, as they caught him up. Olaf was staring from side to side in the new and brilliant light as the cloud ripped clean off the moon.

"Ay reckon I saw something," he said. "It was just behind you."

Sullivan pointed forward. Dark in the moonlight there was a splash of blood. He knelt and put his hand to it, and getting up he slapped his hand against his thigh. "It's something that can be stopped with a bullet or cold steel," he said, with an expression of fierce joy on his face.

Already the drifting snow had covered the blood,

but they had seen it, and the sight sent a new tide of life and spirit into them. They made a tour of the far outside ring of the camp: they saw nothing, but still, when they came back, they felt twice as strong, warmer and encouraged. The wind was dropping fast, and the moon was higher now: yet there was a dark band in the sky behind it that promised more snow to come. The others were up, and with them was Chang. He was trembling, his tail was down.; but he had caught the spirit that was in the men. He left them, instead of creeping at Derrick's heel, and in a moment he had found the blood. He scratched down to it, threw up his head, and bayed.

"That's better," cried Sullivan, and as Chang went out, away from the hollow, they followed him. "We can cope with these beasts," said Sullivan, half to himself. They all felt that the peril could be faced and overcome now, and there were triumphant faces under the cold moon: but when they turned the yaks' great rock it was as if a great hammer had struck them all. There were no yaks.

There was one, ten yards from the shelter; but it was dead, dismembered and mangled horribly. Yet still, faintly in the drifting snow, there was the deep-ploughed track of the rest. It was a path that forked, one branch going up the valley and a fainter one leading down towards the old valley and the glacier.

Olaf, from high up on a rock, shouted, "Ay seen one, Cap'n, way down on the glacier."

They leapt up after him, and there, far away and

often obscured by the racing shadows of the clouds, they saw the black shape of a fleeing yak just turning the corner right-handed down the old valley on the glacier.

"You and Li Han go down and catch it," cried Sullivan. "Don't go too far over the ice. Look lively. We'll go up and find the rest."

He turned and ploughed up the valley through the new-fallen, loose and drifted snow along the fast disappearing trail. The others followed him.

But they never saw their yaks again. They had scarcely got out of sight of the camp before the great dark bar in the sky reached the moon and put it out. They struggled on in the darkness, but five minutes later the first howling blast of the blizzard took them in the face. It was a wall of flying snow, so thick that they could hardly breath. Sullivan turned about at once, shouted an order to make a train, each holding the other and started back for the camp.

The snow fell as they had never known it fall before. Their backs were loaded with it: they could not see their hands before their faces: the tracks that they had made so short a time before were already out of sight.

Hours later they reached their camp, almost unrecognisable now. They had found it by feel alone, and they fell into it utterly exhausted. A few minutes later and it would have disappeared.

The blizzard howled on all the rest of the night. Time and again they had to creep out of their coverings and clear the huge banks of snow that eddied into the shelter that they had hollowed out. When the next day broke it showed but a thin and feeble light through the never-ending clouds of drifting flakes that stopped their view a few feet from the camp. The day merged into the night and in the night the temperature rose: they were almost warm, huddled there in their furs and protected by the pall of fallen snow.

"This is much better," said the Professor. "If this goes on, and a good cold wind follows the snow, we shall have a fine crust to walk upon."

The next day it seemed to them that there was less falling, and that the snow that still filled the air was mostly driven from the enormous drifts by the wind, which had changed its quarter to a little east of north. Still they could not get out, and Sullivan spent his time copying the map that had been destroyed and tunnelling towards the slaughtered yak. It was exhausting work, but to some degree it kept them from thinking of the fate of Olaf and Li Han. They reached the yak at last, and Chingiz cut it into strips in the Mongol fashion. The flesh was stiff, and it would keep as though it were in a refrigerator.

"At least we shall not have a repetition of the heights above Hukutu," said Sullivan, as he arranged the strips into solid packs and roped them down.

The snow stopped. It stopped suddenly, as if it had been turned off, and it was succeeded by a night of the most appalling wind, a wind that reached the intolerably high shrieking note of a hurricane in its last tremendous gusts as it blew itself out a few hours before the dawn.

In the morning they dug themselves out and stood on the hard, firmly frozen snow, under a pure sky, a great blue bowl with the sun already shooting up rays of light into it from the east: there was no wind at all, only a limitless silence all around them.

They instantly organised a search for Olaf and Li Han, but after the first hour or so they had very little hope. The vast face of the glacier was one smooth, unbroken table of fresh snow: not one of the deep crevasses could be seen. Chang did his best: he knew very well what they were looking for, but he could not pick up a hint of scent, not the slightest vestige of a trail.

For three days they went on, although time was so pressing and they knew that every hour was essential if they were ever to cross the high pass alive. Already they had lost a week with the blizzard and the search: they knew that they must either pursue their journey or stay for ever. Yet it was with heavy hearts and unwilling minds that they left their camp at last and set their faces to the west.

They left markers, a copy of the map, a compass, as much food as they could possibly spare and a letter in which Sullivan wrote that they would leave clear signs all the way along their route.

"They have probably got snowed up," he said as they left, "and it will take them some time to dig their way out. I know that they would have had time to catch up with the yak, and they will have all they need. We shall see them soon enough, I am sure." But his words had a very hollow ring, and as Derrick looked back at the glacier for the last time he felt the tears running down his face and freezing as they ran.

Thirteen

IT was two days now since Ross had gone, and they were still marching. How many days it was since they had left the camp by the glacier Derrick could no longer tell. He had kept count once, but now he concentrated all his energy on putting one foot in front of another. He watched nothing but the ground, deep snow, thin snow, ice or rock, before him, for he knew that if he stumbled and fell it would need a great effort to get up, perhaps more of an effort than he could ever manage again. He stared at the ground and at Chang, moving slowly just in front of him.

They had lost Ross two days before, when they were crossing a maze of tumbled boulders. Sullivan had led him through successfully to the little scratching in the snow that they called their camp: he had brought him through, although the last half-mile took him nearly two hours. For Ross's feet had gone with the cold. He had suspected that they were frostbitten some days after they had weathered out the blizzard, and when, by himself in a hidden corner of the rocks, he had managed to wrench off his frozen boots, he saw that they were already black, he had known that it was

291

only a question of a little while before he would be unable to go on. But he kept up with them in their slow and painful race for the high pass, a race against the winter snow, until he saw that with all his efforts he was still holding them back and that they were making preparations to carry him.

Sullivan brought him into the camp that night, but in the morning he was not there. There was his rifle, his ammunition, his meagre rations for the next few days—there was no more after that—and on top of the neat pile a note for Sullivan. Sullivan had read it and had gone out. Derrick had thought that he was searching for Ross, although a light fall of snow in the night would have made the search almost impossible, but he was not. He was sitting on a rock, out of sight of the others. He sat there for an hour, and then, with a face like death, he came back and slowly began arranging things for the morning's march. Derrick had questioned him: he had not replied. Derrick had repeated the question, and Sullivan had knocked him down: Derrick had not questioned him again.

They all of them understood the agonising decision that Sullivan had made, and they respected it, for he alone knew what Ross had said in that last note that he had managed to scribble in the night.

But that was two long days ago, and since then the weather had been bitterly cold.

Two days, thought Derrick. And how many days before that had it been that they had first come in sight of the tremendous peak that soared up into the sky away over on their left? He could not remember: it must have been many days, perhaps a week by now. They had said that it must be the peak called the Silent One—it was shown on the map as not being very far away. Perhaps it was not very far away: but it never seemed to come any nearer, for now their day's march was pitifully short, although they kept on and on and on, as if they felt that they would never start again if once they stopped. It was Chingiz, as much as anyone, who kept them going now. He had revealed a wonderful, inborn toughness, a resistance to hunger and cold, sorrow and disappointment: even now, as Derrick saw, looking up for a moment, he was helping the Professor along: the old man's arm was on his shoulder, and Chingiz was guiding him over some ice-bound stones. He had a wonderful fund of deep courage, and Derrick, fighting against despair, tried dumbly to imitate him. The Professor was doing his very best: everyone knew that. But in these last few days he had aged very suddenly. He grieved for the losses they had sustained, and particularly for Li Han. They talked very seldom now, but some nights back, before Ross had gone, the Professor had said, as they lay huddled in what coverings they had in the shelter of two sharply-angled rocks, "I had meant to take Li Han back with me. He had a deep and genuine love for learning—a disinterested love—and a very real capacity for it. With all his amusing and endearing ways, he had a true scholar's soul: we would have worked together. . . ." He broke off, and when Sullivan had tried, rather clumsily, to comfort him and had said that Li Han and the jade—for Li Han had been carrying it all, and had done so ever since the Professor's illness—were not lost, that they would both turn up together, the Professor had burst out passionately, "I would have given every last scrap of that wretched stuff, I would have smashed it all with a hammer, to have prolonged my young friend's life. And when I think that perhaps it was the weight of that miserable treasure that might have caused his loss, I . . ." He could not finish.

On and on. This was like the dreadful heights above Hukutu, except that there they had known that there was hope below them, and here they did not. But there, on the other hand, they had had no food; while here they did have a very little still—more than a very little, since Ross's sacrifice.

On and on. It was a good thing, thought Derrick, that there was no wind today, for they were walking high on the side of the valley, not in its bed as they usually did, and a wind, with that slope on the right, would have been very dangerous. They were high up on the valley's side and climbing in order to cross the distant col that might mark the highest point before their descent: it was possible that that was the high pass itself, but they had very little hope of it. However, they kept on as though it were: there was nothing else to do, except to lie down and give up hope—an easy solution and a very tempting one to utterly exhausted men, but Sullivan would not allow it for a moment. He did not persuade now: he hit.

For a long time the valley had been widening; it still wound and twisted, but it was less enclosed, and although it held the silence of the everlasting snows, it was no longer the oppressive valley that they had once known. Ever since that frightful day when they had lost the yaks they had travelled on unattacked; they had seen none of those ominous and terrifying tracks, and occasionally they had seen a few birds. They had all known, without being able to say how they knew it, that the things that had haunted them were no longer there. It had been a strange relief at first, but with time, growing weakness and weariness beyond exhaustion, Derrick, for one, no longer cared very much whether the things were there or not. If one had stood in his path he would have plodded blindly on, straight for it: there was only one thing that was important now, to keep his feet moving, to keep on and on; not to let the others down, but to go on, go on, even if it were for ever.

He was tired as he had never been, as he had never believed that it was possible to be tired. It was so long now since they had eaten properly—they dared not let themselves run out of food—that their energy had drained to its very last reserves. Derrick looked up again, and his heart, already low enough, fell farther still: the southern sky was dark with snow-clouds, and the sombre, impenetrable mass was surging towards them. They could never survive another heavy fall. He looked forward to the Silent One, and high on its southern ridge he saw the flurry of the coming wind that tore a great twisting pillar of snow high into the air, like a plume. "Get on," snapped his uncle from behind. Derrick jerked into movement again, swayed and almost fell. Sullivan gripped and steadied him. "Easy does it, boy," he said, in his old, kind voice.

Derrick went on. He passed Chingiz and the Professor, who were changing places. They did not speak, but gave him an encouraging look.

Now Derrick was in front, and he had to make the first steps in the snow. It was not difficult, fortunately, and he went on with a steady pace over the good, firm crust. The direction was easy enough, too: for a long time now they had been following what must have been a natural fault in the rock that led straight for the col. It looked exactly like a path, and they prayed that it might not peter out before the col and leave them with steps to cut or steep slopes to climb: these natural faults that looked like paths so often did that.

On and on. He kept his head down and went down. There was very little weight on his shoulders now, little more than his sleeping fur: the food only occupied a small corner of it: but still it felt like a great burden, and it was easier to walk bowed. On and on. One of the curious things about this altitude—and now they were very high—was that it played tricks on your eyes when you were very tired, he reflected. Only a little while ago he had thought that he saw a windmill on its back on a sort of natural platform in the side of the valley: it was just one of those illusions like the string of yaks that he could have sworn that he had seen early in the morning. They were rocks, of course, but he had been so utterly certain that he saw them move even when he was so close that he could touch them.

On and on. There was no point in taking any notice of those things: they only excited you and made you lose the rhythm of your steps. Chang was whining and looking into his face. "Oh, shut up, Chang," he murmured wearily. He must not break the rhythm, or he would stop and fall.

The first flakes began to fall quite gently, hissing with a tiny noise as they touched the ground. It was getting very dark. He did not look up, but he knew that the sky was a menacing grey.

"Shut up, Chang," he said, rather louder, but the dog would not be quiet. He whined insistently, ran ahead, came back and whined again.

Derrick did not look up. He was turning a corner to the left, and with the great drop below him on his right he needed all his attention. Chang whined and whined: at last he barked, and Derrick looked up. The small dark man on the path before him waved his umbrella. Derrick took no notice. These illusions, he thought: how absurd they are. This one is a man dressed in yellow cotton robes and carrying an ordinary umbrella—an umbrella, of all things. On and on: get back the rhythm of your steps. Then suddenly he thought it strange that Chang had seen it too. He looked up again. The man was within a few yards of him, looking apprehensively at Chang, who was baying so that the valley rang.

"Are you a man?" asked Derrick, in a dull, toneless voice. He was too tired to think in anything but English, yet he was not surprised to hear the man reply, "Yes. Please call off your dog."

They were sitting in a small, bare room in the lower buildings of the lamasery before a glowing fire. "I don't know what to make of it at all," said Sullivan, looking at his bandaged hand: he spoke in a low voice, not to be heard outside.

"Does it hurt?" asked the Professor.

"No, I don't mean my hand—it doesn't hurt in the least —but the whole situation. How does it look to you, Professor? Are they going to keep us here, or is it something else they have in mind?"

"Well, I am not sure of the answer to that. But the general position as I see it is this. We are in a lamasery of the strictest, most ascetic order in Tibet: that is why we have never been taken to the higher building, which is where the masters live—the Great Silent Ones, as Sita Ram calls them. They dislike our presence, of that I am sure. Sita Ram, who is, within certain limits, our friend, mentioned that they had been very much disturbed by the coming of that unfortunate refugee in his flying-machine; and when I asked what had happened to the man, he became evasive, and replied that he did not know, that he thought he had been removed. What he meant by removed, I do not know. But it appears that Sita Ram has no authority to make a decision—he is not allowed even to speak to the Great Silent Ones—until the arrival of another Hindu, whose name is Coomaraswarmy."

"You have the impression that these are genuinely ascetic lamas?"

"I am sure of it. In my walk yesterday I wandered up in that direction, and I saw one of them sitting motionless in the snow: he was dressed in nothing but a thin fold of cotton. Furthermore, the extreme isolation of this place is a proof that they wish to live utterly retired from the world. These are very strange people indeed, Sullivan."

"That's true enough. But if they are all they appear to be, surely they could not have any evil intentions—though I must admit that it looks as though they had."

"It does not follow at all, I am afraid. There is no trusting to this crazy piety. I have never thought highly of men who run to extremes, whether it is an alleged Christian who spends thirty years on top of a pillar or a fanatic who lies on a bed of spikes: in my view—though I may be mistaken—it has nothing to do with religion whatever, and such people, however austere they may be, are just as capable of cruelty as other men; perhaps even more so. But it all depends on this Coomaraswarmy."

There were steps outside, and they stopped. In the long stone passage they heard voices, one loud and bullying, the other soft and apologetic.

"The quiet one is Sita Ram," whispered Sullivan.

The door opened, and a tall, burly man walked in, followed by Sita Ram. The big man looked sharply round the room: the whites of his eyes were blood-shot, and his dark face was congested. It was obviously he who had been talking so angrily, but now he mastered himself and smiled.

"Professor Ayrton?" he said, advancing into the room.

"Good afternoon," said the Professor, rising. "Mr. Coomaraswarmy, I believe."

The Hindu was about to reply when Chingiz's long, evil-looking dagger caught his eye as it lay on the bench. He turned to Sita Ram with a flow of angry words, and then he said, "I must ask you to give up all these things. I wonder that it has not been done before. They have no place in a house of peace."

"Before we go any further," said the Professor, handing them over, "I should like to ask you, with the utmost urgency, to let a party be sent down the valley to search for one of our number who had to be left behind. He may still be alive if your people use the greatest dispatch."

"Which way did you come?"

The Professor described their route. "No, no. You are lying," cried the Hindu with an insolence that made the Professor redden.

"I am not in the habit of lying," he said, in an even voice.

"I have seen the English in India," said the big Hindu, "and I know when to believe the oppressors of

300

my country. They all lie. You say you are Professor Ayrton. I know it is false. I know Professor Ayrton: he is in Hyderabad: you are not the same man."

"You are thinking of my brother, the mathematician," said the Professor, keeping his temper admirably.

"The gentleman is Professor Ayrton," murmured Sita Ram. "I often saw him at Oxford."

"Well," said Coomaraswarmy, "that may be true. But he is lying when he says he came up the forbidden valley."

"If you mean that we could not have come up because of the things you have placed there," said Sullivan, striding up to him and glaring down into his eyes, "I tell you that you are mistaken."

The Hindu dropped his eyes and stepped back.

"And tell me, Coomaraswarmy," said Sullivan, unable to keep the rasp out of his voice, "are those things that you employ down there fit agents for a house of peace?"

"They kill nobody," faltered the Hindu. "They have their orders . . . they are only guards. The Great Silent Ones love their peace." Suddenly he dodged out of the door, and they heard him running down the corridor, with their weapons clattering as he ran.

"I should never have spoken," muttered Sullivan, furious with himself.

Sita Ram was still standing there. He was pale, and he wrung his hands with distress. "Oh, what a pity it is," he cried. "Mr. Coomaraswarmy does not like you."

"We gathered that," said the Professor. "I do not think we liked him, either."

"But what will he do? What will he do?" said Sita Ram.

"The lower men are to come over the pass tomorrow, and then what will he do? There are only a few attendants now, but tomorrow there will be many—very many. And what will he do?"

Sullivan whispered in the Professor's ear, "Shall I get out the gold?"

The Professor very slightly shook his head. "Please listen to me, Sita Ram," he said. "I know that you are a good and a religious man: I do not think that you will throw our lives away. Help me to see the abbot."

"Oh, no, that would be quite impossible," said Sita Ram, silently closing the door and coming a little closer. "Mr. Coomaraswarmy would never allow it. He says that you are here without permission, that you are committing—what is it?—a wicked trespass, and that you are all spies and men of war and blood. I must not betray the Great Silent Ones. I must not. But I wish you could go away. The pass is not very far, and then it is easy: but the lower men are coming up. I cannot advise you, and I should be submissive and not wish that you could go away." He fell silent. After a pause the Professor said encouragingly, "We would never ask you to betray good and righteous principles, but I see that Mr. Coomaraswarmy is inflamed against the English because they occupy India. Perhaps he may be right. I do not like the idea of ruling over other people against their will myself: but whether he is right or not, it has distorted his views; there is the red mist of anger in front of his eyes. But you see more clearly, and you know that he would be sorry afterwards if he were to commit a violence. You know, even better than I do, that there is a higher obedience."

"But I must be obedient," said Sita Ram. "I must not stay here. I must not wish that the flying-machine would work to take you away. I must not tell you that it is only a little way down the valley. I must not say that this door will not be locked at one hour before the dawn." He said these last words in a whisper barely audible in the room, and then, unhappy, nervous and almost distracted he bolted out of the door. A few minutes later they heard an angry voice calling his name and the stamp of heavy feet coming down the corridor. They paused outside the door. Sullivan crept to the door, crouched by it and gathered himself: but the Professor waved at him and shook his head. A moment later there was a little sliding noise at the door, and the feet walked quietly away. Sullivan pulled gently at the door: it was locked.

"No," said the Professor, when they had listened for a while. "I do not think that violence is in place here. It could only end with disaster now that we are disarmed. I remember my dear old father telling me, when first I went to school, 'Do not bark unless you can bite,' and our teeth have been drawn. We must rely on this flying-machine."

Sullivan nodded. "He said it was down the valley,"

he whispered, listening at the door again. He beckoned to Chingiz, and said in Mongol, "Listen at this hole, and if you hear anyone coming, wave your hand." Then, to the Professor, "But first we have got to find it. And then what sort of chance is there that it is not in a thousand pieces? It must have crashed: no plane could possibly have landed there and still be in a state to take off."

A sudden illumination flashed into Derrick's mind. "Uncle," he said, "I believe I saw it. I thought it was nonsense because I was tired. It must have been the thing I thought was a windmill fallen over."

"A helicopter!" exclaimed Sullivan. "Now that is something like a possibility."

"When Sita Ram first mentioned it," said the Professor, "he said that the man floated down and walked out quite safe. He did not say that the machine was damaged in any way—indeed, I had the impression that he considered it quite workable. But whether he had his information from the unfortunate flier or not, I cannot say."

"And yet," mused Sullivan, "how on earth could a helicopter get here?"

"From what I gathered," said the Professor, "the unhappy man was escaping from Russia. Presumably he stole the machine, or acquired it in some other way, and flew until he thought he was in safety."

"That's possible," said Sullivan, with renewed hope. "Let's hope that the poor devil did not fly until he had used all his juice."

Chingiz held up his hand, and they fell silent. It was getting dark. Presently Sullivan walked over to the fire and stirred it into a blaze. "Well," he said, "we may as well have a make and mend and then turn in. Heaven knows what they are going to do with us, but I for one shall sleep until noon." He spoke in a natural voice, quite loud, and yawned. The Mongol's hand was still raised. Sullivan sat down in front of the fire, and by the leaping flare he began to repair his rig as well as he could with his bandaged hand.

The others, except for Chingiz, joined him. Their clothes and their boots were in a shocking state, but they could not bring any sort of heart to their work.

Chingiz dropped his hand, and from the door whispered, "He is gone."

"Good, Chingiz," said Sullivan, "then come to the fire. There is no more for us to say tonight. We must try to sleep."

The night wore on, and they lay about the floor, warm, with their bodies at ease and relaxed; but even Sullivan, old hand though he was at going off, could not sleep. One by one the stars crept by the small high, strongly barred window: Sullivan reckoned them off, judging the progress of the night, and by the time he heard a gentle rustle at the door he was up and ready. He opened it silently, and Sita Ram glided in. He was trembling with agitation, and he could hardly speak. "Here is a little food," he said, sliding a parcel from under his robe. "I should not do it: it is very wrong. There is a little money in case you need it. If you can

305

get over the pass it is down and down all the way until the country of the common people. Take care, take care. I will try to find your friend." He glided out again like a shadow, and the door closed quietly behind him.

"Muzzle Chang and follow me," whispered Sullivan. Derrick already had Chang muzzled: he too had watched the stars, and he had feared that Chang might bark. They crept silently out of the door, down the long passage and out on to the crisp snow, shining under the first hint of light from a cloudless sky.

Down the path they went, bent double with caution. In ten minutes they were out of sight of the lamasery, and they ran with huge flying steps down the path that they had so painfully climbed before.

"Whereabouts is it?" asked Sullivan.

Derrick stared about him in the growing light. "I think it was round the next bend," he said, with a hideous doubt in his mind, "rather lower than those rocks down there."

They went on, and all at once Derrick gave a cry of delight. There, exactly as he had pictured it a thousand times during the night, was the thing he had taken for a windmill. It was standing on its platform, its huge vanes intact, and looking now he could see the shape of its body under the snow.

They hurried down the slope, sliding recklessly on the snow, and began to dig the snow away.

"Why in Heaven's name did they not move it?" asked Sullivan, as the body came into view.

"It happened the day Coomaraswarmy was going," said the Professor, "and he left orders that it was not to be touched until he came back. How very fortunate that there were no strong winds up here between that time and this. Surely, this appears to be a door, and is not this the handle?" He pulled, and they stared into the cabin.

"It is the largest helicopter I have ever seen," said Sullivan, "not that I've seen many."

"It is certainly a Russian machine," said the Professor, getting in and looking at the instrument panel.

They dug feverishly, and presently the whole of the egg-shaped fuselage and the long tail was showing. With every fresh scoop of snow they expected to find some damaged part, and when it was nearly all uncovered without any sign of a crash appearing they hardly dared continue. But eventually it stood there, free of snow, and apparently, to their inexpert eyes, as good as new.

Then suddenly a thought struck them. "Who is going to fly it?" asked Derrick and the Professor both at once.

"I am," said Sullivan, after a moment. "I've navigated some queer craft in my time, but none so queer as this. The first thing to do is to see whether there's any gas aboard." He climbed in and peered at the dials. "Professor," he called, "can you translate for me?"

"This is petrol, or gasoline, as you would say," said the Professor, pointing at one. "It reads zero."

"Perhaps there's a little in," said Sullivan. "We only need enough to reach the top of the pass, and then the thing will go down slowly, like a parachute."

"Without any petrol, Sullivan? Are you sure?"

"I think so," said Sullivan, uncertainly. "Anyhow, let's try to start her up."

"How?"

"Doesn't it say on these instructions?"

"Let me see . . ."

Derrick had followed them in, and he was looking about the back. "What's this?" he said, holding up a can. Sullivan unscrewed the cap. "It's gas," he cried, and then, looking further, "Why, the whole thing is filled with it. Let's fill her up."

They found the tank and filled it to the brim, throwing the containers out into the snow. By this time the Professor had read the long printed list.

"It is most unfortunate," he said, "that I do not understand the technical terms. I am afraid I do not understand them in any language. I cannot translate them. But it seems that there is a bent piece of metal that must be turned rapidly in a clockwise direction."

"Derrick," said Sullivan, "it's getting late. You and Chingiz go to the next bend and watch the path. When you hear the engine fire, run back. If they come for us, they'll regret it."

He turned to the engine and studied it. "I'll try and start it like a car," he said. "Do you understand anything about cars, Professor?"

"Nothing whatever," said the Professor, "but I have

found the place where the tools are kept. Perhaps this is the starting handle."

"It looks like one," said Sullivan, "and this looks like the place where it goes in. I'll try." He engaged the crank and turned. The vanes above them jerked and moved slightly round. The Professor stood back expectantly. Sullivan heaved, heaved and heaved again. "I wish to God I had both my hands," he said, pausing, and wiping the sweat away.

"May I have a try?" suggested the Professor. He grasped the handle and turned. He turned, gasping with the effort, took a new grip and turned again. The vanes moved, but nothing more. Half an hour later they were still standing there: Sullivan had ripped the skin off the palm of his one good hand, and the Professor was exhausted.

Derrick came running down. "Coomaraswarmy is coming down the path," he reported.

"Right," said Sullivan, "I'll come and cope with him. You stay here and try to swing that crank."

Derrick seized the handle and swung madly. He had swung a car several times, but this handle was awkwardly high, and the compression was enormous. He swung with all his force, with more force than he had ever exerted in his life, for there they stood, with their safety in front of them, unable to use it. If only he could make the engine fire, everything would turn from night to day, from death to life. He swung until the blood clouded his eyes: but the engine would not fire. He darted into the cabin and wildly altered all the knobs he could find. The Professor stood helplessly by him.

Again he swung, and again, and again. The vanes quivered and turned, but that was all: the engine would not fire.

Chingiz joined them. "He is waiting for him," he said, with a grin. "Are we going soon?"

"Chingiz, turn this," cried Derrick, panting and wiping his bloody hands in the snow.

Chingiz tried. He tried with all the strength of his body, for he had suddenly understood from Derrick's pale face that everything depended on it. He swung, he swung until he could swing no longer, and then he too sank down to breathe.

They heard a noise like the beginning of an avalanche and started up. It was near, only a little way up the valley: but it did not swell into the full and horrifying roar, and after a moment Sullivan appeared again, running.

"He is dealt with," he said, gripping the handle again. Round and round he forced it, with all the weight that he could muster, round and round and round.

He fell back, and the blood was pouring from his nose. "If only poor dear Ross were here," he muttered, "he'd have the thing going like a shot. He always hated engines: but he could make them do anything he liked."

The sun was in the valley now. One by one they went up to the bend to watch the path, and one by one they came back to wrestle desperately with the crank.

Sullivan tried everything he knew. He cleaned the plugs, warmed them in his clothes, scraped the contacts, flooded the carburettors: he thumped the engine, climbed on the coping and turned the vanes by hand, and unscrewed and refastened everything that might be dirty. None of it was any good. He stared at the thing, gaunt and haggard. He felt that it would break his heart.

Derrick was coming down the path for his turn again, and Sullivan looked up impatiently as he heard Derrick give a hail, "Shut up, you flaming fool," he cried. "Do you want to bring the whole pack down on us?"

But Derrick hailed again, a long and extraordinarily loud ahoy that came flapping back from the farther side. He raced past Sullivan and the Professor, tearing down the slope. They stared after him in amazement.

He had seen what they had not, and his heart was almost bursting as it thumped with joy. When first he had seen the three yaks and the two walking men he had been coming down to report that the path was still clear: the sight had pulled him up: he had waited a minute to see the yaks and the men clear into sight round the corner before he ran down to make his report of their number and strength, and in that minute he had recognised a tall, lumbering form and one short, slight one with a black Chinese cap.

He sped on, tripped and took a frightful plunge

down fifty yards of snow: he picked himself up unhurt and came to a steeper slope again. He squatted, edged on to the slope and slid the whole length of it, shrieking "Olaf, ahoy! Li Han. Ahoy, there, ahoy." He was half-way down the slope and moving at a terrifying pace when he saw that there was a form on one of the yaks, a form that waved an arm. "Ahoy, Mr. Ross," he bawled. "Ahoy!" He went smack into a soft drift and plunged straight through it to the other side.

In another moment he was shaking hands, having the breath knocked out of his body by Olaf's huge slaps on the back, asking questions, answering them and at the same time hopping with delight.

There was nobody at the helicopter now. They were all racing down, and Sullivan was the first up after Derrick. After a single, powerful handshake with Ross and a quick word with him, he said, "Olaf, here's all the ammunition left. You see that machine up there? There are five men coming down towards it. If they approach, one shot over their heads. If they come nearer, shoot to kill."

"Aye-aye, Cap'n," cried Olaf, setting off at a run.

"We must hurry the yaks up there at full speed," said Sullivan, unlashing Ross. "Now get on my back, Ross. I'm going to carry you up. There's an engine that you must start."

All this time Li Han had been darting towards the approaching Professor, stopping every moment to bow and darting on. "Rest assured," he cried as they drew near, "rest assured for treasure, respected sir. Is all safe. Is all on person intact."

"Confound the jade," said the Professor, shaking him by both hands. "Come quickly and shed a little blood, Li Han. They are attacking the helicopter."

Derrick and Chingiz, urging the yaks with all their force, heard a single shot. They listened, motionless, but nothing followed. Sullivan was far up the slope beyond them already. He had taken the path, and he was running in the beaten track, running as though there were nothing on his back: it was an astonishing spectacle. For a hundred yards it would have been an extraordinary feat, but he never slackened, never faltered, never stumbled until he was on the edge of the path above the machine. "Now," he said, in a hoarse, unrecognisable voice. "We've got to slide you down. Olaf! Bear a hand."

Ross winced once or twice on the journey down, and he stifled a groan as he crawled into the cabin. He looked at the instruments, nodded his head, and looked under the deep panel. "Man, man," he murmured, "it's the ignition, nothing more." He leant down and turned a key, altered the controls and said, "Try now."

At the same moment Olaf shouted, "They're coming on."

"Give me your gun," said Sullivan to Olaf, "and swing that handle there. Swing it hard. Swing it with everything you've got."

Olaf spat on his hands, gripped, swung, and was

flung flat on his face as the engine roared, filling the air with snow and the valley with noise. The helicopter rocked: Ross throttled back, and the engine slowed to a steady thrum. Gently Ross increased the power: the helicopter rose a foot and settled back as he experimented with the controls. He looked out of the cabin, wiping the frosted screen. "I'm ready when you are," he said calmly, and eased himself back in the pilot's seat.

Chingiz and the yaks had stopped dead at the prodigious roar. "Come on," said Derrick. "They've got her started. We'll run up with the pack. We won't need the yaks any more." Chingiz stood hesitating: he had not expected this. "Come on," cried Derrick again, unslinging the yak's light burden. Chingiz clutched his charm, took half the load, and they hurried up the slope. He blenched again as they stood by the helicopter, battered by its wind.

"The yaks are all right," shouted Derrick, as he handed in the pack. "I cast off their head-stalls." But nobody heard him above the roar. He flung the unwilling Chang into the cabin, hauled the hesitating Chingiz up by the arm, wormed his way in and slammed the door.

"Will she lift with this load?" asked Sullivan in Ross's ear.

"She may," said Ross, "and she may not." He eased the throttle forward. The roar increased in a mounting crescendo and died away again. In the crowded cabin, with hardly room to move, there was a frightful sense of disappointment and anticlimax. Ross swivelled round. "You'll have to take your dog's tail out of the controls, young man," he said, "if I am to use my helm at all."

Derrick hauled Chang on to his knee, and the roar grew loud again. It stayed loud and high, and in a minute the Professor leaned forward and asked nervously, "Do you suppose, Mr. Ross, that the machine will rise? I am very willing, if there is too much weight—"

"She has risen," interrupted Ross. "We have been a couple of feet off the ground for some time. I am just getting the feel of it."

As he spoke the ground slid sideways and down. Chingiz gave a gasp and closed his eyes. Derrick wormed his way to the side and saw the whole valley lying out below them, with the lamasery and the pass clearly in view.

Gently the helicopter tilted forward and began to rush at an astonishing speed for the pass. "Shall you clear it? Shall you clear it?" asked Sullivan, clutching his fists as he stared forward at the ground as it swept towards them.

"We may," said Ross coolly, "or we may not. I am not well acquainted with these machines, though I understand the principle. As I see it, we have little possibility of gaining much more height. Perhaps I'll go round again."

In a somewhat jerking curve the helicopter circled and rushed for the pass again. "It'll be a close thing on the starboard bow," observed Ross. "Do you see all those people coming up from the other side?"

"Yes," said Sullivan. "They were due a little while ago. They'll stop us if they can."

"I wonder if they have guns," said Ross. "However, we shall soon see. Stop us, will they? The contumelious dogs. I'll shave their heads."

He brought the helicopter upright a hundred feet from the pass, steadied it, and then, with the concentration of a man steering between two rocks in a high wind and a heavy sea, he tore towards the pass again. The angry faces swept nearer with shocking velocity. "Watch the starboard bow," he cried, and plunged at the thick of them. There was a shriek, a distant bang and a scrape as a lance scratched across the undercarriage. Then below them was a vast expanse of cloud, with a few peaks rising through it.

"The contumelious dogs," cried Ross again. "Shall I go back and give them another dose?"

"No, no, I beg you will go on," shouted the Professor above the roar. "I cannot tell you what pleasure it gives me to look down on these clouds on the other side of the pass. Pray do not turn back, Mr. Ross."

"Well, it's as you wish," said Ross, a little discontentedly. "What's the course, Sullivan?"

"West-nor'-west," said Sullivan, consulting the compass. "What's your log-reading?"

"About a hundred knots," said Ross. "A couple of hours, or maybe three, will show a very different face of things."

They had been cruising steadily for hours. They had all got used to the steady, well-nourished roar, and they had exchanged their news. Olaf and Li Han had indeed got snowed up, but they had been snowed up in a shallow crevasse. They had caught the yaks almost as the blizzard hit them, and trying to lead the beasts back they had felt the snow give way under them, and the next minute they were ten feet under the surface. But their feet were on rock, they were shaken, but unhurt, and best of all, they had the yaks with them. Very soon the snow reformed its bridge over their heads, and with the warmth of the yaks they did not do do badly at all. They had plenty of food, and they piled snow between them and the ice to make them relatively snug. The great difficulty was getting out, but after dragging great quantities of snow into the shallowest part of the crevasse they gradually built up the floor. They finally emerged about twenty hours after they had been given up altogether, and hurrying to the camp they had found the note and the stores that were left for them.

They had pressed on, finding the markers left at almost every camp: they had once thought that they had seen a horrible shape among the rocks, and they had spent far too much ammunition on it. Then, by a wretched mischance, a commonplace hole in Olaf's pocket, they had lost the rest: but otherwise they had had a very good journey. Three, times they had come in sight of the others, when they were on straight stretches, but always at a very great distance, too far for hailing with the wind in the wrong direction. At first they had not gone as quickly as the others, because of the slowness of the yaks; but as Sullivan's party slowed down from weariness, they had gained, so that they came up to the place where Ross was sitting not much more than ten hours after he had been left. They had had to stop quite a long time then, for he was in a very bad way. Olaf built him a snow-house over his yurt—the smaller yurt had come along with the yaks—which had kept him warm and dry while they fed him. His legs and feet were bad, very bad, but worse than that was his near-starvation. For days and days he had secretly been putting back more than half his ration into the others' loads: he recovered very quickly when Li Han fed him with strong broth and when he was certain that there was enough and to spare for all. Then they had taken the strongest and most docile of the yaks and had arranged him as comfortably as they could on its back: from that time on their marches had been slow, but they had been quite confident that they would get through in time; the only worry was whether they could reach civilisation in time to save Ross's left foot, which was the worst; and until they had reached the helicopter it had seemed not so much doubtful as impossible. More than once Ross had been on the point of deciding to have it off, to prevent the infection mounting. "And I believe," he said, throttling back a little, "that if we had not met today, tomorrow you might have met with a wooden-legged mariner, instead of an interesting case for the nearest saw-bones. Do you think, Sullivan, that there would be one down there?" He tilted the helicopter sideways, pointing to a broad and straggling village or little town below them.

"I doubt it," said Sullivan. "I doubt if it would have even so much as a single juke-box in it. But with this tearing wind following us, we should get you to all the comforts of civilisation in an hour or two. And that," he said, turning round and talking to Derrick, "includes school."

Derrick nodded, and looked out. Down below them, through the scattered patches of lower cloud, the hills were giving way to flatter country, all spread out like a map. A broad river, whose green banks they could see even at that height, showed up sharp and white; and all along its sides, spreading far out to north and south, there was the patchwork of fields. The cloud shadows floated below them, racing over the distant ground as the strong wind pushed them from behind: and here and there the drifting smoke of villages made a faint mist below the clouds.

The Professor was looking out beside him. "Yes, there it is," he said. "Yes, I am sure that that is it. Down there, Derrick," he cried, stabbing downwards with his pointing finger towards a thin, incredibly remote line that stretched as far as they could see, "there is the road to Samarcand."

Center Point Publishing

600 Brooks Road ● PO Box 1
Thorndike ME 04986-0001 USA

(207) 568-3717

US & Canada:
1 800 929-9108
www.centerpointlargeprint.com